SECOND CHANCES

SECOND CHANCES

MARC CULLISON

SECOND CHANCES

This is a work of fiction. All names, characters, places, and events are the work of the author's imagination. Any resemblance to real person, places, or events is coincidental.

Cover Art designed by Rebecca Dugan for Imzadi Publishing, LLC.

Interior formatting for print and digital publications by
Anita Dugan-Moore of Cyber-Bytz, www.cyber-bytz.com.

If you would like permission to use material from this book for any reason other than for review purposes, please contact the publisher at: imzadipublishing@outlook.com.

Published by Imzadi Publishing, LLC
"Our Only Limitation is Your Imagination"
www.imzadipublishing.com

Printed in the U.S.A.

CONTENTS

FREE PREVIEW

The Other Vietnam - A Helicopter Pilot's Life in Vietnam

THANKS

A special thanks to the talented team at Imzadi Publishing. They have made this book a reality and brought life to a story of family struggles, regrets, and resolve.

And my undying gratitude to my wonderful wife who take better care of me than I could myself.

WHEN IT ALL BEGAN

February 1948

Those days long ago, born of wonder and steeped in curiosity, seemed to wander by in a cryptic mist of innocence uncharted by young minds constantly reveling in discovery. It should have been no surprise, then, that I watched from the doorway to the hall as my little brother, Alan, two, marched across the living room floor toward my older brother, Dennis, five, who was peacefully sitting among the Sunday comics, and smacked him on the head with the meat tenderizer. That's when it all began; a spontaneous happenstance when Alan found in his small hand a meat tenderizer and, at two years of age, unable to discern the nature of right and wrong, especially when confronted with the opportunity to put a tool to its intended purpose, stood over Dennis and smacked him in the head with benign intent, thus fulfilling the meat tenderizer's destiny.

The sudden wails brought Mom to the front.

"What happened?" she ordered with fierce anxiety, her green eyes with a sharp focus toward the sudden shriek of terror. She had grown accustomed to these outbursts and was no longer prone to fits of panic but rather a kind of deference that eventually overtakes the anxiety and timidity of the novice parent. It was the abrupt and unfamiliar piercing outcry, however, that put her hackles up.

With his face awash in tears and his contorted mouth trying to utter an explanation that he couldn't quite articulate, Dennis turned to point toward Alan. He wanted to say something, to assess blame for the dastardly deed but his speech seemed to be frozen by the enormity of the situation. In his mind, he had been mortally wounded, not that he recognized it in such proper terms, but he knew that he had been unduly and savagely attacked with a lethal weapon.

Of course, I knew something big was up, but I had never witnessed such an act of violence, especially between my two brothers. I remember thinking at the time how odd that such a small boy could inflict such damage on one so much older. It was not until Dennis' scream broke my concentration that I realized what had happened.

"'Eee 'it meee," Dennis bawled. Then he let loose with even more robust wailing.

"Hit you?"

Mom's head snapped toward Alan. She looked at the meat tenderizer dangling from his small hand, the tool she had just used to hammer out the cheap slabs of chuck in the kitchen. Dad saw no reason to waste good money on real steak when cheap cuts of beef pounded into a bloody pulp were just as good, according to him.

"Alan, what did you do to your brother?"

Naturally, the two-year-old had no idea what he had done other than mimic what he had just seen Mom do in the kitchen. Dennis' head appeared to offer a good target to test his skill.

She pulled Dennis' hand from his head, and inspected the wound, a little blood blended into his brown hair and good-sized dent in the skin below. She dragged him to the kitchen sink to attempt to stem the flow of blood from his scalp. From a drawer, she snatched a clean rag that she dampened under the faucet and held to the wound over his dark hair, consoling him as well as she could. The cool compress arrested the bleeding, and his crying turned to whimpers. She pulled him into the dining room, more of a breakfast area, and sat him in a chair.

"Hold this rag on your head," she told him.

It was a shame that Dennis hadn't inherited more of Dad's easy-going manner instead of the hot-headed brashness of Mom's side of the family. It seemed as if all she did was quell arguments and confrontations between the two boys with authority and dispatch. Classical sibling rivalry. For some odd reason, I was rarely a target, I suppose because I was a girl, a year younger than Dennis, two years older than Alan. The middle child often recedes into the shadows, unnoticed and ignored.

Then Mom turned to the scene of the crime, Sunday comics still spread out over the floor. She stared at Alan, shy and quiet, looking at her, dumbstruck as to what the commotion was all about, both of them oblivious to me standing in the doorway.

She looked at the meat tenderizer dangling from his hand. The metal points on the thing, though not exactly sharp, were pointed enough to wreak a fair amount of damage on a boy's fragile noggin. What stumped her, though, was working out how on earth Alan had gotten hold of the thing.

She was on him in two steps, yanking the heavy tool from the tiny hand as a hawk would snatch up a field mouse from the ground. Shocked from the sudden assault, Alan then burst forth in tears and wails while Dennis, who had been peeking around the corner, looked on with vengeance in his eyes. She leaned over Alan and from a good two feet above his upturned face, her short stature not affording her a loftier stance, like a dragon about to scoop him up with large, sharp teeth, and shook the tenderizer at his face.

"How did you get hold of this?" she asked, as if a two-year-old could thrust away the intimidating gesture with the tenderizer and provide a coherent response.

Alan, frozen to the floor, his feet unable to move, gazed up at her, eyes wide with fear and trepidation, oblivious to what he had done. My attention was trained on the encounter but with the bafflement of a four-year-old attempting to understand the meaning of the transgression.

Mom waved the meat tenderizer again in front of Alan's face, and with a mouth that exaggerated the words, "You hurt Dennis."

3

A huff. "You leave this alone," she almost yelled. "It is not a toy." It was then that she saw the blood on the metal points.

Alan blinked, then his face wound itself up into a knot, and bawling again filled the room.

In the meantime, Dennis had recovered from the shock of the unprovoked assault, and now merely nursed an injured ego. Sitting on the chair, his legs swinging above the floor, he seemed ashamed of the fact that a little twit like Alan, three years his junior, could take advantage of him. How embarrassing. I knew Alan would not get away with it. Still peeking around the doorjamb, I privately reveled in the brazen act by my little brother, notwithstanding his inability to conceive of its genesis or significance.

From that day forward, Alan's world became a labyrinth of anxiety-ridden ordeals with hazards, triumphs, and defeats. Mostly defeats. He would be the shy one of the family, and with the burden of his brother's machinations, his path would grow more obscure, hidden beneath uncertainty and lack of experience. Alan had no idea what was in store for him.

Dennis would find himself in a tenacious contest for superiority, often sacrificing his own victories for a small measure of prestige and finding failure instead of success.

I, on the other hand, would become lost in the struggle to keep my balance on the fence between my two brothers.

CONFESSIONS TO MY NEIGHBOR

December 2001

As I approached the front door of my apartment, my neighbor, Melinda Bentley, a tightly wound soul with a petite, but shapely figure, and a vast store of opinions that would test anyone's patience, was leaving her own apartment. Our eyes met.

"Hi, Melinda," I called out.

She stopped momentarily and turned toward me. "Oh, hi, Sue."

"Where are you going?"

"To the liquor store. I'm out of Scotch."

To my surprise, a kindred soul.

"Listen, I've got a bottle of single malt. Why don't you come over and we can share it."

She dropped her shoulders in relief. "Oh, god, thank you."

Melinda sat across from me on the patio behind my apartment under the metal roof that was dinging with temperature contractions. We were discussing our families, and I have to admit, she must come from a timid bed of wilted wallflowers.

"But Sue, you can't be serious," she said, waving her glass of Scotch through the air, her hazel eyes in bewilderment. "Nobody can be that bad."

The Dallas sun began searching for the horizon and the red line in the thermometer on the wall began diving toward the bulb at the bottom. I grinned at her and leaned back in my chair.

"Our family is a typical American family, if you considered typical American families to be dysfunctional." I took a sip of Scotch. "Not that we are incapable of presenting a normal appearance. That's something we are very good at. Everyone thinks we are such a nice, friendly family."

Melinda blinked her eyes in feigned surprise. "But I've met your brother and his wife, and they're very nice."

I shook my head. "I have an older brother, too. And I don't believe you would have the same opinion of him."

"Why not?"

"Just trust me on this."

She let out a huff of disapproval and took a drink of her Scotch.

"Well, what about your parents. They're dead, aren't they? What were they like?"

"My mother, Madeline Carter, the core of the family unit, held it together like so many mothers do, a maternal glue that binds and nurtures. She did everything except make repairs to the house and car and bring home the bacon, although her time spent working at Dad's store could be considered just that."

"Was that the hardware store?"

"Yes. Our bread basket, so to speak. Mom was all; of four-foot-eight, a live wire with tremendous resolve, enough to deal with family squabbles, an irate husband, and nosy neighbors. She had these brilliant green eyes that could look holes through us and bore into our brains to see what we were thinking."

"Yeah," said Melinda. "My mom was like that."

"There wasn't much we could get away with. Even though Dad ran the family, Mom usually had her say-so in it."

"See, your mom sounds just like mine. And we had a good family."

"Just wait," I said, sipping my Scotch. "There's more. Mom was the one who was always there for me. Well, usually. Since she and I were the only two girls in the family, we had to have some special bond. It wasn't like my brothers. When Dennis, my older brother, was harassing me, she would step in and squelch it, not that Dennis ever got a reprimand for it, but at least I was spared a lengthy ordeal. Mom always told me I had to stand up for myself, because no one else would. Of course, she didn't exactly adhere to her own advice. Dad called the shots and Mom acquiesced. For me, though, her advice has served me well. I wouldn't be the manager of a prominent women's shelter had I not forged ahead with my rejected application. The director claimed that my lack of experience disqualified me. I did some research into shelters, and I found solutions to many of the problems at this shelter and offered those suggestions to the director. She was impressed and gave me a chance to prove myself. I'm still there."

"That's impressive. I never knew that. Good for you."

Another sip of my Scotch. "And then there's my father, George Carter. He was the tightest son of a bitch in the world. He was the only man I ever knew who could pinch a penny hard enough to make it squeal."

Melinda broke down in laughter.

"I can remember Mom patiently waiting for him to hand over the meager allowance he gave her to buy food for the week. If anything broke or wore out, he would work himself to death trying to fix it. I have to admit that he was pretty good at that. Of course, whatever he had operated on bore the marks of expedient alterations, but it worked. I know Mom would have preferred to just buy a new one, but given our financial situation, to her, anything that worked was better than nothing at all, regardless of what it looked like. For a man with an eighth-grade education he certainly knew a lot about things. Not so much about people, unless it involved money. He always knew when someone was trying to jerk him around."

"He sounds like a very smart man," she said, bringing the glass to her lips. "My dad just kind of watched the world go by."

"He must have been pretty easy going," I said.

"Oh, he was. He never got excited about anything. Even when my brother wrecked his car, he didn't get mad. He just didn't let him have another car."

"Well, that seems reasonable. Dennis wrecked two cars and Dad replaced the first one, but not the second."

"Your dad doesn't sound as bad you make him out to be."

I laughed. "I guess he really wasn't that bad. He was just tight with money. I suppose that's the way a lot of fathers are."

We settled back in a moment of silence, listening to the roof ding.

"My brothers and I," I continued, "were just kind of there, if you know what I mean. The obligatory children expected of a married couple. Dennis spent his time teasing Alan, I followed Mom around helping her, and Alan spent his time avoiding Dennis."

Melinda finished her Scotch and looked at me with a puzzled face.

"Oh, teasing's not so bad. My brother did that to me all the time."

I polished off my Scotch, too.

"Well, Dennis' teasing wasn't just teasing. It was more like humiliation. And Dennis never teased me much. It was all Alan. And he didn't do well with it."

"Sounds like Dennis was kind of mean."

"He was, in a way. To look at Dennis and Alan, you'd never guess that they were brothers. They were so different, in looks and demeanor. Alan seemed to favor Dad, easy going, green eyes, straight nose, light brown to blond hair, light complexion. Dennis favored Mom, shorter, dark brown hair, an almost straight nose, darker complexion, but with hazel eyes. I'm not sure I favored any of them with my blonde hair and medium complexion. And blue eyes. Yes, a blue-eyed blonde."

"That's what's so attractive about you, Sue. You don't see many blue-eyed blondes around here."

"Thanks, but I know I'm no knockout. Another drink?"

"If you're having one, sure. I don't have to work tomorrow."

I took our glasses and refilled them. I thought about Dad and what he would say if he saw me drinking Scotch. He'd die. Him and his cheap bourbon.

I put the glasses on the table and sat down, smiling at Melinda.

"Was your family well off?" I asked.

"We were pretty well fixed. I know I had a lot of things other kids never had. Dad even bought me a new car when I turned eighteen."

"You're lucky. My dad was old school. He and Mom had gone through the great depression and their lifestyle reflected it, tending towards extreme conservatism. They would always tell us about their trials and tribulations, usually as lessons about frugality. Of course, World War II was tough on everyone, given the use of ration stamps and all. Mom had devised substitutions for basic foodstuffs to use when cooking, since many staple products weren't available. And when Dennis was a baby, since they couldn't afford a crib, he slept in the bottom drawer of the dresser when it was pulled out, or that's what Mom always told us. And Dad had become an expert at jerry-rigging things to make them work without proper replacement parts. These enlightenment sessions became important only when we reached the age when we left home and had to fend for ourselves."

"Wow," she said, leaning back in her chair. "You must have had a hard time growing up."

"Well, it wasn't all that bad. We would take family outings, if they weren't expensive. We took a trip nearly every year. Dad would pack our car with the portable gasoline cookstove, blankets, army surplus folding cots, and other things. Mom would stock the ice chests with bacon, eggs, butter, and other food we would eat on our trip. She would replenish things along the way. Each of us kids had a small suitcase of clothes."

"God, Sue. It sounds like you were moving."

A sip of Scotch.

"Yeah, I guess we were, kind of. We went to places like Yellowstone National Park and stopped at Dodge City, Kansas, on the way. And we went to Pike's Peak. We went other places, too. Dad always drove. Mom could drive, but Dad couldn't stand to just sit still and watch the scenery pass by."

"You know," Melinda said as she leaned forward, again. "We never travelled much. I never got to see those places. We did good just to get out of town."

"Really? I thought everybody took trips. Why didn't your family go anywhere?"

"My dad was too busy with work. He worked all the time. He was a salesman, and the company kept him on the road. I guess he's the only one that ever got to go anyplace."

"That's kind of like my dad and his store, but he did take off occasionally. It was the trip to Carlsbad Caverns that was the best. I was about eight, and Alan was six. Dennis would have been nine. We didn't have air conditioning. We had an old Ford, black. It was hot, and I sat in the middle of the back seat between Alan and Dennis. They were constantly fighting about something, usually Dennis picking on him. We got to the big cave and everybody was consumed with it. Even Dad seemed surprised by it. Mom was really amazed by the whole thing. Dennis, not so much. But Alan. He was blown away by it. I think he would have stayed there if we had left him. I still remember all of that."

"I've never been there," she said, a gaze of envy in her eyes.

"We had stayed at a motel in some small town, one of those motels with a string of detached cottages as was normal back then and packed up early in the morning to start driving. It was probably an hour later that Dad pulled off the road onto a grassy area. The view wasn't much, just sand and brush and cactus. Dad set up the gas stove, and Mom prepared food."

"You mean you cooked breakfast out like that? Like camping?"

"Yeah, I guess it was like that. Alan was busy watching lizards. Dad finally set up a cot and we kids sat on it. The bacon and scrambled eggs tasted so good."

"That sounds like so much fun. I wish we had done things like that. I've never been camping."

We both hit the Scotch, again.

"Henry," she continued, "he's my brother, always got everything. The girls got crap. I still resent that. It was so unfair."

I laughed. "If any of us received any attention, it was Dennis, especially when he was old enough to do things that Dad liked to do. Like hunting.

I never really knew what their hunting trips were all about. I don't even remember them bringing back anything that they had killed, to Mom's delight. It was never a big deal to the rest of us. Dad's interest in Dennis was just something that we took for granted, him being the oldest."

"Yeah," said Melinda. "I can understand that."

"As we got older, Dennis discovered girls. That's when the family dynamic changed. His harassment of Alan seemed to darken a bit. Teasing was no longer enough. The attacks became personal and cruel, like humiliation. He was ignoring me by that time and focused all of his aggression on Alan. It was fortunate for Alan that Dennis' interest in girls kept him out of the house much of the time. "

"That's so sad," she said, frowning. "Poor Alan."

"Since I was a girl, Mom took me shopping, not that she ever bought much, unless I needed some school clothes. We could never afford to buy much when we lived in Milton. I would help Mom prepare meals, and if I wasn't playing with my friends, I would be enlisted to help clean house. Southwest Oklahoma was layered in red dirt and populated with horned toads and red ants. It seemed like it rarely rained. The dust storms would blow the dirt through the cracks in the window frames and doors and leave piles of fine, red dust on the sills and all through the house."

"Yes, I've seen Oklahoma's red dirt. Yuk! I remember visiting my cousin in Elk City. It was really dry and red dust was every-where. We didn't play outside. She let me try on her makeup. My mother about had a heart attack."

I laughed. "Mom actually showed me how to use makeup. It kind of promoted the feminine presence. It really surprised me, seeing as she never indulged in makeup and such. It was an unnecessary expense, she said. What little makeup she had was reserved for church or other formal occasions. But I still learned the basics of how to apply lipstick and rouge."

Melinda was thoroughly enjoying my history. I wondered if she had ever talked about hers much.

"How old were you?" She asked.

"I was in high school. All the girls wore makeup to dances and things like that. At least Mom understood."

"You are so lucky. I couldn't use makeup until I was in col-lege where Mom never knew what I was doing. It was my first period that threw my mother into turmoil."

"What happened?"

"She first noticed it when I stood up from a chair. The back of my dress was spotted. I thought she would come unglued. Anyway, she went through a lengthy lecture on sanitary napkins and all of that stuff. I was so embarrassed. I guess she was too, having to tell me about it."

"I discovered my first period while in the girls' restroom just before fifth hour. I stuffed toilet paper in my panties and asked Mrs. Ottley, my fifth hour history teacher, if I could be excused. Of course, it was so embarrassing, but she was very understanding and took me to the office and called my mother at Dad's store. Mom picked me up and took me home. She told me all about it and got me calmed down."

"Your mother must have been really neat. I wish my mom had been that cool."

"Well, that afternoon when Dennis got home, he saw the back of my dress laying on the big shelf on our screened in back porch. The washer and dryer were in the basement. He unleashed a barrage of crude remarks that stabbed me to the bone. Mom unleashed her own wrath on him, and the incident went away."

"I guess I was lucky, since Henry never seemed to notice. But he did take notice when I started getting breasts. At least he didn't tease me about it."

I sipped my Scotch and smiled.

"My experience was a lot different. Dennis would continually snap my bra and pinch my nipples and tell me I was a titty baby. I finally got over it, but the hurt is something I will never forget."

"That's terrible," said Melinda. "How on earth did you deal with it?"

I sighed, sipped my Scotch and smiled at her. "You just learn to ignore it. After a while, you become numb enough that it doesn't hurt as bad."

"Well, what about your other brother. Alan? Is that his name?"

"Oh, poor Alan. A completely different sort. His existence in the family was largely ignored, unless he excelled at something, which captured Mom's attention, then she would mention it to Dad. If the achievement met with his approval, he would grunt and make some obscure remark of subtle praise. That was the best Alan ever got."

"Jesus, Sue. I'm beginning to believe your family really *is* dysfunctional. Did Alan grow up to be a misfit or something?"

"No. He was largely left to his own devices. He spent most of his time with his network of friends from school. He was the kind of kid everyone wanted to be friends with. Quiet, considerate, smart, and willing to be a part of any activity. He was happiest with his friends."

"Well, it seems odd that your family would ignore him."

"Oh, he was fine with it all. He was also happy when left on his own. He was quite creative. He loved assembling plastic airplane models. He had a whole wall full of them. And he was always building things. Mom would bring home wooden fruit crates from the grocery stores to feed his passion for making birdhouses, garages for his toy trucks, and even a crèche for Mom to display at Christmas."

She sipped her Scotch and almost laughed. "I guess I got the wrong impression about him. He sounds like someone I would like."

"Yes," I said. "I think you would."

"What about Dennis?"

"Dennis was inclined to just hang out with his band of friends, some of them questionable, but it kept him away from the house."

Melinda seemed to melt into the chair, the glass of Scotch in her hand. "You know, I had a terrible time leaving home. My mother cried and cried. I think it almost killed her to see me go."

I chuckled. "Well, I had no problem with that at all. When we grew up, each of us kids had gone his own way, much to the relief, I suppose, of Mom and Dad. Especially, Dad."

"Why would your parents be relieved? I'd think they'd be sad."

"Remember, my dad was a cheapskate. The grocery bill was cut, no extra cars in the driveway, the water bill decreased drastically, and he could enjoy the peace and quiet. There was no more college tuition and other expenses to pay and no more teenagers running through the house."

She looked at me in disbelief.

"Once Dennis, Alan, and I left home, our lives diverged. Dennis attended college for a year until he flunked out. Then he enlisted in the army for two years, married Jackie, and moved to Southwest Oklahoma and joined a commercial credit firm. He went to night school to get his associate degree in business management."

"Well," she said, "it sounds like he did all right by himself. What about Alan?"

"Alan also attended college and stayed in ROTC. He joined the flight training program. He was commissioned a second lieutenant at graduation and reported for duty at Fort Belvoir, Virginia, then flight school, and a year and half later, he was sent to Vietnam to fly helicopters."

"Oh, my God. Really? I can't imagine what that would be like. He wasn't hurt, was he?"

"No. When he returned, he worked on a dam with the Corps of Engineers for two years and married Carol. Then he got his master's degree in architectural engineering and became a professional engineer in Oklahoma City."

"What's an architectural engineer?"

"He designs the structure for buildings."

"I've never known anyone like that."

"I hadn't either until he told me what it was. I don't think Mom and Dad completely understood, either."

I finished my glass of Scotch and was totally relaxed. Then I wondered why I was telling all of this to Melinda. I never talked about myself like this. But it felt so good to get it all out.

"Several years later, he and Carol relocated to Harrison, Oklahoma, where they built their own log house."

"Seriously? A log house? Oh, Jesus. I've always wanted to live in a log house."

"You'd like this one. I certainly do."

"I guess you've stayed there?"

"Oh, yeah. Several times. I love it. I could live there forever."

"You are so lucky." Melinda finished her glass of Scotch, too. "So, what did you do after college?"

"After I graduated, I found a job as a social worker in Oklahoma City, and later moved here to work at the women's shelter. I found a nice small apartment for a couple of years, then moved here."

"Your family seems so…self-sufficient. I still rely on my folks for a lot of things. Fortunately, my sister and brother live nearby. We see each other quite often."

"I'm glad for you. My brothers and I were aimed in very different directions. We lost touch over time. We hardly call or see each other. Well, I see Alan more than Dennis. Even family gatherings on holidays became victims to our indifference."

Melinda frowned at me. "That's just so sad. How do you do that? Not seeing your brothers?"

"Oh, we've had our share of get-togethers. But when the folks got older, they had their share of health issues, Dad with his heart condition. A triple bypass. And Mom with her diagnosis of Parkinson's Disease that was complicated by the onset of Alzheimer's Disease. I wasn't able to help, due to my work here, and Dennis and his wife, Jackie, had little inclination to upset their lives to offer any assistance. I really don't think they understood the complexity and burden of the diseases that forced Mom into a world of confusion and fear. That left Alan and his wife, Carol, to shoulder the load, along with Dad."

"Oh, Sue. I'm so sorry. I had no idea."

"Anyway, when that became too difficult for Dad to handle alone, Alan suggested that they moved to Harrison where Alan and Carol lived. They could look after them. They put a mobile home on Alan's property. They lived in the country, so there was plenty of room."

"That was so good of Alan to do that. I wonder what will happen when my parents get really old."

I sat up a bit straighter and looked at Melinda.

"I was always skeptical of Dennis, though. He and Jackie wound up with two kids, Brent and Becky. After Dennis got his degree, they moved around the country chasing higher paid jobs and more perks and benefits. Dennis began gaining weight and developed a hideously large stomach that gave him the appearance of a short, fat shyster, as Dad would have called him. Jackie also put on her share of weight."

"Gosh, my brother is skinny as a rail. And my sister is, too."

"Alan, bless his heart, managed to maintain his appearance

and became an exercise fanatic. Later, he delved into healthy eating, and gave frequent lectures to us, which we promptly ignored. I was content to maintain the status quo of my lifestyle and leave everyone else to his own devices. I was happy with my work and proud of myself to be able to help so many women and their children."

"You should be proud of that," said Melinda. "You're doing good work."

"I like to think so."

"Sue? I'm amazed that you turned out as special as you did. If I'd had to live with all of that I'd have been a raving lunatic."

I looked at her, smirking. "Ah, you're not too bad, Melinda. At least you've been patient enough to let me vent."

"Well, I have to admit, I've learned a lot about you in the last hour."

"Has it been that long?"

"Yes, dearie. Look at where the sun is. Or almost isn't."

She was right. The long shadows had all but disappeared, the light was fading. I hadn't noticed that it had become cooler. The dinging of the roof had increased its tempo. And I had just bared the soul of my family to my neighbor, who I only knew by brief encounters as we came and went from our apartments. I was almost embarrassed at having given up so much about myself, but at the same time it felt comforting, exhilarating, to finally let it all out.

Melinda said she needed to get back to her apartment and make some phone calls. She left in a strangely buoyant mood, very much different from when she first came over. Maybe my confessions had done something to brighten her day. Maybe I had given her something to satisfy her curiosity about me. And maybe she was just happy. I wish it was so simple.

I continued to sit there, Scotch in hand, thinking about our conversation. I suppose our family wasn't that much different from any other. Who knows what really goes on in the privacy of their homes? Maybe it's just my wishful thinking that we could have been more affectionate, more considerate. But that's not the way our folks were raised, so that's not the way we were raised.

They raised us to leave home, to be independent, on our own. I'm pretty sure they didn't want us hanging around mooching off of them all of our lives. I don't think I would have wanted my kids, if I'd had any, to do that, either.

I spent the rest of the evening watching a corny Hallmark movie and promptly went to bed.

THE CALL

December 2001

The damn phone! My hand wandered over unrecognizable items on the nightstand until it finally landed on something that felt like a cell phone.

"Hello." I finally said, louder than I should have from within my sleep-induced stupor. Why didn't I clean the bedroom last weekend? I hate housework of any kind, but sometimes the filth just got too bad to take. I glanced at the clock beside the bed; it was just after two o'clock. In the morning. It was dark and cold as hell. Was the heat even on? Hell, it was forty-five degrees outside when I went to bed. That cold front must have arrived.

I could hear it; the cold, that is. The bing and bonk of the metal roof over the patio as it contracted in the cool air. It would do the same when the sun came out in the morning, if it came out at all. Hell, who needed an alarm clock?

"Sue, it's Jackie."

My sister-in-law. Dennis' wife. The one with the voice that sounded like a dull saw chewing through words, if that's possible, with an occasional squeak or two for emphasis. I had two of them. The other one was Carol. Alan's wife. A sweet thing, but with a good head on her shoulders. Down to earth. At least she kept Alan grounded and out of trouble. Most of the time.

Two sisters-in-law to keep my competitive skills sharpened. Two brothers would have been enough, at least, for the kind of brothers they were. So different from each other. I'd never married. I didn't place much hope in finding a man that wasn't fucked up with too much ego. Although, if Alan hadn't been my brother, I would have given him a second look. Besides, I was too busy with my career, dedicated, consumed with planning for the future. I thought it was a smart move. Kind of like Alan, I suppose. I just wish Dennis had been busy with his future, but he couldn't seem to keep a job long enough to stabilize.

After a day of facing heckling attorneys and bill collectors at the women's shelter that I managed, I had already resigned myself to taking whatever disagreeable news might come from the call. What the hell did Jackie want? She didn't call that often, thank God. Hardly ever. Two o'clock. The only time the phone rang at this hour was to bring bad news.

"Hi, Jackie. Good to hear from you."

"Sue…"

Of course, there was always some reason for her calling, usually to tell me they wouldn't be able to attend a family get-together.

A series of noises burst over the phone. Was she choking?

"It's Dennis," she said, finally, her voice weak and unsteady.

My brain stopped. I said nothing, waiting for her to finish whatever she was trying to tell me while I imagined my brother lying dead in some hospital bed or in the street. Not that I'd had premonitions of such a tragedy, but it was the way Jackie said his name, as if she had just seen him for the last time.

"He's had a heart attack," she said between sobs. "They took him to Baptist Memorial."

A heart attack? Wait…a heart attack. There they were, the memories of all the times I had wondered what it would be like to get this call. You think about things like that, but you never really expect them to happen. They just remain things to think about. Until they happen. Dennis' fifty-eight years had caught up with him. That and his smoking and gluttony.

I had no idea where Baptist Memorial was and had no inclination to ask right then. I was still assimilating what she had just said. Aside from thinking about actually getting a call like this. I had often wondered how long it would be before Dennis succumbed to a heart attack. The fat son of a bitch. He stuffed himself with artery-clogging food that was battered, buttered, or fried. He smoked hard, and sat on his ass most of his life for the last three decades; a walking coronary. His stomach had grown to the point that he could no longer see his feet. Uncle Charles always joked about Dennis having "Dunlop's Disease", where his "belly done lopped over his belt." It was funny to a point, but I grew to detest the family making light of his situation.

Then it hit me. My brother had had a heart attack. I knew I should have felt some kind of empathy for him, and especially, Jackie, but I just couldn't get my mind around that. Empathy? Sympathy? What? Feeling something like that for a slob that was slowly killing himself and didn't care?

Well, there was this fleeting moment where I felt some kind of …what? Sorrow? Grief? Fear? I don't know. I just felt my chest tighten for some reason I couldn't explain. Oh, it was Dennis' heart attack, all right, but I couldn't say how I honestly felt about it.

What was I supposed to say? What did Jackie want me to say?

"How bad is he?" I finally asked.

"Bad," Jackie fired back. "The doctor said he needs a heart transplant."

Fucking hell. A heart transplant? What had just happened?

"What do you mean?"

"They said his heart is working at only twenty percent capacity." There was another pause filled with sobs and choking sounds. "They've put him on the transplant list."

A heart transplant. The second salvo hit me. A mere heart attack, hell, people had those all the time, and I'd even expected it at some point in the future. But a heart transplant? I recalled visions of heart transplant documentaries I'd seen on television; the chest laid open like a field-dressed deer under masked faces, sweat being wiped from foreheads, bloody hands with shiny instruments plunging into that most personal cavity of a body. Watching those shows never bothered me, but then, as I envisioned Dennis lying on that table, surrounded in green sheets and smocks, masks, and glove-covered hands, it felt like someone just kicked the air out of my lungs. I imagined it was like the baseball hitting Alan in the chest in the sixth grade, knocking the air out of him. He just stood there, looking dazed, not breathing. Finally, it passed and he was okay. I had thought he was dying.

I'd have to call Alan. Then I could ask to take off work and plan to travel to Oklahoma City, if that's where Baptist Memorial was. It wasn't something I wanted to do, but, after all, Dennis *was* my brother, not that *that* had ever motivated him to give a shit about Alan or me. Dennis never seemed to give a shit about anybody.

"Christ, Jackie." I had to give her something. "Are you okay?"

A sniffle. "I'm okay, Sue." Another sniffle. "I just don't know what I'm going to do if I lose him."

Upon hearing that, I instantly thought of several things she could be doing to drag her out of the complacent idolatry she showed toward Dennis. She could go back to school. She could get her realtor's license renewed. She could do any number of things to improve her life. None of those things would have occurred to her right then, not in her state of mind. But then I thought about her real situation and why she had married Dennis in the first place.

Then I caught myself. He was my brother, for Christ's sake. I had to get off of that tirade.

And, what about Becky and Brent? Her two kids should be able to help, if they would. Their family was no closer than ours had been.

Jackie was never an independent spirit. Not particularly beautiful but pleasing to look at. Tall. Taller than Dennis, and outgoing, like he was. Brown eyes, big nose, and hair sweeping down beside her face ending in outward curls. The sixties. What a time that was.

When I met her for the first time, I had recognized the empty ambition. She really had none, or so I thought. I knew she would depend upon my brother for all of her emotional needs, not that Dennis was capable of providing that kind of reassuring support, unless he found some way to reinforce his own station in life as a result of it. That had become the mainstay of their marriage.

"Where is the hospital?"

"It's at the Northwest Expressway and I-44."

Oklahoma City, as I had thought.

"Listen, I'll make arrangements to get up there."

"Okay. Thanks, Sue."

"Do the kids know?"

"I called them. They said they'd be here when they could."

I hoped they would. It's not like they were a close family, but then, none of us were that close.

Jackie's call came a week after Dad's burial, and I was thrown into a state of chaos. Arrangements would have to be made for probate. I wondered how Alan would take the news about the heart attack. I could almost see him gloating, smiling that scoffing grin that says, "I told you so." He and Dad both had issues with Dennis. I think Dad always felt he was a disappointment, and Alan thought he was…now that I think about it, I'm not sure what Alan ever really thought about his older brother. I always tried to look at Dennis as someone who had come to terms with who and what he was and was happy with what he had accomplished. But then I wondered if maybe he hadn't come to terms with it at all, and maybe he wasn't that happy. I know I damned sure wasn't.

Family dynamics are funny. A dysfunctional family doesn't usually realize that they're dysfunctional. They just can't see what should be so obvious to everyone else, even when they play their roles as an everyday, ordinary family to perfection. We have kidded ourselves our entire lives, thinking we lived the same lives as everyone else. Now, I saw it. I recognized it for what it was. We were so fucked up.

THE SECOND CALL

December 2001

Before I called Alan, I sat motionless on the bed allowing my mind wander into that treacherous field of introspection. Would I lose Dennis? Had his life been purposeful? Noteworthy? Was mine? I had endured a family with two brothers, a father that had no clue as to what to do with me, and a mother that fell a bit short in passing down her knowledge of how to deal with all of that. But I persevered and earned a bachelor's degree in social work. I worked my way up the ladder to a management position at a women's shelter, and I've loved every minute of it. I have made a good life for myself, as much as my work allows, and I consider myself successful. Although I never married, I'm content.

Dennis, the oldest, in spite of his short attention span and insecurity, flunked out of college after one year, enlisted in the army for two years, then married Jackie. After his discharge, he put himself through college at night school and got his associate degree in business management. He has a family that supports him and has made a good life for himself and his family. If you overlook their arrogance and air of superiority, you'll find a typical American family swathed in opportunities for success. It's just that they have overlooked so many of them. Dennis had his redeeming moments that Alan and I often overlooked. Maybe it's that our expectations get in the way of our perspectives. I know he deserved better than what we gave him.

And then there's Alan. The enigma of the family. He was always shy and reserved, but an astute observer. And smart. Well Dennis was smart, too, but not like Alan. Learning seemed to come easily to him. He hardly studied in school, and when he did, he was focused on that and nothing else, excelled in college and stayed in ROTC, including flight training. Upon graduation, he was commissioned as a second lieutenant. After officers basic and flight training, he was sent to Vietnam to fly helicopters in a war that had ravaged and killed so many. When he came back, he was stationed at a dam with the Corps of Engineers. Somehow, he found the wonderful woman he married. After his discharge he got his master's degree in architectural engineering and became a professional engineer. He and Carol had a brilliant child who inherited the best of both of her parents. If it hadn't have been for Vietnam, there's no telling what Alan could have accomplished. Those dark memories and demons seem to have bridled his initiative and held great accomplishments at bay.

I didn't know what to expect when I. called Alan. I braced myself as I dialed the phone.

The phone rang tree times before a voice said, "Hello."

I was surprised Alan sounded…not exactly alert, but not groggy. I guess that's what the army does to a person. Once you start getting up before dawn, you don't linger in bed for half the morning.

"Alan, it's Sue." I gave him a minute for that to sink in. "Sorry to wake you."

"Sue?"

I noticed the alarm in his response.

"Jackie just called."

"At…" A pause. "At two-thirty in the morning?"

Before I could answer—

"Oh hell. Dennis?"

"He's had a heart attack."

"Shit."

"He's in Baptist Memorial in Oklahoma City."

"Is he okay?"

"Jackie says it's bad. He's on the heart transplant list."

All I heard was breathing.

"Alan?"

"What the hell?"

I could almost hear him thinking about Dennis and all of the times Alan had thrown his lifestyle in his face.

"A heart transplant?" I heard heavy breathing "Seriously? A heart transplant?"

"According to his doctor. He's on the transplant list. Jackie said his heart was working at only twenty percent capacity. I figure he's lucky to be alive."

"What hospital did you say he's in?"

"Baptist Memorial."

"I know where that is. We'll get there sometime later today."

"I'm planning to drive up. Could I stay at your house?"

"Of course. We'll wait for you to get here. We might want to wait until tomorrow to go."

"I think that will be all right. I might be a bit rushed today."

I listened to the silence for a moment.

"Sue?"

"Yeah, Alan?"

"Do you think he'll make it?"

I didn't know what to say to that.

"I really don't know, Alan. I really don't."

Another break in the conversation.

After a sigh from Alan's end, "The stupid son of a bitch."

Oh, God. There he went.

"What the hell," he said.

More silence.

"I knew this was going to happen," he said. "Hell, we both did."

"Yes," I said, "and it has."

"So, what do we do?"

"We go see what we can do."

"How is Jackie taking it?"

"It's hard to tell. Of course, she sounded awful. Crying, I imagined. Stressed. Worried. We really need to be there for her."

"What about Becky and Brent?"

"Jackie said they were coming."

"Good. At least she won't be alone."

"Who is it?" I heard Carol in the background.

"Jackie," Alan said to her. "Dennis has had a heart attack."

"Oh, no! Is he okay?" Carol asked in the background.

"He's at Baptist Memorial. He's on the transplant list."

"A heart transplant?" Carols' shocked voice sounded closer this time.

"Listen, Sue, let us make arrangements to get to the city. We'll be waiting for you. We'll talk then. I'm going to call Teresa at college and let her know."

"Okay, Alan. Sorry about Dennis. I look forward to seeing you all. Bye."

That had gone better than expected. I just hoped Alan didn't get on his high horse and start preaching about the virtues of healthy lifestyles. I knew I could change some of the stupid things I did, but sometimes it just didn't seem worth giving up things I do as a habit. It was too far from my comfort zone.

I sat back down on the bed and my eyes caught the photo of Alan graduating from college, standing straight as a board in his army uniform. God, he looked good. I was so proud of him. That's when he got his commission as a second lieutenant, about sixteen months before he was sent to Vietnam. We were all on pins and needles during that time, wondering if we would ever see him again. Of course, we all watched the news reports about the Vietnam War every night and I know each of us worried. It seemed like more and more soldiers were being killed or went missing in action. We were all so surprised when he showed up at Winfield eleven months later, not a scratch on him.

Then I saw the picture of Dennis in his army uniform. He was a good-looking man, handsome, fit. It was such a disappointment when he dropped out of college. I imagine it was all of the partying at his fraternity.

God, I remember that fraternity at Oklahoma State University. Alpha Tau Omega.

I had just opened a letter from Oklahoma State University, College of Human Sciences. That's where I got my bachelor's degree in human services. Like Alan, I entered college right after high school. Dad was footing the bill, so I took advantage of it.

I'd always wanted to do social work, helping people. I was never sure what prompted my interest in it, but I suspect it might have been watching Alan suffer through his childhood. I don't think my own childhood was any worse than anyone else's. I had endured a family with two brothers, a father that had no clue as to what to do with me, and a mother that fell a bit short in passing down her knowledge of how to deal with all of that. But I persevered and earned a bachelor's degree. I worked my way up the ladder to a management position at a women's shelter. I love every minute of it. I have made a good life for myself, as much as my work allows, and I consider myself successful. Although I never married, I'm content.

Then there's Alan. Alan had extenuating circumstances that shaped his character into someone who was driven and, I suppose I could call it angry. I felt so sorry for both of them. That's who we are. No one really has much choice of who they become. Some of it is luck. Some of it is a result of choices. I think most of it is what life does to you. Or for you.

Life must go on, and our lives are still moving forward through whatever is thrown at us.

THE DRIVE TO HARRISON

January 2002

During the unsettling drive to Harrison, I could focus only on memories. The early times I had spent with Dennis. High school had been difficult for both of us. Dennis had to work hard, when he had a mind to, to keep even a C average. Had he spent less time harassing Alan and me, might have done much better. But, he did manage to graduate and then off he went to college. As it turned out, he had much the same problem there with his grades. In fact, it was a bit worse. I suspect most of it was due to his fraternity.

After the family visited Dennis at his fraternity at Oklahoma State University one fall during his first and only year there, I became enchanted with the campus. The fraternity, Alpha Tau Omega, didn't impress me, nor did the sorority houses that lined University Avenue. The members of Dennis' fraternity certainly didn't give me any reason to believe that they were any better than any other students there. I was never sure why Dennis decided to join. He really didn't fit the frat-pack style and seemed intimidated by it all. He had invited the family to dine at his fraternity house one Sunday. I think it was required of all the new members. We showed up in our Sunday finest, Dad in a suit he hadn't worn for years, Mom in one of her Sunday dresses she had made over, me in my Sunday outfit, and Alan in a black suit and white shirt that Mom had just bought for him two days before, and one of Dad's old ties.

We met the house mother, a sweet old lady named Beatrice. She looked after the boys and did the cooking for them.

A fellow named John presided over the dinner, and he had Dennis introduce Mom, Dad, Alan and me, to the fraternity brothers, who sat leaning over the table in expectation of food. Being a senior in high school, I had already taken notice of boys and quickly learned the subtle art of taking their measure. Most of the boys in my school were not exactly the exciting type and seemed to be possessed with an obnoxious silliness, a holdover, I suppose, from their childhoods. But the young men sitting around the table gawking at me with lascivious stares ignited my adolescence. I felt like jumping up and strutting around the room to elicit whatever hungry attention I could garner from their lustful anxiety.

After the precursory scrutiny of my desirability, they all examined us, one by one, most of them smiling when their eyes met Alan's.

I suspected that the smiles were a reaction to their assessment of his character. Not necessarily smiles of approval, but more like smirks. They probably thought he was a wimp. He *was* kind of a baby-faced kid. He stared back at them with a blank look, the one he gave Dennis whenever he made a derogatory remark, his only defense. What a bunch of pussies. It would be only three years before Alan would be in that same university knocking the socks off of their mediocre academic accomplishments.

Dad surveyed the lot of them with skepticism. Since he had left school after the eighth grade to help support his struggling family, higher education was foreign to him, and I figured the upstarts, there, at the table, appeared to him to be spoiled brats. He wasn't expecting the young whippersnappers to talk to him. Then one of them did.

"Mr. Carter, what do you do?"

"I, ah..." George put his fork down, leaning back in his chair with a regal look on his face. "I own a hardware store," he said, pride bursting forth. I knew he was proud of what he had accomplished. I was, too, and dad was not bashful about letting other people know, especially his neighbors. He would survey the surrounding houses for signs of a neighbor outside, then amble over to offer unsolicited advice, which, even though the person dreaded to hear it, the advice usually worked. He was not that popular in his neighborhood. What friends they had was because of Mom.

One of the other young men chimed in.

"So, you're in retail."

"Yeah," replied George. We'd never thought of it that way. It sounded impressive. His chest ballooned out just a bit.

"What's it like," asked another, "owning your own business, I mean."

Dad seemed stumped. He'd never really talked about what it was like. He merely took care of business, day by day. Merchandise flew out the door and money flew in. That's what it was about. There was no need to labor on the meaning of it all, just do it.

"Well, ah..." Dad was still stumped. He struggled to find words. "Well, I manage the inventory, keep the books, and make my own decisions. It's been pretty profitable."

The inquirer's eyes opened a bit wider, and his mouth opened in a bit of awe. Silence seemed to drift around the table as Dad's words slowly sank in. They were all probably thinking, "Gets to make his own decisions. It's profitable." That was something they could all get behind. There, in the new world of freedom and inspiration, making their own decisions and making money was held in high regard, an almost sacred privilege.

Small talk consumed the table with no one uttering any words of significant value to the conversations. Alan ignored them for the most part, focusing, instead, on Dennis, who hunched over his plate like a vulture over carrion. A fork he clenched in his fist like a toddler, laboring to heave huge gobs of food into the gaping mouth that closed around it in a strained manner necessary to allow some amount of chewing to take place without spewing its contents back into the plate. Being a southpaw, his elbow, braced in a horizontal plane just level with the fellow's shoulder on his left, jostled the young man and the food was jarred form his fork. Dennis paid it no mind and thrust the wad of food into the dark crater behind his lips. .

Alan watched in fascination and disgust, apparently wondering how his brother managed to cram so much food into his mouth and still process it without choking. It was embarrassing, knowing that others must certainly be watching, too, and probably thinking what a gross specimen he was. I remember thinking, why did we have to have *him* for a brother? Why couldn't we have had a brother that was actually a brother? Of course, I'd rarely had good luck to begin with, and that explained a lot. Later, I would chastise myself for thinking such a thing.

In the meantime, Mom was also watching Dennis make a fool of himself with his primitive eating habits. She'd tried everything she could think of to correct his repulsive manners, but to no avail. It was like trying to teach a cow how to dance. She swallowed her frustration and, I thought, hoped the meal would not last long. I hoped people weren't staring at her, wondering how she could have raised such a crass simpleton.

Dad, on the other hand, was watching the table, eagerly awaiting more inquiries about his "retailing" expertise. I bet he thought he could show those young bucks, as he called them, a thing or two about how it was done, because that's what he usually thought about everybody. These young, snooty bastards, he would call them, probably didn't know the first thing about salesmanship or running a business. He would be telling them, "Hell, I didn't even go to high school, much less college, and look at what I've accomplished?"

It was true that he'd built a business from near bankruptcy into a thriving retail store that held much acclaim with the folks who shopped there. He was putting a son through college and paying off the mortgage ahead of time. Plus, he'd just bought that brand new 1963 Buick LeSabre with a 265 horsepower V-8 sitting out by the curb. Yeah, he knew how to do it.

Alan noticed that everyone's plates had been emptied while he had been daydreaming, and everyone was now sitting back silently waiting for the first brave soul to signal a formal end to the dinner and leave. John finally stood and announced that the dinner was finished.

That's when Dennis almost jumped out of his chair and rushed around the table to escape outside, hoping the rest of us would follow. We did.

"That was a good meal," Mom said. "Do you eat like that all the time?"

Dennis looked at her, a funny half grin on his face.

"Well, not all the time," he said, thrusting his hands into his pockets. "Mostly when company comes."

"Say," Dad broke in. "I noticed some of those young bucks in there were dressed pretty fancy."

"Oh, they're the ones that try to show out for everybody," Dennis told him. "The rest of us just wear regular stuff."

I started wandering away and one of the frat boys caught up with me.

"Hi," he said, his voice uncertain. "I'm Simon."

"Hello, Simon," I said. "I enjoyed the dinner."

"Oh," he gave a chuckle. "We do that whenever we have company." We walked on a bit. "Hey, do you live in a dorm?"

I looked at him. I could see anticipation in his face, lust in his eyes.

"Me?" I asked, raising a hand to my chest. "Heavens no. I'm a senior in high school."

His eyes grew curious. "Oh, well, here in town? I mean, it would be nice to see you again."

I felt my heart flutter, its rejoinder to the affections of an older man. I hardly could speak.

Alan suddenly appeared in front of us. "Hey, Sis."

Simon looked at him, a bit of anger in his eyes.

"You're Alan, right?"

"Yeah," Alan replied, a smirk on his face.

"Actually," I said, turning toward Simon, "I'm just visiting. But I hope to go here next year."

Simon flashed a big smile. "Great. I'll look you up."

We nodded and he left.

"Was that guy hitting on you?" Alan asked.

"Yes, he was. It was very sweet."

"What a jerk."

I looked at him, almost upset. "Why do you think he's a jerk? I thought he was very nice."

"God, Sue. Didn't you notice? He had a hardon the whole time he was talking to you."

The shock took me out of my reverie. I couldn't believe Alan said that, the little shit. For a few moments I had tasted some of the fruits of college life and an excitement that had burst through me like electricity. Yeah, this was the place.

We walked on down the sidewalk a ways. Alan, while taking in all of this, surveyed the surrounding buildings, all more elaborate than the ATΩ house. He stopped, arms crossed over his chest.

"Do you think this place is okay? I mean, look at all of these other houses. They're a lot more ornate than this one. I mean, it's like a cottage more than a frat house."

I took a look around. He was right. Then I thought about Dennis and his grade point average.

"Well, I doubt that it's the best fraternity. Dennis didn't have the best grades in the world, you know. I doubt the more prestigious houses would take him."

We both looked at the trees dripping yellow, red and brown leaves on the sidewalk.

"I suspect this fraternity is just a party place that gives its members an excuse to drink and have stupid bashes.

My eye caught the shimmering golden leaves of huge trees a couple of houses down the street. Alan saw it, too. The view, filtered through leaves drifting to the street and walks gave the impression of an almost hallowed place, a haven of knowledge, a sanctum of learning. The campus was emblazoned with an indelible aura of what I had dreamed of. Then, I wondered, what was Dennis doing there?

I made up my mind right there that I was going to Oklahoma State University. My grades were good and my determination even better. The next year would be filled with studying.

"I'm going here," Alan said, all of a sudden, looking at me with a determined face. "This is where I want to go to college."

I looked at him with admiration. I wasn't surprised. I knew he would make it in college. He would probably excel at it.

"Yes, Alan, I'll bet you do."

At least he wouldn't have Dennis around to hamper his efforts.

Denis and Alan had looked so sharp in their suits. It had been a very pleasant day, and I had enjoyed being with my brothers. In spite of whatever conflicts arose between them. Strangely enough, *that* hadn't happened that day.

More memories entered my mind, an already crowded conglomeration of images and thoughts and feelings stepping over each other, Dennis in the foreground.

ICU

January 2002

I had arrived at Alan's the night before. It would have been a shorter trip to meet him at the hospital, but I wanted to be with him before we traveled to the hospital.

We took my car that morning; Carol sat in back so Alan and I could talk.

"So," Alan said, "do you think it's really bad?"

"Yes, I do" I told him. "Jackie was stressed. If Denis' heart is at only twenty percent capacity, well, that pretty much tells the story. I think he's lucky to be alive."

Alan just shook his head.

Carol leaned forward. "Brent and Becky will be there, right?"

"She said they would. I just don't know when."

We rode in silence for a while.

"I didn't know what to tell my boss," I said. "I have no idea what all we'll be getting into. We kind of left it open, for now."

"Yeah," said Alan. "I don't either. I took off a few days. I'll see how it goes."

Alan directed me to the hospital, and I pulled into the east parking lot in front of the main entrance. Due to limited parking, I let Alan and Carol out at the door and looked for a place to park. I ended up parking in the south forty. I had spotted a space close to the entrance, but just as I approached it some asshole in one of those small smart-assed sports cars zipped in front of me and took it. I honked and gave him the finger. As he locked his car, he turned toward me and laughed. He kept laughing on his way to the entrance. I was in no mood to be fucked with. I pulled up behind his car, found a screwdriver in the glovebox and got out. His license plate was easily removed. Getting back in my car, I searched for another parking space, finding one in the next lot over about a five-minute hike to the entrance. As I approached the main doors, I dropped the license plate into a trash can sitting just outside the building.

The fetter of antiseptics hovered in the bland, soulless foyer of the hospital, a warning to all who passed through to not look for happiness within its walls. However, the horizontal metal channels or tubes that ran across the ceiling did present a more attractive surface than the usual tacky suspended ceiling tiles. Irregularly placed walls in various colors failed to define the large space as anything other than a hospital. Footsteps, voices, trolleys, telephones, and the swish of elevator doors echoed from the hard surfaces characteristic of modern architecture. All they did for me was to stir up memories of the hospital where my mother died, a vision I can never forget.

I saw Carol at the elevator in her usual gray winter flannel pants, black moccasin shoes, and white sweater top. I had paid no attention to her attire in the car. She was the same height as me but with longer legs, her auburn hair, long and straight, curled under at the ends, and the bright green eyes, belied her forty-eight years. Carol's somewhat countrified look and awkward smile seemed to calm me. I had worn slacks, as I usually did, with a sweater top.

"So, are you ready for this?" I said, approaching. We had talked about it in the car, and our conversation included the shelter where I worked and Teresa's experiences at college.

"I almost dread seeing him," she said. "I feel awful about this."

"No need," I told her. "It should have been a shock, but you know what? Alan and I have been anticipating this for years. We just never knew when it would happen."

Her reaction startled me. There was a question in her eyes, and I knew what it was.

"Carol, you know as well as I that Dennis didn't exactly take care of himself. It was bound to happen eventually."

She sighed and nodded, then turned to go to the elevators.

"Alan is waiting upstairs," she said. "He wanted to see Jackie."

Our shoes scuffed the white and gray floor, echoes following us, toward the elevator. I pressed the button for the eighth floor to the intensive care unit.

"I'm anxious to talk to Jackie," I told her. "She sounded terrible on the phone." I looked at her, a slight frown on her face. "What about Alan? Has he said anything to you about it?"

Her eyes had that vacant look, the one she had whenever she didn't understand something.

"That, I don't know for sure."

"No indication of how he feels?"

"I can't read him. I can't figure out how he's handling this."

I knew only too well what she was saying. Hell, I grew up never knowing how the little shit felt about anything. As the years passed, I watched him change from an emotional billboard when he was not yet in school into a forbearing, introspective bastion of anger, frustration, and contempt, never once yielding to the need for retribution. Even deaths in our family couldn't break through the stone-cold façade.

Carol looked straight at me. "Well, I think I know what he's thinking, and you probably do, too. But I'm not sure how this is really affecting him."

We both studied the silence, broken only by the hum of the elevator and the dismal lighting that turned everything into a presage of death. I knew exactly what she meant. Alan had a poker face that could win a world championship poker game. He never showed any hint of what was on his mind.

"Well," she continued, "Alan never did show a lot of emotion when his parents died. Kind of stoical, detached."

"Yes, I remember him just staring into space." In a flash I recalled sitting there in Mom's hospital room, him on one side of the bed, me on the other, each of us holding one of her hands. He never cracked a smile, a frown, a grimace or a tear. Nothing. Even when she finally gave up and passed away, nothing.

Even at Uncle Harvey's funeral Alan just hung in the background with that almost disengaged look on his face watching everyone else blubber and carry on as if the world was ending. I knew he was affected by our uncle's death, and maybe he was just angry that it had happened. But Carol was right. Alan never showed much emotion.

The doors opened onto a desolate and depressing hallway, white and gray floor, yellowish-brown walls, ochre, maybe, and there, in a dreary, upholstered rigid-backed chair, obviously selected to complement the hospital's death-provoking décor, Jackie was sprawled like a deadpan drunk after a long night of celebration. Alan was standing in the hall, hands in his pockets, looking like a trapped animal wanting to be somewhere else. Average height and slight build, it would have been a challenge for anyone to guess that he had been an army pilot flying helicopters in Vietnam. He seemed so...normal, or at least that's what anyone would assume. He still had a bit of that military bearing, having never quite given it up. His time in Vietnam wore at the family's stamina, our parents the worst. He always carried himself proudly even though he never talked about his time there. His eyes, though, let me know that there were many stories behind them, things he'd never want to talk about. Even his cute mustache signaled secrets.

I hadn't seen Jackie or Dennis since Christmas two years earlier, when they begrudgingly made the trip to Alan's house in Harrison to partake of the holiday boredom with our parents. Jackie had put on weight. A lot of it. Even though she was a tall woman, she was looking more like Humpty Dumpty. The artificially blonde, frazzled hair hung to her shoulders like a lifeless pelt thrown over her head. Her long face was not necessarily attractive, but pleasant in an amicable sort of way. Dennis selected her so that he would look good beside her.

"Oh, hi, guys," Jackie said, forcing herself up from the chair with feeble arms. It reminded me of one of Carol's brother's lame cows that couldn't get up from the ground; he'd finally had to shoot her.

"Thanks for coming," she said, almost panting from the effort, her long face fuller than I remembered.

Jackie and Carol did their girl thing with a brief hug, while I watched Jackie perform the charade of strength as Carol talked to her. During a lull in their conversation, I moved in for a hug. Alan remained aloof, carefully watching everyone. Jackie's emotional control surprised me, and it occurred to me that she might be able to survive this tragedy with a minimum of damage.

"How bad is it, really?" I asked Jackie.

"The doctor said his heart is only working at about twenty percent capacity. Apparently, he's been having mini-heart attacks all along. Dennis just thought it was indigestion."

I remembered the last Christmas dinner with them. Dennis was in a chair in their parents' mobile home at Alan's place. After dinner when Dennis fell into a chair, he stiffened and grimaced, holding one the arms of the chair. He must have been having one of those attacks then.

"He's in room three," Jackie told us. "You can go on back. They only allow two visitors at a time, so I'll stay here."

I went over to Alan. His eyes trained on mine with a look of… what, desperation? I couldn't really tell, but I knew he had to be worried.

He let out a big sigh. "He finally did it."

I nodded. "I just wish it had never happened."

He looked down at the floor. "I do too."

"You've seen him already?"

"Yeah. Just for a minute."

"How is he?"

"He looks like hell. I'm pretty sure he feels like it, too."

"You want go back with me?"

"Sure."

Alan and I left Carol in the hall with Jackie. From the foot of the bed, I could see only the huge belly rising from it like a snow-covered knoll, Dennis' face hidden behind the huge bulge. A forest of poles with bags hanging like dead vermin surrounded the head of the bed, and other poles held electronic equipment that beeped and chirped in an arrhythmic symphony. Alan hung back while I approached the bed, my mind not on any sympathetic note, but rather thinking about why Dennis had allowed himself to get in this condition. I also toyed with the idea that I should be having some kind of concern for my brother's survival, but that's what a logical mind does to a person. It removes that core of compassion that a normal person would demonstrate. I was pragmatic, if nothing else.

If Dennis survived this, it would be a miracle. And being the agnostic that I am, I did not believe in miracles.

"So, what the hell happened to you?" I looked down on his bloated face, a striking resemblance to an aged William Shatner. It was the kind of face that was full of fun and personality, or it should have been. It almost fit him. He was a couple of inches shorter than Alan and his huge belly seemed to make him look even shorter.

I should talk. I'm not exactly a beauty queen, but I have my moments.

"Hey, Sis. Glad you could come," he mumbled, his voice weak. "I'm not in the best of shape, right now."

"You doing okay?"

His belly jumped from a half-hearted attempt to laugh. "No. I feel like I've been run over by a truck."

"That might have been preferable."

Another belly-jump. "I'm pretty much out of commission, here." A pause for breath. "All I have to do is wait for those darned nurses to come in and jab me in the butt." Another gasp for air. "I can't even sleep." Gasp. "They're in at all hours of the night checking this and that." A large breath. "I feel like one of those lab rats."

"I imagine the food sucks," Alan said. "I still remember my appendectomy. I starved to death waiting to get home to a decent meal."

"Yes," I confirmed. "Hospital food sucks."

Only one of Dennis' eyes was open, the left one, a large green iris reminding me of an aggie marble the boys used to play with. The other one swollen shut. "Well, at least you don't have to get up and go to work in the mornings."

"I think I'd rather do that than lay here in this damned bed."

"Yeah," Alan grunted. "It's the pits"

I moved closer and took his hand. He squeezed it.

"How's the staff treating you?"

"Most of the nurses are pretty good. There's one spic that comes in at night."

I noticed Alan's head drawing back and a scowl burned itself onto his face. I knew it had to come out sooner or later.

"She's always on my butt about something."

I wondered how he got along with the hospital staff. His idea of joking was usually a string of personal insults, surprising most folks before they figured out how to respond. He could possibly be hastening his own death, there, in that bed.

"Well, we won't stay long. Just wanted to check on you, see if you needed anything."

We all looked at each other, none of us knowing quite what to say.

"Any idea when the transplant will happen?" asked Alan.

"All I know is I'm on the list. They said it could take weeks or months. They just have to find the right donor."

I saw a flash of a grimace on Alan's face. It felt to me like someone had punched me in the stomach. I wondered if he could even last that long.

Dennis finally broke that awkward silence.

"Thanks for coming. Jackie's taking it kind of hard. There's not much I can do for her from in here."

"Jackie seems to be doing okay," said Alan. "We'll do whatever we can for her."

Alan left to return to his wife.

"So, you've caused quite a stir, haven't you, big brother," I told him.

"Not by choice."

"No." I let that go, deciding not to contradict him, the drone of beeps and chirps settling in a bit. "Alan seems to be taking this hard."

"Yeah, well, here's another imposition that he'll never forget. He's like that, you know." A few gasps filled in the silence. "The little shit never forgot one thing I ever did to him." A deep breath. "He never brought them up," gasp, "or tried to shove them down my throat," gasp, "but I knew he was always thinking about them." Another breath. "He's tougher than I thought. No matter what I did," gasp, "he always managed to do something better." Gasp. "The little bastard just couldn't leave it be. He had to outdo me." He trained his green eye on me, a bit of regret in it. "I guess I was never good enough, and Dad never let me forget it, either"—a gasp—"with those off-hand remarks he always made when Alan was around." He closed his eyes as if trying to sleep.

It was quite a monologue for a short-winded man, full of bitterness and contempt. But, of course, I'd seldom heard anything else from him concerning Alan. The only times I could remember any kind remarks were when he was bragging about being the brother of a Vietnam vet, a helicopter pilot, or a professional engineer.

"What the hell brought all of this on?"

His eyes flew open. "Are you going to stand there and tell me your little brother isn't feeling a superiority complex right now?"

"Dennis, I'm not taking sides in this. Whatever quarrel you have with Alan is between you and him."

"Huh. You never could commit one way or the other, could you?"

"Why should I? We're family. None of us should have to take sides against the other. Whatever regrets you have about your life were because of your own choices, not Alan's. You had every opportunity he did."

"You bleeding-heart liberals are all alike."

"You know damned well I'm not a liberal. I'm registered independent, just like Alan. We don't have to have someone else do our thinking for us. We were all put here on Earth to help one another, not fight."

He rolled his eye, and I could see the pain seeping back into his body.

"I should leave and let you get your rest. I certainly don't think that's going to happen while I'm here."

There was no response as I slipped out the door. One of the nurses met me.

"How is my brother behaving?" I asked her.

She smiled and said, "Oh, he's a darling."

"Wait a minute? Are you talking about him?" I said, pointing to the door I just came out of.

"Yes. He's charming. He's one of our favorites."

Words had abandoned me, and I just stood there in a daze while the nurse continued on her way.

I returned to the hallway where Jackie was pouring out her heart to Carol.

What an ass. So, that's what it was all about? He thought he was competing with Alan. I guess it did kind of look that way, but deep down, I knew Alan wasn't trying to outdo his brother. Both of them had great talents. Alan just chose to use his to his advantage. Dennis squandered his on boasting and arrogance.

And what the hell was *I* trying to accomplish? I certainly wasn't competing with either of them. Hell, I couldn't. Being the girl of the family, I was in a completely different league. One they knew nothing about. Dad didn't, either. I wonder if he ever thought of me as successful. He never said one way or the other. Of course, except for Dennis, he never said anything about Alan, either.

All I had left was Dennis and Alan. I didn't want that to change. I don't think I could withstand the loss of Dennis. When your legs are unsteady in life, you need two crutches. One just won't do.

We stopped for dinner on the way out of the city. The ride back to Harrison was long and mostly silent. None of us knew what to say. It's funny what apprehension can do to a person's mind. I tend to withdraw into a vortex of derailed thoughts. I can't seem to focus on any one thing of importance.

The drive back to Dallas I don't even remember. At least it saved me the memory of a long boring trip.

CONFRONTATION

January 2002

It had been over two weeks since we saw Dennis in the ICU ward. He had remained stable and had been well taken care of, according to Jackie. I drove up to Harrison once again to join Alan and Carol for another visit to the hospital. It had gone well. We were all in good spirits and no hostilities broke out. Dennis was optimistic, although concerned about how long he would have to wait for the transplant. Some people had been on a waiting list for nearly a year. Some, even more. I wondered what kind of stress he was under, keeping in mind the financial burden they would be faced with. We didn't stay long and headed back to Harrison that afternoon.

The drive back to Alan's house was quiet, the exhilaration over Dennis having drifted off to parts unknown. It was the kind of quiet that you can hear, like the silent ticking of a clock. A sobering quiet that allowed me a period of introspection.

Alan's stern focus on the road left him with little inclination for conversation, his body rigid behind the steering wheel, which was held captive by clenched hands. Carol, too, seemed out of sorts, her head turned toward the window beside her. Maybe the visit to the hospital hadn't been as smooth as I had thought.

I was happy to have the back seat to myself so I could re-play all the shit that had happened since Jackie's phone call two weeks ago.

As kids, none of us ever considered ourselves to be deprived of love or the necessities of life. What kid thinks about those things, unless he *is* deprived of them? We played, we teased, we squabbled, we cared for each other, although that might not have been apparent to others. We cared in our own way, more of a benign understanding.

And, like other families, we had our battles and skirmishes. Sibling rivalry, they call it. Dennis delivered most of it, and Alan received most of it. What could I have done differently when we were growing up? Was part of it my fault? Could I have helped Alan? Stood up for him more? Tough questions to ponder.

We pulled into Alan's drive and parked in front of the detached garage. In spite of the harsh afternoon sunshine, we were a gloomy lot. I remembered Alan bragging about his shop and all of the things he could do there. I had no reason to doubt him, since he'd built his own house, the log house that hovered over us near the driveway. Two stories, it was, with a porch around the front and part of one side. Maybe having the garage took his mind off whatever was bothering him, like Dennis. Vietnam.

"How about showing me your workshop," I said as we got out of the car, hoping to lighten the mood.

He looked at me as if perplexed, pausing, I supposed, to let my suggestion sink in. He shrugged.

"Sure. Why not?"

Carol and I followed him into the side door of the garage. I breathed in the sweetness of wood, bare wood, that hearty, earthy aroma of wood, Tools lined the walls along with a big lumber rack and storage cabinets. Bits of sawdust, wood shavings, and pieces of wood littered the bare concrete floor.

"So, what are you working on?"

"He's making a cabinet to go over the washer and dryer," Carol said, sitting on a stool. "We've been planning it for a while. He just hasn't had time."

"There's this guy I work with," I said. "Tim McGowan. He's a Vietnam vet. He does woodworking, too. Says it keeps his mind off of Vietnam."

Alan turned to look at me, pensive, almost vacant. Then a brief silence.

"Yeah," he finally said. He took a deep breath and let it out slowly. "That's one way to do it."

Carol eyed him suspiciously.

"Did you ever talk to Dennis about it?"

His eyes caught mine, a question in them.

"Vietnam, I mean."

His jaw tightened. "No." He turned away.

"Did he ever talk to you about when he was in the army?"

Alan laughed. "Oh, yeah," he said. "He told us a bunch of crap that…well, I really don't think even Mom and Dad believed him."

Carol pulled over a stool and sat down taking all of this in.

"Like what?"

"Well, you know he was Spec 4 and assigned to some communications outfit or something like that."

"Yes, I remember. He said he worked with the NSA."

Alan raised his eyebrows. "Did you believe him?"

I thought for a moment. "Well, at the time I guess I did."

"And now?"

I bit my lower lip. "Now, I'd say he was probably just blowing and going like he always did."

"He was with the 101st Airborne, wasn't he?"

"Yeah," Alan said. "The Screaming Eagles."

"That's right," I said. "I remember him bragging about that."

Alan looked sideways at me.

"You know, he never really said if he actually jumped out of a plane. I never saw any evidence of it."

"No, I never heard him say so, either." I let out a sigh. "But at least he was in the army. He served his country."

Alan sighed. "Yeah, I'll give him credit for that."

Carol said, "I never knew Dennis was in the army."

I smiled at her. "Yes, our dear brother did his duty when he flunked out of college. He wasn't exactly a hero, but he did his duty."

"Was he ever in combat?" She asked.

"Not that I ever knew," Alan said.

"So why did he say those things to you?" Carol asked Alan.

"What things," I asked.

Alan snapped his head toward me.

"Hmph," he said, a wry grin on his face. "He told me he thought I'd had it easy over there, flying helicopters and all. He said I probably didn't even get my boots dirty."

Alan was not unlike Dennis in his tendency to overreact.

"Alan, you know how Dennis goes on about things like that. You don't really think he believed that, do you?"

"Hell, Sue, I don't know what to believe anymore. That son of a bitch has tormented me my entire life." He leaned against a sawhorse and took a deep breath, then dropped his head. Then he looked up at me from raised eyes. "I have no reason to believe that he didn't mean it. Just one more way to humiliate me."

I closed my eyes, trying to think how to quench the glowing embers. I knew how Alan felt, and I also knew how Dennis had treated him when we were growing up. At times, he treated me the same way. But I knew Dennis would not have belittled Alan for his military service.

I grabbed Alan's arm.

"Alan, Dennis was not humiliating you. He was jealous. He always has been. Don't you see that? He's spent his entire life trying to compete with you because he knew you had accomplished things he never could. Even when we were kids. Remember when he got that trumpet? You could make a note on it and he couldn't. You always got better grades in school. No matter what you did, he couldn't match that. You graduated from college. You got commissioned as a lieutenant in the army. You went to Vietnam. Teresa was an All-State high school graduate. God, Alan, how can anybody compete with that?"

He picked up a piece of two-by-four, looking at it as if it held an answer to some ethereal question.

"And," I told him, "you've never exactly been complimentary about what he's done in his life."

I watched his jaw clench while the pressure built into something like a boiler about to burst. His breathing, picking up steam like a racing locomotive, almost hissed from his rising fury. He threw the two-by-four toward the wall, and while it ricocheted off of tools and bounced across the floor, Alan stomped toward the door leaving Carol holding her breath as she jumped up from the stool.

I looked at her. Stared at her. She didn't look at me. I saw the manifestation of some long-standing divergence from a marriage of feigned unity. I had obviously touched a nerve.

"Carol," I said, quietly, "I'm sorry if I spoke out of turn. I didn't mean to cause such a reaction."

She raised her damp eyes toward me and shook her head slowly.

"It's all right, Sue," she said with a sigh. "He needed that."

I wasn't sure what she had just said. Then it clicked.

"What do you mean?"

"Oh, Sue…" she sat back down on the stool. "I've known for a long time something was bothering him. It always has. It wasn't just the animosity between him and Dennis. There's something else. I just don't know what it is."

"And he won't talk about it?"

"No."

"Well, Alan was always the silent one when we were kids. Even when things seemed impossible for him. He would never say a thing."

"But why? What happened to him to make him so…I don't know. Withdrawn?"

I had to think back to ancient history, when Alan began showing signs of withdrawal.

"I think it must have begun when Dennis started school. Not kindergarten. The first grade. Alan would have been…three? That's when the teasing started."

"So, it's true. Dennis *did* tease him."

"I'm afraid so. It sometimes went beyond teasing. And Mom and Dad did little to prevent it. I think, at times, they were amused by it. Some of the things Dennis said to him."

Carol merely stared at me, a pitiful look in her eyes I somehow felt as if she were casting blame on me. Of course, I probably had to share some of it. I tried to stand up for Alan sometimes, but nothing ever did any good. Without the support of Mom and Dad, nothing I did was worth a hoot.

"Carol, let me go talk to him. Maybe I can…well, say something that will calm him down."

She shook her head, and I left.

"So," I said, approaching Alan, standing by the front porch, "That was quite a show."

He turned to look at me, a scowl on his face, shoulders slumped, hands in his coat pockets. Then he pulled his mouth to one side like he did when he was embarrassed.

"Yeah," he mumbled. "I'm sorry."

"It's not me you should be apologizing to."

"I know," he said with a sigh. "I'll go talk to her in a little while."

"Alan, this isn't the Civil War, you know. Dennis is not the enemy. He's a jerk. I know it and so does everyone else. But he's still your brother."

"Hell, Sue. I know that." He turned back around, away from me, his hands flew out of his pockets and batted the air. "I guess I deserved that. But I just can't erase a lifetime of the bullshit he gave me." Waving a finger in the air, he said, "and I can't forgive Mom and Dad for what they did." He took a deep breath "Or, what they didn't do."

I couldn't really say anything. He had a point, after all. Mom was never sympathetic to Alan about Dennis' bullying. She would just tell Alan, "Well, just fight back." That to a small boy three years junior to his brother who was taller and heavier didn't make a lot of sense. And Dad, well he just ignored it all. He was too busy with his business. All Alan had was me, and that wasn't saying much.

We were standing near the porch, so I sat down on the edge and looked up at him.

"Alan, you can't keep doing this."

He slowly turned his head toward me, another scowl on his face.

"Do what?" He spat out with restrained anger.

"You can't keep blaming everyone else for what's wrong with your life."

He turned away from me, hands in pockets, probably pouting.

"And, by the way," I said, "just what is so terribly wrong with your life that makes you so unhappy?"

I waited for some response. There wasn't one.

"My life hasn't exactly been a picnic. And Dennis…well, his hasn't either."

Carol wandered up at that time and positioned herself in front of Alan. His hands came out of his pockets and fell to his sides.

"Alan," she said, a cautious, soft voice. "You're not the only one who hasn't had a perfect life. You know about my family when I was growing up. You know how tough all of us had it."

She took his hands.

"We all have things in our lives that we wish we could change. But we can't, can we?"

He shook his hands free.

"No," he said with some regret. "We can't."

We all looked at each other until Alan spoke again.

"You know," he said, sitting down beside me. "Even Vietnam wasn't able to erase all of the hurt. The damage. I thought by volunteering for ROTC, the army, flight school, I could build myself into something I could respect. Something better than a shy wimp. Well, it did to some extent, but I still have all of the baggage."

I looked at him, his head low, eyes searching the ground.

"Oh, Alan," I said, "you don't need to prove anything to any-one. You never did. Not to me or anyone."

He didn't acknowledge what I'd said.

"Hell, you fought in the Vietnam War. You're a hero."

He turned his eyes to me, a look of puzzlement.

"A hero?"

Then he laughed.

"Fuck, Sue. I'm no hero. I just did my job like every other sucker over there."

"Alan, over 50,000 soldiers gave up their lives in that war and never made it home. You were lucky. You came back to us. You're lucky you weren't one of those that didn't come home."

I saw the fire ignite in his eyes, anger building inside, ears becoming red. He slowly turned his fiery gaze to me.

"Well," he growled, a finger pointing my way, "just maybe I should have been one of *them*."

Then, an intense silence slithered through the air, a deafening stillness devoid of any hint of life. A silence so complete that it left my brain in harrowing anticipation of sounds that would not come.

The sudden vacuum surrounding the house echoed Carol's white face, shock stiffening her body, frozen in one of those poses you see in movies, where muscles harden and the face morphs into an abstraction of fear, horror, and disbelief.

Her despondent eyes followed her husband as he stood and started to walk away. As I managed to pull my mind out of its stupor, I replayed Alan's words in my head. I remembered the only time he had said anything about Vietnam, the crews, the Viet Cong, the inept leadership, and the feeling of helplessness they all had. It was when Mom had died and we were waiting in the hospital for the funeral home men to arrive.

Of course, it was all just a story, like something I had read in a book. It was then that I knew I might need to understand the turmoil in Alan's mind. I turned toward Carol, her face in tears.

She took a step to follow Alan and paused before turning to face me. Our eyes studied each other searching for some sign of what to do.

"What did he mean?" she stammered. "What was that."

Having never been married, no obligation to another human being other than my coworkers and the women we sheltered, I saw in her the tragic result of true love.

"Let's go in the house," I told her. "I could use a drink."

We slowly made our way into the front door of the big two-story log house, it's solid walls echoing a need for the barrier Alan required against the realities of life, the confusion, the frustration, the embarrassment. I'm sure Carol had no idea what purpose those thick logs served.

I found a bottle of Pinot Grigio and poured Carol a glass. I also saw a bottle of Talisker single-malt Scotch. I poured myself a healthy glass, and we took off our coats and sat down at the dining table at the large bay window.

"What does he mean, Sue?"

Her innocence was almost heartbreaking. She had no idea. I honestly didn't either.

"Has Alan ever talked to you about his time in Vietnam?" I asked.

"Why, no. He hardly talks about it at all."

I felt so sorry for her. Married to a man with a hidden past, unknown to her and troubling to him.

I was in the same predicament. Alan had never revealed many hints of what he endured over there to anyone in our family. None of us really knew what had happened, but I knew enough to suspect that he had been a part of something that would never leave him in peace. Some of my coworkers had spouses that had served in Vietnam, Iraq, and Afghanistan, some of them harrowed with PTSD. I'm sure Alan had not been affected that seriously, but I also knew that he'd had issues when he came home.

"Carol, Alan was always quiet about himself. Sensitive. Compassionate. Of course, Dennis' bullying didn't do him any good. But Alan managed to get past that and become a decent person." Then I thought, no. "An amazing person."

I sipped the Scotch and let the slow burn work its way down to my stomach,

"He was always a loner, spent a lot of time by himself. But he always had time for me."

Damn that was good Scotch, I took another sip.

"He could be understanding when he wanted to be. And smart. But you know that."

Another sip.

"He seemed to understand my difficulties and always knew the right things to say."

Another sip. Carol was nursing her wine carefully, her attention glued to my disclosure of her husband's secret life.

"He was always nice to Dennis in spite of all the things he did to him."

The Scotch went down smooth, it's bite lingering in my mouth, teasing my palate.

"Then he went off to war."

I nearly emptied my glass.

I thought carefully about what to say next. I looked out the big bay windows in front, the huge oak trees standing guard over the house. Squirrels romped on the porch.

"Mom had a difficult time with Alan in Vietnam. Oh, she didn't dare show it, but I knew it was there. I think it really bothered Dad. He put on a good show of indifference, but it bored into his stoical façade. And, of course, Dennis hardly gave the event notice."

Carol finally polished off her glass of wine, and I emptied my glass. I refilled both glasses. She sat there, morose, her face blank as if she were staring into space.

"Day after day the folks would sit at that kitchen table, watching the news on their little tv, I'm sure, fearing they might never see Alan again. I think Mom must have aged ten years in the time Alan was over there. Oh, they would write to him, and he would respond, but not very often. Each time they got something from him, I could see the relief in their faces, if only for a brief time. Then it would start all over again until the next letter or tape recording came."

We both sipped our drinks.

"Anyway, when Alan came back from Vietnam, he'd changed."

We sat looking at our drinks, reticent, an uneasy air hovering over the room. I could hear the squirrels running across the porch outside.

She looked into my eyes, a drawn expression, almost one of hurt.

"But…what did he mean, Sue?" Her eyes began to tear. "That he should have been one of them. What was that all about?"

I closed my eyes and took a deep breath.

"Carol," I started in a low, soothing voice. "I'm not exactly sure." I lifted my glass for another sip of Scotch. "But I suspect he might feel guilty."

Carol slammed herself against the back of her chair.

"Guilty?"

Her eyes wide and her mouth open.

"What on earth would he feel guilty about?"

I closed my eyes and lowered my head. She had no clue. I set my glass down on the table.

"You're going to have to ask Alan that question," I said. "No one on Earth knows the answer to that except him."

IT FINALLY COMES OUT

February 2002

Two days later the storm of emotions had blown over and an air of civility had settled on the log house. Carol had dragged out some old photos, and the three of us spent a lot of our time going through them. I was never into reliving history spawned by pictures myself, but I had to admit that seeing them there, in the presence of Alan and Carol brought back many reminders of who and what our family had been. I also learned many things about Carol's family. Since Alan was usually the one with the camera, he did not appear in most of the photos. I watched Carol become a bit subdued as she surely became aware of that same thing. There was little to document Alan's life other than his military memorabilia. I saw Carol give him a pensive look. Maybe she had her own regrets.

We all had mixed feelings about Dennis' future. Carol displayed a greater propensity than either Alan or me, most likely since she had a reserved relationship with Dennis. She had certainly been the brunt of his tasteless efforts to be witty, but she ignored them for the most part. In spite of the news about his need for a transplant, I was fearful of what might happen. It had been over a month since Dad had died. And now the possibility of Dennis. It seemed inconceivable that nearly our entire family could be gone.

Alan, even within his stoical facade, showed few signs of distress. He continued to act as if a heart transplant meant nothing. It was no wonder. What with his inner turmoil about whatever Vietnam had done to him and the notion of losing a brother, it would not be uncharacteristic of him to push it to the back of his mind like he did Vietnam. I'm not so sure I would have been in much better frame of mind, although I was scared as hell that either Dennis would die or Alan would trip out and go nuts. I suddenly noticed Alan's clenched jaw and the targeted gaze of his eyes. At that moment, I knew he was deeply worried. I was surprised to notice it.

I spent the nights there, in the comfort of the benign and sweet aroma of wood. The walls, the ceilings, the floors. All wood. A log house has a special smell and ambiance. It wasn't like a hunting lodge or anything similar, but it was a log house. No grotesque animal heads hanging on the walls. No bearskin rugs. Just a simple and comfortable home. And the setting was so beautiful. Six acres of trees and lawn, a small creek running through it. The nearest neighbor a quarter of a mile away on a dead-end road. I could have lived there. If Alan had invited me, I would be tempted to accept. But we both needed our space.

The days passed slowly, dragging on into the evenings pouring over old photos and reminiscing about our shared events. Alan had rescued the photograph albums from the folks' trailer. I had never seen these pictures. Even Alan, as complex and pragmatic as he was, joined in the conversations and stories. I was struck by how much of my life had been forgotten. Pieces of it tucked here and there that evaded my daily life. It was uplifting to see those segments of my life that had lain undisturbed for so long.

That is when I began to understand what Alan had been going through. If it was that easy to lodge memories away in some secret vault of your mind, it would have been just as easy for him to do that with his memories of Vietnam. Unless some word or event triggered a memory, it would remain buried. Although the memories of the photos on the table had been a delight to experience, I was sure some of Alan's memories were very painful.

After two days of photos, boredom set in. I spent the rest of the day in isolation, walking down the gravel road to the cemetery at its end and sauntering down the edge of the lake to just sit on the bank and think. About Dennis. About Alan. About me.

When I returned to the house, a somber mood prevailed. After the blow-up two days before and a sluggish morning and a dismal lunch of hamburgers no one really felt like eating. The bottle of Scotch appeared, as a catharsis for our tangle of emotions. A bottle of Pinot Noir put Carol more at ease with it all.

We sat at the table in the bay window by the kitchen. The fading light became a salmon-colored dusk, shadows stretching across the yard and the temperature descending into a frosty chill. Across the road in the field, a doe ambled out of the woods followed by others. I counted twenty in all, their slow graceful gait a soothing delight. Then the buck showed himself, standing tall, alert, a beautiful pose. I sat there spellbound, immersed in admiration. Yes, admiration of such beautiful creatures that wandered freely across Alan's domain and admiration of Alan's domestic habitat, a reflection of the ideals he had always presented to the world. Peace, harmony, and nature. What a glorious place to put one's mind at ease.

I had always wondered what had possessed him to retreat to the rural outskirts of civilization and sequester himself in isolation like that. Then I knew.

I looked at Alan. I wanted to know about Vietnam.

"I'm curious, Alan," I said. "Why do you never talk about Vietnam?"

They both froze, Carol in mid-drink and Alan…well, Alan was already frozen in his stoical prison, bars of aloofness and trepidation separating him from the rest of the world. I was determined to shake Alan out of his mental cave. I looked him straight in the eyes.

"What is it that you Vietnam vets don't want anyone else to know about?"

He was still looking down, but I could see his eyes close. He took a deep breath and blew it out, leaned forward and let his body nearly hang over the table. I leaned toward him.

"I don't want to talk about it," he said, in a rebuff.

I leaned toward him over the table.

"Well, baby brother, I do!"

Those green, piercing eyes of his launched a barrage of anger toward me.

"Was it so terrible that you think we can't take it? Is that it?" I returned his angry stare. "We want to know."

I didn't let up.

"We need to know," Alan. "We deserve to know," I almost shouted.

"You wouldn't understand," he snarled, as if to cast it all to the side, unimportant, trivial.

"I know I don't understand," pleaded Carol. "But I want to. Why can't you help me understand?"

"Me, too," I said.

He sat there, smoldering, his ears turning red, his jaw set like a vise.

I stared at him.

"What can be so terrible that we can't understand?" I asked.

Carol and I stood and moved beside him, our eyes bearing down on him. His hands, resting on the tables drew into fists, clutching at the frustration and anger in the air. I leaned over him.

"Alan, what the hell is this all about?"

He jumped up from the table, his chair nearly tipping over backward. He snapped his head toward me, green fire in his eyes, lips curled in a sneer.

With a raised finger thrust toward my chest, he said, "You… don't…understand," he yelled, a jab of the finger emphasizing each word.

I reached out and shoved him. He stumbled back into his chair.

"Then MAKE us understand," I screamed at him.

After the shock of my assault wore off, he turned back toward the window, away from us, and blinked his eyes, lowering his head, and scooted his chair back to the table. He put his hands around his glass of Scotch. Then he took a deep breath.

"You know, whatever happened over there happened," I told him.

Another deep breath.

"Maybe it happened to *you*. But that doesn't change the fact that you have a life to keep living. You have a family to keep loving. Life has to go on. If you keep burying it, it will continue to consume you."

He slapped the table with his hand and snapped his head toward me, again.

"You don't understand," he grumbled. "You *can't* understand." Determination stole over his face.

Carol put down her glass and leaned over him, too.

"No, Alan," she said, softly. "I don't understand, but I want to."

"So do I," I said. I studied him, hoping he would break loose.

"We both would Alan," said Carol reaching for his arm on the table.

Her touch must have been like an electric shock to him. He jumped. He sat there for a few minutes, all of us quiet, him twisting his glass on the table, his jaw working itself back and forth. Finally, he leaned back, pulling away from Carol's hand and slumped in the chair. He put the half-full glass to his lips and swallowed it all in one gulp. His face squeezed itself into a knot from the burn of the Scotch. He was so calm, almost like a mannequin in Alan's clothes. He slowly placed his glass back on the table but did not look up. He worked his mouth, speaking no words.

He sniffed and twisted his glass on the table again.

"You know…" He shook his head, "…at the time I was there, it all seemed so easy. Get up in the morning, eat breakfast, hit the crapper, go to the line, fly the mission, then come back, get drunk, forget about what you did that day, and go to bed. Nobody wanted to have time to think about what was really happening or why. If you thought about what could have happened on the mission, the next one might be the one that killed you." He kept twirling his glass, and Carol and I sat down. "We were just there, kind of in a…I don't know." Here, he paused, longer than I expected. "Maybe a paradox where you think you're doing the right thing but then people die because of it, anyway."

He continued to stare at the glass on the table, his hands slowly twisting it around. Carol and I were both afraid to say anything. His face turned sullen.

He nodded his head. He reached for the bottle of Scotch and refilled his glass. "Yeah, people died. A lot of them." He twirled his glass again. "And I flew them into it."

The glass stopped and silence fell heavily a few minutes.

"We took troops into an LZ on a combat assault." He looked up at the window. "It was clear, they told us. Clear. No VC in the area. Five ships. Twenty-eight GIs."

His hand shook as the glass met his lips. He drank about half of it then let out a big wavering breath. The glass made a clank as reached the table. Then his eyes narrowed.

"They waited until we were all on the ground unloading. Like sitting ducks." Silence again. "Then all hell broke loose. We took fire from all around us. Bullets were flying everywhere. The men jumped out of the bird and scattered, diving for cover, and the flight leader told us to get the hell out of there."

He just stared through the bay window.

Then in a kind of monotone, as if in a trance. "Both of our 60s were firing and the radio was pure chaos. Nobody could understand a damned thing coming over it. There must have been hundreds of VC out there waiting for us. They must have known we were coming." Another sip of Scotch with a trembling hand. "We made it out of there, all right, and headed for the staging area. One of our ships was hit bad and had to return to base. We were all glad to get out alive."

Another shaky sip and his face turned to anger.

"Then, we got orders to go back and extract the guys we just put in."

Alan kind of snorted. "So, we turned around and went back in. By that time a couple of gunships showed up and started pounding away at the tree line." He let out a laugh. "But two gunships didn't do shit. Oh, they helped, but there were just too damned many of them. We made it back in and the guys scrambled to make it to the ships. I had five on board. We didn't see anything else moving in the LZ." Another sip. "I hesitated a moment to make sure, then lifted up to take off with the others. That's when the gunner got hit."

He swallowed. Hard. His voice was quivering.

"Then the peter pilot took a round in this head. My crew chief got hit in his leg but kept firing. Three more GIs made it on board. I don't know how we made it out of there, but we did."

He polished off his glass of Scotch, his hands still shaking. He refilled it, again, the neck of the bottle clinking against the rim of the glass.

"When we got back to the staging area, all four of our birds were shot to hell. Two of them, we left there. They weren't fly-able." Back to the trance. "A couple of medevacs came to get the wounded and take them to Qui Nhon. My gunner had taken three more hits. The crew chief took four more."

Another hard swallow.

"They didn't make it."

He looked down at the table again, banging his fist on it. "They didn't make it," he almost shouted, his face contorted, tears flowing down his cheeks.

"Twenty-one men died that day. Twenty-one." His low voice became bitter. "Because the intelligence team fucked up. It happened all the time. I was the only one of my crew that didn't get hurt or die. Me."

He poured another drink, most of it landing in his glass. He threw back his head and shook it.

"Just me. I should have done more. I just don't know what."

Tears continued to roll down his face. Carol stood behind his chair, tears rolling down her face, too, and put her arms around him. I had my own tears to deal with.

"Oh, Alan," she said, crying. "I wish you had told me about that."

She kissed the top of his head.

"Ever since I've known you, I knew that you were special. Someone who…had compassion. And secrets. I know you had secrets. We all do. I just wish I had known about yours."

Alan placed his hands over her arms. His bleary eyes blinked. He sniffed.

I shook my head. "Alan, no one can blame you for what happened. It wasn't your fault. It was war. That's what happens in war. People die."

He looked over at me and tightened his hands on Carol's arms.

"But why?" he asked, shaking his head. "Why?"

Carol and I consoled him, trying to convince him that he wasn't at fault. The way he described it, there is no way anyone could blame him for what happened.

Alan turned back toward the window. Carol found a box of tissues and set it in front of him. He dried the tears from his face and just sat there, his mind, I suppose, trying to digest all that had been said.

"That's easy for you to say," he finally said, his voice low and insecure. "Some things you just can't forget. Not this. I'll always remember it. And I'll always feel guilty. I can't feel any other way. That's my cross to bear, as they say. It has nothing to do with either of you. It's just me."

I left the two of them there, at the table. I went outside to think about what had just happened. I couldn't imagine what seeing his crew killed had been like for him, but I began to see why he acted the way he had. Why he never talked about it, I don't think I could have if it had happened to me. At that point I almost wished I hadn't pressed him to reveal what he had.

Some twenty minutes later, I returned inside. They were still at the table. It appeared that he had begun to understand the significance of what had just occurred. I think he was finally able to weigh his guilt against innocence and find a way to abandon his self-condemnation and come to terms with reality.

He straightened up and wiped his eyes with his fingers. A deep breath, then he stood.

"I'm sorry," he said. "I should have said something a long time ago." He looked at Carol, then at me. "I'm okay. It's just that after forty years, some shit just kind of weighs you down."

"Is it that way for all Vietnam veterans?" Carol asked.

He looked at her and smiled, then leaned back against the table, the Scotch taking effect.

"Pretty much. For some, a lot worse. Each of us has his own demons. What you and everyone else sees and hears is what we want you to see. We say and do whatever we think is expected of us to fit into society. We try to act like everyone else. Everyone who has never seen and done what we have. The ones who've never been in the dark places we've been. The rest of who we are is what hangs below the surface. It's where we fight with ourselves. Did we do enough? Did we screw up? What did we accomplish? Why were we there?"

He poured more Scotch.

"All I was there for was to fly men to their deaths."

He picked up his glass and stared at it. Then he took a sip.

"Questions," he continued. "Doubts. Regrets. Oh, yes, lots of regrets. We were stupid enough to be duped into believing South Vietnam was worth saving. What place do schmucks like us have in society?" He took a drink. "Why in hell would anyone feel compelled to brag about that?"

Carol said, "What about the shadow box I made for you with all of your army things in it? No matter what you think, you did your duty and served our country."

Alan closed his eyes and sighed. "I know. I really appreciate you doing that for me. I know I should be proud of it. Of all the things in there."

"Well, I'm proud of them. I'm proud of *you*."

I edged away from the table and left the two of them to work out this difficulty. I couldn't help but think that it would be all right. Alan was a pragmatic sort of man. He always had been. That's what I had admired about him. I knew he could overcome his misconceptions about Vietnam.

THE ANNOUNCEMENT

February 2002

It was still dark when I heard the phone ring. The clock beside the bed read three-twenty-four. In the morning.

I got up and ventured into the hall. The half-moon allowed enough light into the stairwell to see where I was going. The dark stillness seemed to amplify the smell of the surrounding wood walls. I peeked into Alan's bedroom.

I listened while Alan talked to Jackie on the phone. I wasn't sure if the news was good or bad. He showed little emotion as he talked. Like a poker face, the kind that just stares at you or something else in space, not a muscle moving, not even a twitch. I just never knew what he was thinking.

Carol was also listening with avid interest and an expectant look on her face.

He hung up the phone and turned to Carol. Then he noticed me at the door. With a sheepish grin on his face, he said, "He's getting a heart."

Carol and I both stared at him, silent, not quite believing what we just heard.

"Yeah," he said, as if presenting an obligatory speech. "It seems that it was foggy this morning at the airport. Some kid was killed in a car accident during the night. He was an organ donor, and he was a match for Dennis. The kid's heart was supposed to go to

Chicago, but all of the airplanes are grounded due to the fog. Well, the heart is a match for Dennis, so he's getting it."

An enormous weight suddenly lifted from my chest. Carol seemed to be in her own state of bewilderment mixed with puzzled excitement. It seemed so bizarre. He hadn't been on the list but about a month. Most patients on the list waited months or years. He was darned lucky. Imagine all of these little things happening right then: the accident, the heart, the fog. Oh, but that poor boy who died. I wondered what his family was going through then. I wondered if they knew that Dennis would be getting that heart instead of the one who was supposed to? And what about him? Or her. I couldn't imagine the depressing disappointment that person suffered.

I had thought about returning home that day, but with this news, I just couldn't. I tried to talk Alan into going back to see our brother. I wished he would lose his pitiful routine. He needed to get over that. It was done, over with. He needed to get on with the rest of his life. Our lives.

Dennis wasn't so bad. Oh, he could be overbearing and insensitive at times, and he didn't think very highly of himself, at least not internally. And I've seen the way he treated Alan. Well, really, he treated just about everyone that way. Like he was better than they were. But, deep down, I knew he was a good person. Jackie told me how he bragged about his "little brother" to other people. He did have respect for him. I just wished Alan could see that.

I was darned sure going to insist that we go see him after the operation. Alan had to quit being such a jerk toward Dennis. Okay, so his childhood wasn't all roses. Well, mine wasn't either. But I don't hold that against anyone. Hell, I suspected that every person on this planet had a crappy childhood in one way or another.

And Jackie. She must have been going through hell. I couldn't imagine what I would do if anything like that happened to Alan. At least I had our family for support. All she had was her kids, and well, they weren't exactly responsible. Surely, they would help out. If not, well, I'd see if I could get Alan to go back sooner.

A MEMORY AND CONTEMPLATION

February 2002

So, big brother was going to get a new heart. Just thinking about that warped my sense of reality. Take out a heart and put in a new one. Like replacing a battery in my car. Medicine has become incredibly advanced. Yesterday's science fiction has become today's reality.

While thinking about Dennis and his heart, I couldn't help thinking about Mom. It had been a little over a year since Mom and Dad had moved to Harrison to live in their mobile home at Alan's house. At least Mom was able to get some of the care she badly needed. Dad was totally incapable of providing any kind of support or care.

Mom's Parkinson's and Alzheimer's had progressed to the point that she required round the clock care. Dad had become worn out trying to cope with it. I could tell even from infrequent visits that she was failing rapidly.

That's when Alan and Carol suggested that they move to Harrison. Dad could buy a mobile home and park it on one of the six acres near the house. That way Carol and Alan could look after them and give Dad some breaks from Mom.

Of course, at first Dad balked at the idea, a perceived failure of his ability to provide for Mom. It took a good half year for Dad to realize he had to do something, so he called Alan and made plans for the move. Afterward, things went well for a while, but eventually, Mom's condition grew so bad that Dad begrudgingly hired a home health nurse to stay with Mom during the day. Dad had become so abusive toward her that Alan and Carol moved her into their own house along with the nurse, who had begun staying around the clock.

One day Mom began aspirating while trying to eat lunch and had difficulty breathing. The nurse called for an ambulance.

At the Harrison hospital, the doctor managed to stabilize her, then sent her on to St. Edwards Hospital in Fort Smith Arkansas, about a half hour away.

It was there that she stayed for two days, never regaining consciousness. On the second day, I drove up from Dallas and Dennis and Jackie came from Okemah. Of course, Alan and Carol were there. We all knew Mom was dying. I was nearly in tears. I could tell Dad was upset, but his stoical nature did not allow much sign of it. Carol was almost beside herself and I could tell that the situation was affecting Alan. Even with his experiences in Vietnam he showed subtle signs of grief, little things that didn't appear obvious to anyone else. He constantly stared at Mom, or the wall, or the window, but never at anyone else.

Dennis and Jackie? Well, I believe Mom's condition had little effect on them. They dominated every conversation bragging about Dennis' job at the local veterinarian clinic, and Jackie was riding the wave with him.

The nurse had left after telling us that it was only a matter of a short time until Mom was gone. I felt sick. Alan's face dropped. Carol took a deep breath. Dennis and Jackie just stood there, blank, unfettered, as if the nurse had said nothing.

It was nearly lunch time. Carol had to return home to tend to her mother, who had just had a knee replacement. Everyone else except Alan and I left to eat at a restaurant across the street from the hospital. They didn't see the urgency in what was happening.

Alan was on one side of the bed, and I was on the other watching the small chest barely rise and fall beneath the blanket. Her open mouth sucked in a minute bit of oxygen from her mask covering her face. The chirps from the monitor were slow, mo-

notonous, almost annoying. After a few minutes, they came farther apart, gradually slowing like a battery growing weak. The
nurse popped in again with a representative from the staff to help
us prepare for the mortuary to collect the body. I stood by, frozen
in confusion as Alan gave her the information about the funeral
home and Mom's wishes for her cremation.

It was real. Mom was going to die right there in front of me.
There would be no last hugs, no good-byes, no opportunity to
connect with her. No way to tell her how much I loved her. I
just hoped she would somehow know. Alan, his face hard and
alert but solemn, was breathing heavily. I knew he was hurting,
charged with conflicting emotions, like my sorrow for the loss,
but grateful for her passing from her turmoil. Each of us took
one of her hands, the small, cold, boney hands that had caressed
us, bathed us, cooked our meals, and waved to us when we left
home. I can't say for sure what I felt at that time. It was all so
distant, like an apparition, a veil of an event that may or may
not be happening. I watched Alan's eyes focus on her, his face,
having changed slightly, now at ease with the coming death. My
god, what had happened to him over there? Not a tear, not a sign
of sadness or distress. How in the world did he do it? My tears
were flowing freely down my cheeks, and I was holding Mom's
hand tightly. I might have been shaking.

Then the monitor's chirps were even farther apart, one after
the other, until they stopped all together in a continuous tone
leaving cold silence cloaking the room, nothing stirring except
the green line moving steadily across the monitor. Mom was finally gone.

Alan and I were alone with her. Just us two. The others were
sitting in some restaurant stuffing their faces, laughing, most
likely, without a care in the world about Mom. The thought of
it infuriated me. How could Dad just leave his wife there to
die alone? How could Dennis just leave his mother there to die
alone?

"Sue."

I heard Alan's voice through the torrent of anger that swarmed
my mind. I looked at him.

"Sue," he said softly. "It's all right. Mom didn't die alone. We were with her. I'm sure she knew that." I smiled at him.

"Oh, Alan."

He smiled back.

"You were always the caring one."

The smile left his face, anger creeping in behind it.

The nurse came back in and offered her condolences, then disconnected all of the paraphernalia. She told us they would take care of our mother. After she left Alan and I just stared at Mom lying there, tiny, inert, finally free from the horrid diseases that had ravaged her.

"Why the goddamn hell did they leave?" Alan asked, in-flamed and bitter. "They knew she was dying. That she didn't have much time left."

He looked at me with those glaring green eyes that could turn my heart cold.

"What the hell is the matter with this fucking family?"

I didn't know what to tell him. I wondered the same thing, myself.

"Well," I said at last, "You're right. Mom didn't die alone."

He looked up at me again, a look on his face so strange, eerie, as if he had just had an epiphany.

"She knew we were here," I said. "She knew."

We both looked down at our mother.

"Yes," he said, "I'm sure she did. I remember her talking about when Aunt Verda died."

"Oh, yeah," I said. "I remember you talking about that. How long had she been in that nursing home?"

"I think about four years. I imagine it was a pretty long time for her. I mean, being alone and everything. Hardly anyone went to visit her except Mom and Dad. Carol and I went a few times. Took her out to lunch one day. The next time we went, the staff there told us she had bragged about that for a week."

"Mom was upset that she had gone to that nursing home. I know she'd wanted Verda to move in with them. But Dad wouldn't have tolerated it. I think it's sad that the bastard couldn't have given Mom's sister just an ounce of compassion."

Alan's head jerked up.

"Hell, Sis, he can't give anybody any compassion. Where the hell is he now?"

The nurse returned to inform us that someone from the funeral home was on his way to collect Mom's body. We could contact them when we got home.

Alan called Carol to let her know about Mom.

Then the rest of the family came back, laughing and carrying on as if nothing was wrong. They all looked toward the bed. It finally dawned on them that Mom had died.

I saw Dad's face tighten into a knot. He either felt some measure of grief, or he could have felt relieved; I'm not sure which. It could have been both, but I couldn't know for certain. It should have been guilt.

Dennis didn't move a muscle in his face. He looked the same as he did when he first arrived. Jackie still had the remnants of a smile on her face. I honestly didn't think she understood what had happened. After a couple of minutes, reality must have hit home, and the smile dissolved, and tears formed in her eyes.

And Alan? His eyes were fixed on them like an M-16 ready to fire. Usually, his ears turned red when he was angry, but his entire face was red. Flame red. I had to get him out of there.

"Let's go, Alan. I'll drive you home."

He insolently brushed past Dad and Dennis, who were still trying to make sense of what was happening. I followed him out of the room at a slight trot and to the elevator.

Once the doors closed, he looked at me, his head down.

"It's pathetic. I'm ashamed of my own family."

I felt the same way, but I wasn't going to enable hatred within my kin. The feud between him and Dennis was enough to handle. All I could muster was a sigh.

"We need to go by the mortuary and make some arrangements," I said. "Didn't you tell me Dad had already had a headstone made?"

"Yeah. One for each of them. They just need dates on them. I'll make sure it's finished and ready. They both want to be cremated and the ashes buried in the family plot in Harper."

"We need to sit Dad down and get all of this straight."

"Okay," he said. "I guess we can do that tonight. You staying for the burial?"

"Yes. Let's get arrangements made and I'll start letting people know."

The folks at the mortuary were very helpful. They were friends of Alan's and they seemed eager to help. We gave them information for the eulogy to be put in the local paper, and they said they would arrange for the death certificate. It would be two or three days before we had Mom's ashes.

When we got to Alan's house, Dad's car was parked in the driveway to his trailer. Alan and I went over to talk with him.

"Well, huh," Dad said. "Come on in."

CNN was blaring on the television just like it always was. Dad was in his recliner, stoical as ever. Dennis was in another chair, half-closed eyes glued to the television. Jackie was in the kitchen getting drinks.

I walked over to Dad.

"Sorry about Mom."

Alan sat on the sofa. He said nothing. Jackie brought Dennis and Dad their drinks.

"Would y'all like something?" She asked.

"No thanks, Jackie," I said. "We just want to talk with Dad for a bit."

"Alan and I stopped by the mortuary. They've got everything in order. We should have the ashes in two or three days. Dad, you had a headstone made, right?"

He looked up at me, his eyes puzzled, maybe even a touch of grief. For all the emotions he couldn't show, his eyes made up for it.

"Oh, yeah. Uh, an outfit in Oklahoma City has them."

Dennis perked up.

"Yeah, I can pick it up and take it to the cemetery. When do we want to do that?"

Alan stood up.

"Let me call the cemetery and ask what we need to do. Dad, do you have the plot number for the cemetery?"

"Why, ah, I've got the plot number. I don't know the phone number."

"I can find it," Alan said. "When I get some information, I'll let you all know."

Two days later, Alan picked up Mom's ashes and the death certificates. The next morning Alan drove Dad, Carol, and me to the Harper Cemetery in Kansas where we met Dennis, Jackie, and Brent, their son. A small hole had already been dug for us on the plot. We waited until the few remaining family members from Dads side of the family found their way to the gravesite.

There weren't any left of Mom's family. No memorial was planned, and none was wanted by Mom or Dad. Mom never believed in big ostentatious showings. She never really wanted a funeral. So, Dad, Alan, Dennis and I agreed to a simple graveside service.

The small group lingered until Alan finally suggested they start whatever ceremony there was to be. With all of us standing under the overcast sky, a warm breeze skimming around us, Alan spoke first.

"Mom was a simple woman. She liked simple things. I'll miss her."

I spoke next. "Mom was one hell of a mother. One of a kind. What I know today, I learned from her. Now she can be at peace."

No one else ventured an oration. Not even Dennis or Dad. I shot a scowl toward him, but he was fast absorbed in his own world.

Dad awkwardly stood over the small hole in the ground, held the box of ashes above it, then dropped it in without fanfare. I saw Alan's eyes look toward him in contempt. Mine did, too. The stingy son of a bitch couldn't even say a kind word about his wife of over fifty years.

Mom had been his life. Anything they did was because she had planned it. Any friends they'd had was because she made them. Any real happiness our family enjoyed was because of what Mom made possible. Without her, Dad would be lost. He seemed confused, disoriented. We were all standing there waiting for someone to do something.

Finally, Alan said, "How about let's all meet at the Hiway Diner for lunch?"

A collective sigh of relief gushed from the group, and after a moment of silence, we all left in our cars for the diner.

I had never been to the diner, a nondescript place mainly frequented by locals that favored the home-cooked dishes. The menu was fair with inexpensive meals. Our family group sat at a long table. Dennis couldn't resist bragging about his raise at the local vet's office where he kept the books. And Jackie was her usual robust, obnoxious self. Dad was quiet, almost withdrawn, which I understood.

After we had finished the meal, Alan got up and went over to one of the waitresses and gave her a credit card. She processed it and brought it back to him. Then he sat back down at the table.

Dennis had been watching. He had that perturbed look he often got when he suspected something wasn't right. He went over to Alan, standing beside his chair.

"What was that all about?" he asked.

"I paid for everyone's meal," Alan told him.

Dad looked at him as if he had gone crazy. I knew what he was thinking: "Why waste your money on everyone else? Let them buy their own food."

After the surprise left his face Dennis said, "How much was it?"

Alan looked at Dennis, eye to eye, with that masterful arrogance of his.

"Don't worry about it. I got it."

Indignation flushed over Dennis' face.

"Don't be like that. How much was it? I'll split it with you."

Alan, in his cool demeanor, said, "All right. A hundred."

"I'll chip in, too," I said.

Dennis relaxed. "Okay, I'll give you a check later."

When I heard that I thought to myself, well, maybe he will and maybe he won't. Dennis was always quick to make promises, but slow to follow up on them, if ever. At least a confrontation had been avoided.

As we got ready to leave, I noticed others in the group asking for checks and being told that they had been paid. They looked toward Dad and waved. Dad waved back. We left.

***

I don't know now much sleep I lost during that episode of memory lane. I just couldn't bear the thought of Dennis dying on us. I'm not sure I could go through that again. But the news of a new heart brightened my spirits, and then I was too excited to sleep.

THE TRANSPLANT

February 2002

The transplant operation was scheduled for five o'clock in the morning. Breakfast came early, although we knew the surgery would take several hours. We waited in the dim glow of a single lamp in the living room of the log house, the gray dawn not yet seeping through the windows, a news broadcast quietly emanating from a television on the wall.

"Jackie must be in a fit." Carol in her robe and pajamas said, her face devoid of color and absorbed in worry as she sat down on the sofa and leaned forward toward Alan who was standing in the in front of the fireplace in his lounge clothes holding a cup of coffee, his expression battling between worry and disgust.

"Well, I'd hate to be in her shoes." Alan answered and looked at her. "Hell, I'd hate to be in *his* shoes, too."

She looked at him with those questioning, green eyes of hers. "I wonder if he had any idea this would happen?"

"I don't know how he couldn't have known." Alan sat next to Carol on the sofa, coffee cup in hand. "I mean, the man was having heart attacks all along and didn't even know it? That just doesn't add up."

I was sitting across the room from them in my own pajamas and robe listening to their assessment of the situation. "Don't take this the wrong way, but as arrogant as our brother is, don't you think he figured it couldn't happen to him?"

I still held onto some string of hope that Dennis wasn't as big an ass as I thought. Optimism had always been there, needling me into giving in to him or giving him the benefit of the doubt. It had crippled my rationality and kept logic at bay since I had been old enough to be aware of his shortcomings. I drained my coffee cup and got up to refill it.

Carol sat up. "Don't you think that's a bit cruel? He *is* your brother. You grew up with him. Surely, he wasn't *that* bad. I'm sorry, but I feel bad for him."

I got a refill, went back to my chair and jumped in the discussion to avoid Alan making a fool of himself.

"Dennis had his moments. I can't say that I had that many bad experiences, but I know Alan got the brunt of his harassment. Our parents tended to overlook it. They never realized what Dennis was actually doing. Mom was too busy trying to make ends meet with the little money Dad gave her, and Dad, well, he was too busy with that damned store of his. Dennis could be just as nice as could be occasionally, usually when he wanted something from you, but those times didn't happen often. But still, Dennis *is* our brother."

"I know, I know" Alan admitted, waving a hand in the air. "I shouldn't be an ass, too."

"You've never really talked much about you growing up," said Carol. "What really happened back then?"

Carol and I both looked at him, Carol with expectation and me with trepidation. I just hoped Alan wouldn't launch into a long harangue about our childhood. It was bad enough just to have to deal with the memories of it.

He set his coffee cup on the table beside him. "We were always at odds," he started, head lowered, arms crossed over his chest. "Well, at least after we moved to Milton. I had friends who had brothers, real ones. Brothers that acted like…brothers." He looked up at me. "They seemed to have this emotional attachment to each other, each of them knowing what the other was thinking. Always sticking up for each other. Laughing, joking, playing with each other. Even as a kid I was able to recognize that much."

"Alan…"

He waved me off.

"I never had that. The only thing I'd ever gotten was humiliation and degradation. I always wondered what it would be like to have a real brother. He usually ignored me. Any other time he was berating me."

He took a drink from his cup and looked over at me, again.

"Nothing against you, Sis. You were the one that showed me the only empathy I got, not that you could have done anything about it."

"Alan, you don't need to go on a pity trip. I don't believe you had it as bad as you think. Dennis was always expected to be the star of the family, being the oldest. He had a lot of pressure on him. Pressure you never had. At least, not pressure from the folks. You made your own pressure. You made it hard on yourself because you always tried to be better than Dennis. He knew that."

I let that sink in during the silence and under Alan's arrows that were flying from his eyes, his arm flew up and an angry finger jabbed out toward me.

"No, Sue. I never tried to be better than him."

I stared back at him, and his arm dropped.

"You know, he was very envious of you. You accomplished things he never had. Things *I* never had." He lowered his head, I hoped in a bit of shame.

"I was envious of you, too. And proud. It's not every girl that has a war hero for a brother."

He snapped his head back toward me, his body suddenly rigid. "Stop it, Sis."

"Why? Are you going to play your modesty game?"

He relaxed a bit, and the military Alan came out.

"Modesty has nothing to do with it."

Back to the placid, detached expression, as if he were looking through me and into some distant place unknown to any of us.

"Vietnam was just…Vietnam. I did what I signed up to do. Nothing more. Sure, I dodged bullets and did what everyone else over there did. I was no hero."

He stopped and swallowed hard.

"You should know that from what I told you yesterday."

Then he perked up and continued.

"Yeah, we did our duty. Did anyone give a damn? No. When I got home there were nothing but scowls and angry faces. Even Dennis tried to make light of it. All I got from Dad was goofy look that could have meant anything. No, I was no hero. A lot of the guys were, but I wasn't. I never wanted to be. I never wanted to go. But I didn't figure I had much choice. I just didn't want to wait to be drafted. I made up my mind to go the way I wanted."

Carol and I watched him test himself; trying not to lose control, trying to hold it all in.

"Look, I'm sorry for Dennis. I'm sorry that he fucked up his life. I'm sorry for his family. I'm sorry that he didn't get everything I did. Or you. I know you didn't exactly have a picnic being our sister. I knew the folks neglected you. I felt sorry for you but what the hell could I do about it? What the hell could I do about Dennis?"

The room fell silent, the grandfather clock ticking away the minutes, and I sat there wondering if I should say anything. Carol was almost in tears. She fidgeted with her hands while staring at Alan. Then he continued.

"Look, he had every opportunity I did. Most everything I accomplished I did by myself." He raised his arms, palm up. "I had to." He propped himself an arm against the sofa's arm. "There was no one there to help me. No one who had the time or inclination. At least Dennis got some of that. He just never saw the opportunities."

I looked him in the eye. "Alan, no one is blaming you for what happened to Dennis."

Alan finally calmed down enough to stop talking. That's when Carol took over.

"I never really knew what it was like for you growing up. From what I know of Dennis I'm sure it wasn't pleasant. Even your father seemed to be a bit detached from all of you. Your mother must have had a hell of a time managing your family with that tightwad. From my own family's experience, I can imagine what she went through." She placed her hand together in her lap and continued.

"My family was hard enough to grow up in."

"Dickens was right," said Alan. "All happy families are alike; each unhappy family is unhappy in its own way."

I always thought that was so profound. Now I understood why.

Carol looked straight at Alan. "Do you want to go back to the city?"

He looked at her. "No. There's really nothing we can do there. Not now, anyway. Jackie is probably worried, but their kids ought to be able to offer some support."

I thought for a moment. "Nothing we could do would change the outcome. Dennis is going to get a new heart and he'll be well taken care of."

"Okay," Carol said, "You're probably right."

"Besides," Alan mumbled. "I wonder if he really would want me there."

"Alan!" Carol almost yelled

"What?"

"What a terrible thing to say."

"Well, it's the truth."

"Alan, you've got to get over this. He's your brother."

From behind his scowl, "He never seemed like it."

I heard Carol let out a terrific sigh.

"Look," Alan told her. "We've never been close. Hell, even when we were kids, I was just something to provide entertainment for him."

"I know," she said, annoyed at his behavior. "You've told us about all of that hundreds times. I still can't believe that he was so mean."

"Well, believe what you want. That's the way it was."

"Are you sure you just don't feel sorry for yourself?"

He turned toward her. "So, what if I do? That doesn't change our history. He's an asshole. He always has been."

Then a pause. I took solace in the brief silence between them.

"Are you sure you don't want to go?"

I could tell he was thinking about it.

"I really don't. Just let the doctors get on with whatever they're going to do. We can see him afterward. Who knows? A new heart might change his entire personality."

"That's not funny, Alan," I said.

"Maybe not, but it's possible."

I'm pretty sure he was fully aware of my irritation. He always knew when I was upset about something. He was the one who would be near me and share in my sorrow. But I also knew that even his soft heart would not tolerate the life he had been dealt in our family. The chip on his shoulder had grown too large, another burden for his already screwed up mind. But I had no idea what I could do about it.

Carol scooted beside Alan, hugging him.

"Well, I suppose that's the best thing, right now. I don't think any of us can do anything for him until he's in recovery. Maybe we should just stay out of it for now."

Alan got up and put another log on the fire. The heat radiating from the open fireplace doors felt so warm and comforting. I wanted so much to help Alan with his ambivalence. I knew that's what it was. I knew he was torn between harboring contempt for Dennis and showing him an iota of compassion. I also knew that, given a little time, he would make the right decision.

WAITING

February 2002

The morning's dreariness huddled over me like a shroud, the skies, heavy like cement, almost black, and what little light broke through gave the place an illusion of dusk. I listened to the wind howl at the doors of the log house, the limbs of the huge oak trees thrashing the air. The few oaks that still had leaves reluctantly turned loose of them as the wind tore them from their moorings. They fluttered across the yard like tiny birds fighting for purchase in now dormant grass. The lack of shadows gave the yard the appearance of desolation. It seemed to fit my mood. Would Dennis survive this? Would any of us?

I was sitting by the small bay window in the den when Carol wandered in.

"Good morning, Sue. You're up early."

"Couldn't sleep."

"I couldn't either. I got tired of fighting it." She sat down across a small table from me. "Have you had anything to eat?"

"No, I'm not hungry right now. But I could use some coffee. I know you don't drink it, but if you show me where the stuff is, I think I can manage."

"Alan uses the French press. I'll show you where it is."

"I'm familiar with those. Alan gave me a lesson some time ago."

We got up, and I followed Carol to the kitchen.

"I'm just so nervous about Dennis," Carol said, pulling the coffee press from a cabinet. "I've never been involved with anything like this."

"I haven't, either," I told her. "My brain is so screwed up with things bouncing around in there. I keep thinking about our growing up. It's kind of pathetic, dredging all of that up now."

Carol pointed to the coffee grinder.

"I don't think so," she said. "I think about my family all the time."

I set the grinder and turned it on. I waited for the loud growl to stop, then measured coffee into the press. Carol had put on water to boil.

"You know, it's funny how tragic events stimulate the brain. It seems to dredge up memories that we didn't know we had. All of the things that had happened in my life seem like yesterday."

Carol looked at me. "Yeah, I've been thinking about things, too."

I poured boiling water into the press and put on the lid.

"Can you imagine Dennis stretched out on a table with an army of doctors and nurses carving out his heart and replacing it?"

"No," she said, wincing. "I really can't."

"And what about Jackie?" I asked. "Jesus! I'm glad I'm not in her shoes."

The four-minute timer went off and I pushed down the plunger of the press. I poured a cup of coffee and headed for the dining table.

"Well, there is one advantage to not being married. I didn't have to worry about losing a husband."

Carol mixed some chocolate milk and joined me at the table.

"And Brent and Becky," I continued. "What about those two? I haven't seen them at all during this episode of 'Family Carter.' Jackie said they were there the day before, but you couldn't prove it by me."

"I'm pretty sure they'll be there."

"I knew you just tolerated Dennis and don't have a lot to do with Jackie. But I imagine you'd be the first one there to help if they needed it. I'm just glad Alan has you. A man like him, constantly battling the beasts of his mind, his history, his family, and his emotions, needs someone like you."

I think Carol turned a bit red, but I didn't say anything.

"If Dad were still alive," I went on, "he would have been in there telling Dennis, 'I told you so.' Mom, too. The oldest son is supposed to be the favorite."

I took a sip of coffee. "Well, let me tell you, our family just never got the message. I think Dennis had always been somewhat of a disappointment to them. I can't really see that the folks had showed favoritism to any of us."

Another sip. Carol took a drink of her milk.

"Even being the only girl, I didn't get much preference over the boys. But that was Mom's philosophy. Women were supposed to be the silent partner in a marriage. Just do the work to keep up the family home and keep her mouth shut."

"Yes," said Carol. "My family is the same way. That's the way it was when my parents grew up."

"I really resent it. I was glad, in a way. At least I didn't grow up thinking I was privileged just because I *am* a girl."

"I can understand that," she said.

"But if any of us got anything more than the others, it was Alan. Not that he had gotten anything from the folks. Whatever he got was from his own efforts. He always seemed to be one up on Dennis in an almost furtive way."

Another sip. "Like getting a bachelor's degree in architectural engineering. Did you know that's one of the toughest majors in college? Then after the army, going back for his master's degree."

"Yes," said Carol. "I worked a couple of jobs so he could go to school. It was worth it. He's doing well as an engineer."

"Then becoming an officer in the army, flying helicopters in Vietnam. Boy, Dad was so proud of him, even though he never had the nerve to actually tell Alan so. Alan knew, though."

More coffee.

"So did Dennis. Oh yes, Dennis knew. And I think it really aggravated him. I was proud of Alan, too. That took a lot of guts, and Alan had never shown much bravado around the family. Or anyone else, for that matter. He always did have a certain affection for the army."

"I know he always likes shows about the army and war and all," said Carol.

"I think it started back in the old house in Winfield when we were kids. Dennis would lay on the floor in the basement behind the wrinkles in Mom's blanket, the blue and white plaid one, waiting for Alan to move his tiny army men up so he could blast them away."

"It sounds like you lived in a nice house."

"Oh, it was pretty much like every other house on the block."

Carol finished her chocolate milk and got up to take her glass to the kitchen.

"We lived in the country. We didn't have a lot of space in the house. We played in the back, mostly."

I finished my coffee and went to the kitchen for a refill.

"Anyway, Alan always wanted Dennis' army set. That had not been a good Christmas. Alan hated the farm set he got. He never said as much, but I could tell. Why would the folks think Alan gave a damn about a farm set? He'd never even seen a farm. Hell, at five years of age, he wanted to be like Dennis. Alan tried to like the farm set. He really did. But he'd look over at Dennis gloating over the little green army men with Jeeps and guns all kinds of stuff, and he'd almost cry. The fact that Dennis knew and made faces at him didn't help."

"That sounds kind of sad."

"Well, my present wasn't much better. A tacky doll that didn't move and a dress that made me feel like a total freak. I don't know what the folks were thinking that year, but it darned sure wasn't about us."

We both returned to the table.

"Our Christmases were pretty sparse," said Carol. "We were lucky to get something in a stocking. Fruit, mostly."

"Sounds like you had it pretty rough."

"We didn't have a lot, growing up. Just enough to get by."

"So, you've lived here most of your life?" I asked.

"Until I married Alan. Then we moved around some."

"Yes, moving can be a tough time."

"Actually, it didn't affect us all that much. Even Teresa adjusted really well."

"Well, I remember when we moved to Milton, Oklahoma. I was nine. Boy, there was a bump in my life. I kind of feel like that, now, about Dennis. Afraid, but excited at the same time."

"Yeah, I feel the same way."

"It seems like I've done a lot of that. But at least I made new friends. It was a lot easier than I thought. My new friend, Janie, lived in the next block and Martha, another friend, lived on the street behind our house."

I paused to take a sip of coffee.

"The kid across the alley from us, Jimmy Barnes, was Alan's first friend. They hit it off really good. At school, his friends kind of became my friends, too, even though they were younger and boys. It was tough in the middle of a school year, like that. January, the start of the second semester. Fourth grade for me and second grade for Alan. The dead of winter when you don't get around much."

"I've heard Alan talk about Milton. We went there once for a class reunion. It was really a dead place."

"It was a bustling little town when we lived there. Dennis was in the fifth grade. The older kids seemed to congregate in hordes of similar interests. He fell into one of those groups of rowdy boys that gave their parents cause to worry, not that Dennis did any of those things."

Carol took a drink of milk. "I don't remember much about school. I had my friends and my sisters and brother had theirs. We didn't mix much."

"Well, that's when Dennis really started picking on Alan. It was like he needed a punching bag, or something, not that he ever hit him. He just changed, like he was finished being a brother and started being a jerk."

Carol laughed. "My sisters and I always picked on our little brother. He used to get so mad at us."

"Dennis rarely bothered me. I never understood what he was trying to do. Being a seven-year-old kid, Alan was easily confused and intimidated. Every time he opened his mouth, Dennis seemed to be able to turn it against him and make him look like a fool and he laughed. That's what I couldn't stand. His laughing at Alan. It never stopped. Even as an adult, he still tries to make Alan look like a fool, then laughs."

"Yeah," said Carol. "That's what I really don't like about him. He's kind of a bully."

I waved off the comment.

"I've since learned to ignore it, but it still bugs me. Unfortunately, Alan has never gotten beyond that. But I still see signs of compassion, there, beneath Alan's outward display of contempt. I don't believe Dennis ever realized what he had been doing all of those years. None of us did. But Alan managed to overcome some of it. Like wearing shorts."

"Shorts!" said Carol. "What in the world?"

I laughed. "Yes, shorts. Alan never wore them as a kid."

"Why not?"

"Because of Dennis."

"What did Denis do that would cause Alan not to wear shorts. He wears them all the time, now."

"Dennis used to call him girly legs."

"Girly legs?"

"Alan was four. Mom had bought him a new pair of blue shorts. Alan was really proud of them. When Dennis saw him wearing them, he called him girly legs. He used it as another opportunity to rub Alan's face in more of his humiliating taunts."

"That was kind of mean."

"We didn't get new clothes very often. Alan, hardly at all. He just got Dennis' old ones. Of course, being the only girl, I got new clothes. All the time."

"Well," said Carol, "being the youngest girl, I know exactly how Alan must have felt."

"Mom had planned to take us to the park. We all liked the park, even though there wasn't much playground equipment, but Alan was the kind of boy that didn't need all of those metal contrivances. He was perfectly content to explore his surroundings and take in the wonders of nature. He would wonder why trees looked the way they did, or why the grass was green and dirt brown, or what the tiny insects were doing when they crawled across the soil. The park was a haven of curiosity."

"Yes, Alan is still like that."

"When Dennis called him girly legs, I saw his mouth draw up, and tears started. Dennis just kept on until Mom came in. That's when the crying really took off."

"Didn't she stop it?"

"God, no. She scolded Alan for crying about it. I think he knew he wouldn't get any sympathy or help from Mom."

"That's terrible," Carol said. "That's just not right."

"Anyway, Alan ran to his bedroom and hid in a corner by his bed."

"Apparently, he got over it."

"Oh yes. It wasn't until he was in college that he started wearing shorts."

"I can't believe it. He wears shorts all the time, weather permitting," said Carol.

We finished our drinks.

"I suppose I should go ahead and make something for breakfast," she said, getting up and heading for the kitchen. I followed.

"I'm kind of glad Mom and Dad are gone. Dennis' unfortunate situation would have killed them. Dennis having a heart transplant. I know they didn't approve of a lot of Dennis' antics, but still, what a predicament. Mom wouldn't have taken it quite so hard. She could hide her feelings really well. No one would ever know for sure. But, they're gone, now. Mom, then Dad, and now maybe Dennis. If he died, that would just leave Alan and me. Man. What the hell's happening?"

Carol set about preparing breakfast while I helped as much as I could.

Carol looked at me. You don't have much other family, do you?"

"No. Some cousins somewhere, but we don't stay in touch. I have no idea where they are."

"I know your family has never been close."

"Oh, no, we don't dare show our feelings. I think Alan would self-destruct if he ever did."

"That's too bad. I don't know what I would do without being able to talk to my sisters."

"Well, that's our charming family, for you."

While pancakes were cooking and turkey sausage frying, the conversation took a turn. Carol turned to me, again.

"I think ever since Alan's mother died, he's become more… distant from Dennis. I think he did have a pretty good relationship with his mother. Her death did affect him, somewhat."

"Oh, I know it did."

"I think watching her slowly being destroyed by Parkinson's and Alzheimer's really got to him."

She flipped the pancakes.

"After we got his folks moved down here, one night we heard this awful noise outside like a kid crying. It was raining cats and dogs. Alan finally got up to see what it was. Madeline was outside in the rain grabbing hold of a porch post, yelling for help. We got her in the house and dried her off and got her to sleep. This was about eleven o'clock. About two in the morning, George called and asked if we knew where she was."

I flipped the sausages.

"We finally talked his father into getting home health care for her. Of course, all he did was bitch about how much it cost. But it worked out pretty good. She eventually developed sundowners syndrome, and things got worse. It got to the point she didn't even recognize him. The sad thing is that Dennis and Jackie showed no interest in them at all."

"Well," I said, "you remember at the hospital. We all knew Mom was dying, and everyone left to go have lunch, leaving Alan and me there alone with her. Of course, you had your own family to deal with. But Alan and I sat there at the sides of her bed and watched her slowly pass away."

"Yes, I remember that. I couldn't believe they just up and left like that."

"I was crying my eyes out and Alan never even shed a tear. I could tell he was hurting. And I believe that's what turned him against Dennis so badly."

"Well, I didn't have much respect for him either after that."

About that time, Alan came down the stairs. Breakfast was served.

****

I went to my room to change into clothes. And I think. I knew Dennis was a jerk, but he did have his moments as a brother. I just hoped he came out of the surgery. How the hell long were they going to take? Jackie would call when it was over. I wondered what Brent and Becky were doing that they couldn't come?

Oh well, I needed to call the office.

Things were being taken care of and the staff had hardly missed me. It was a shock to my ego, but then I realized that if they *had* missed me, then the office wouldn't have been as well organized and efficient. I wanted to pat myself on the back. I told my boss about Dennis, and she encouraged me to be with my family and be as much help as I could.

****

Even though the sun had finally made an appearance it was difficult to notice, except for the huge oak trees standing guard around the house. They looked so grand, majestic.

Alan spent part of the early morning in his workshop. I figured he was working on Carol's cabinet, and I had no intention of interrupting him. I sat there, in the den looking at Alan's handiwork. He had become quite the carpenter, or craftsman, as he used to say. The two-story log house he and Carol had built themselves was a tribute to their dedication and resolve. A monument to their existence. She had busted her butt to help this thing rise from the ground to its final glory. It was quite impressive, and innovative. I know Carol's family had considered it to be a kind of mansion, and her family looked upon her as a rung above the rest of them.

I had spent many nights in that house, a complete escape from my life. I wished I'd had that kind of escape when I was younger. When we all were younger. At the folks' house, it seemed as though it was little more than a battle ground. Nothing like

Alan's house. Whenever we gathered at Mom and Dad's, some skirmish always erupted, mainly between Alan and Dennis, and I frequently got dragged into it.

I remember one Christmas in particular, the one when all of us were able to be there on Christmas Day, so long ago.

CHRISTMAS AT THE FOLKS' HOUSE

December 1985

That year, the first one in a long time that Dennis had been able to make an appearance, we all had Christmas at the folks' house in Winfield. They had moved back there from Milton after Alan graduated from OSU. I had just started working at the women's shelter in Dallas. Dad sent me money for a plane ticket, a rare show of parenthood, and I flew into Wichita the day before Christmas, rented a car and drove to Winfield.

Brent had just turned ten earlier that month, and Becky was seven, the same age as Teresa. I hadn't seen any of them for some time. I had looked forward to seeing how much they had grown.

Our family had never been big on Christmas, having had few opportunities to spend a real Christmas at home since the folks had moved to Milton, where Dad's store dictated everything we did, including vacations, buying clothes and food, eating at restaurants, which only happened if company came, mainly Mom's two sisters, Verda and Vivian. Since he would keep the store open until eight on Christmas Eve to catch the late shoppers, he would get home shortly after that. Mom would have worked at the store until supper time, then gotten her and Dad something to eat from a nearby restaurant, then she would come home to feed us kids. When Dad got home, we would open our presents, then pack up to go north to Anthony or Winfield for the family gathering on Mom's side. They were always close and enjoyed the holidays, since neither Vivian nor Vera had kids of their own. That gave Dennis, Alan and me a distinct advantage on Christmas. Mom enjoyed the holidays, too, except for all of the rushing to prepare for the drive north. Dennis and Alan and I were just as eager to see our aunts and uncle. We had two uncles there, but one, Howard, spent Christmas with his wife's family. It was usually a fun time for everyone. Dad...well, Dad did have moments of what he would consider fun, but mostly just tolerated it. It was almost as if he wished there was no Christmas at all, except for the fact that sales in his store boomed during that holiday and the money rolled in.

After Dennis, Alan and I left home and started our own families, well; at least Dennis and Alan, where to spend holidays became an issue: Which family would get which holiday, the husband's or the wife's? Mom and Dad were graciously understanding about the other families and didn't insist on our being there on the actual holiday. I know they had been disappointed, but they rarely said anything. This one year, though, we all managed to make it to Winfield.

I was the last one to arrive on Christmas Eve in the cold, blustery wind that blew through the deserted neighborhood with gusto. I was surprised to see Dennis' Chrysler parked in front next to the garage with Alan's Buick behind it. I figured with all of Dennis' "Important" business to take care of, he would have been late. I was glad to be wrong, thinking this was a good omen.

I parked my cheap rental car, with its deficient heating, next to Dennis' car and lugged my bag to the door, opened it and went into the hall, that narrow sound tunnel that broadcast any slight noise throughout the house. The flurry of conversation coming from the kitchen drew me that way. They were all at the breakfast table laughing and drinking.

"Sue," Alan almost yelled. "Hi. Do you have stuff in your car to bring in?"

Mom sprang to life in her chair and Dad just sat there and gave his usual grunt of acknowledgement.

"Hi, Alan," I said. "Yes, the presents are out there. Thanks."

He got up and headed for the door. After a short pause, Mom punched Dennis and he pulled his big belly up out of his chair and followed Alan. "I'll sleep on the sofa in the living room," I said since there were only three bedrooms. "Where are the kids going to sleep?"

"We'll make beds in the basement," said Mom. "They won't be bothered by our talking late at night."

I heard the kids screaming in the basement, their high pitch voices a sheer delight. What a pleasant sound for a change instead of the morose, depressing stories from the women and children at the shelter. Most pleasures I'd gotten out of life amounted to the whimpering and crying of babies and small children caught up in the throes of a difficult life, their mothers often unprepared to deal with the frustration of a frightened child. Knowing I was able to help soothe their fears and comfort them was a great pleasure to me.

But hearing the carefree shouts and laughter of my nieces and nephew unleashed an old excitement that had been buried for a long time. I went down to see them.

Brent, cards in his hand, sat cross-legged on the floor. He had grown so much, a good-looking boy. Much of his father's looks, but a lot of his mothers, too. He was not shy by any means and was quick to be the explorer. Becky, had grown as well, her face getting longer, like her mother's, and a little extra girth around the middle. She still had that adorable face, dark brown hair, rich brown eyes receding just a bit as if hiding from the world. A real charmer. Then there was Teresa, sitting with her legs folded beneath her, fanning the cards in her hand. The almost blond hair whisked back into curls, her light complexion almost shining, and those radiant green eyes that captivated me.

"Aunt Sue," screamed Becky. She jumped up and ran to hug me. Teresa followed, coyly, as if approaching a member of the royal family. And Brent, just turned his head toward me, looking up with one of those smart aleck grins of his.

"Who's winning?" I asked.

"Teresa lost last time," boasted Brent. "She got stuck with the Old Maid."

He and Becky broke out laughing. Teresa kind of withdrew a bit, almost embarrassed.

"Probably because you cheated," I told Brent.

He laughed again.

After a brief chat, I went back upstairs to the kitchen, standing beside Mom, who was at the sink filling a pot with water.

"What can I do to help?"

She looked up at me through those soft green eyes of hers, a smile on her face.

"You can peel potatoes," she said. "I just hate to do that."

I did, too, but I didn't say that. I took a pan from the cabinet, a knife from a drawer, and the bag of potatoes, and set them on the table next to Dad, the only chair not occupied. Jackie and Carol sat in two other chairs, Carol stuffing deviled eggs. I dragged the trash can over by my chair and started peeling.

Dad looked at me. "You want a drink?"

"I'd kill for one," I told him.

His eyes lit up, a kind of smile on his face, then jumped up, grabbed the bottle of bourbon off the counter and poured some into a glass, plopped in a couple of ice cubes and some 7-Up. He brought it to the table and set it down in front of me.

"How's that shelter of yours doing?"

I looked at him while he sat back down, an unusual sincere expression on his face, an expression that one seldom saw.

I took a good hit on the drink. "Dad, we're drowning in abused women. There must be an epidemic or something. We're crowded and there are still women and children who need shelter. We just can't cope with it all."

By that time, Alan and Dennis had retrieved the packages from my car and deposited them beneath the Christmas tree in the living room.

I kept working on the first potato.

"Say, uh...who pays for your shelter?" Dad asked.

I took a deep breath. "It's funded by the city, but we also get a lot of donations and grants. We're not necessarily short on money."

"I would guess not with all the taxpayers' money going into it," Dennis spouted sitting back down in his chair, as if it was a drain on society. "Crap like that is why my taxes are so high."

My anger didn't give me a chance to prepare for that barb. My eyes shot green bullets at him. "And I supposed you'd just leave them with their abusive spouses to be raped and beaten to a pulp. And the kids half beaten to death."

A silence bomb dropped. Everyone looked at Dennis while his face turned red. Alan pulled the kitchen stool to the table and sat.

"Oh," Dennis said, "I didn't mean it like that."

"Then just how *did* you mean it."

"Just forget it." He backed his chair up. "I'm going to play pool." Then he went downstairs to the basement.

I couldn't help but notice that Alan's face had turned into a block of stone, jaws set, brows tightened, teeth clenched. Carol was looking at him, her hand on his arm.

"Alan," she said. "Let it go."

Poor Jackie sat there, clueless, apparently having no idea what to do. I think she honestly believed Dennis' outburst was uncalled for, but she couldn't allow herself to admit it. I picked up another potato and continued peeling.

"I'm sorry. The shelter means a lot to me, and those women have nowhere else to go."

I was so frustrated with the system, my anger swelled up in my gut. "We just don't have the room."

I didn't intend to sound so sharp.

Dad grunted. "Well, how many women do you have there?"

I dropped the potato onto the table and looked at him.

"We have twenty-four women and sixteen children."

Dad leaned back in his chair. "By God, that's a lot. I didn't know it was that big of a problem."

"Well, we don't get much press coverage. It seems to be unimportant to most folks, unless they need our services."

Mom had been listening and said, "I think that's where Brenda's daughter is. She was trying to stay away from her husband. He was abusive to their son."

She stirred something in a pot, looking at me.

"Brenda's is our neighbor's daughter."

"Well," said Dad perplexed, "where is this place? I never heard of anything like that."

"We've driven by it a dozen times. It's that old house on West Elm Drive. Right next to the old ice house."

"Is that the only one here?" Carol asked.

"I guess so," said Mom. "I really don't know."

We eventually got around to supper. It wasn't the most cordial one we'd had, but at least everyone was civil. No more barbs or smart aleck remarks. Dennis was unusually quiet, which seemed to put us all at ease. I don't think I could have withstood another onslaught of his selfishness and crass jokes.

Jackie dominated most of the conversation with a long, drawn-out description of their latest travels. According to her and Dennis, it was the biggest and best vacation anyone could have taken. Alan was seeking escape in his drink and rolling his eyes, Carol was trying to act interested, and Dad...well, he just sat there looking at nothing. The kids seemed content just to giggle among themselves. Teresa sat very ladylike in her chair, her eyes keenly fastened on the adults. Brent was making faces at her and trying to be cute. Becky, poor dear, was fastidiously capping her fingertips with black olives. Such charming children.

It was a blessing when Jackie's monologue ended, and we all relaxed. Dennis, Dad and Jackie went to the basement with the kids to play pool, Carol, Alan and I helped Mom clean up the place, then went down to play pool with the others.

There had been an empty room in the basement when the folks moved into the house and Dad had put in a pool table to while away the evening hours with Mom, who played with him only to humor him. She was not necessarily into pool.

When bedtime came, I was past ready. After the adults filled the stockings hung on the mantel of the fireplace that had never been used in the living room, I hit the sack. I don't think an earthquake could have disturbed me.

****

I heard the early morning traditional banging in the kitchen, cabinet doors slamming and pots and pans skittering on the stovetop. Mom and Dad were up. They never worried about the noise disturbing anyone else. Then I heard a door slam in the hall and Brent giggling. Then a door forced open, and a young voice says, "Peek a boo. Get up. Get up."

It was Brent, again, followed by an angry voice, "Brent, close the door and leave us alone."

That was Alan. The episode repeated itself at least three times.

I got up and ventured into the hallway. Brent opened the door to Alan's bedroom and recited his demand.

"Brent," I said. "Leave them alone. Where are your mom and dad?"

He stood there in his pajamas looking at me with an impish grin on his face. "They're in the bedroom."

"I think you should go join them," I said. "It's very rude to disturb peoples' privacy."

"I don't think so," the arrogant little shit said.

"Well, I do," I almost shouted. "Go!"

He stuck out his tongue at me and ran for his parents' room. I was tempted to yank the little bastard up and spank his butt, but that would only set off fireworks. Not on Christmas.

I retrieved my clothes from the living room and headed for the hall bathroom to wash and get dressed. I damned sure locked the door before the little urchin tried to barge in on me.

Later, I went to the kitchen to help if I could. Mom, spatula in hand, steam, rising into the exhaust hood, was cooking bacon and eggs, the skillets grating over the electric burners like a shovel on concrete. If anyone was still in bed, they darned sure weren't sleeping. Dad, apparently, was in charge of the toaster. I saw that the coffee was done, so I filled a cup of the light brown liquid that Dad thought was coffee. They had one of those Mr. Coffee drip coffeemakers with the pull-out funnel that used paper filters. Dad was one of those people who bent over backward to save a penny. In fact, I figured he still had the first penny he ever made.

The coffeemaker itself was fine but Dad insisted that it used too much coffee, even though he bought the cheapest brand he could find. Some of those brands really had a nerve calling the contents of their cans coffee. So, he fabricated a plastic ring to fit around the wall of the funnel inside the filter leaving only the bottom part of the filter to let coffee pass through. The result was what looked like dirty water that tasted only vaguely like coffee. It was terrible, but better than no coffee at all. The "Great Depression" had really done a job on him.

I had given him a fifth of Evan Williams bourbon one Christmas, something he would never buy himself, since it was more expensive than many other brands. He bought the cheap bourbon, and when the Evan Williams bottle was empty, he would fill it with the cheap bourbon to serve to guests, hoping they would think he was a big spender. He was a real class act, my father.

I took over the toast and set the table. The toast that morning would be real toast, fully buttered. If Dad were making it, butter, or the margarine they used, would only grace the center third of the slice. Margarine cost money, you know.

Breakfast went smoothly, with mild chatter and excited anticipation from the kids, who surprisingly ate their food instead of playing with it. Mom's breakfasts were always my favorite. Alan's, too. Dennis could take it or leave it. Jackie had no trouble digging in, and Carol enjoyed it as well. Then it was time for presents.

The poor, decrepit artificial Christmas tree in the living room, with lights that had survived three decades and ornaments that preceded them, spread its worn, dilapidated green branches over a cache of gifts that could have served the entire block. Brent and Becky plopped down at the edge of the presents spilling from the tree while Teresa calmly sat back and stared at it.

Mom appointed Dennis as "Santa Claus" and the kids as elves. The exchange, mostly for the kids, began.

The presents were unusually appropriate that year, and well received. Teresa was given a big doll that could walk with her holding it up. She immediately grew attached to it, among other things. Becky also got a doll and a charming make-up kit for kids. Dad brought Brent's present in from the garage, a low rider tricycle. Since it was too cold and messy to go outside, they took it down to the basement. Brent mounted it and took off in circles around the large room, the plastic wheels roaring on the concrete. It was good to see him enjoying himself. In fact, everyone seemed satisfied with their gifts.

Later, after things calmed down a bit, I ventured into the hall to go to the bathroom. Passing by Alan's bedroom I noticed the bed neatly made and clothes hung in the closet. I heard Alan and Dennis arguing in Dennis' room.

"Dennis, Brent has no business barging into our room," Alan said. "What if we'd been having sex or something?"

I heard Dennis smirk. He always let out this little grunt when he smirked.

"So, what if you were?" Dennis said.

"You think this is funny?" Almost yelled.

Dennis laughed. His "why don't you go pound sand down a rathole" laugh.

"Oh, don't get all bent out of shape about it."

A momentary lull.

"Just teach your damn kids some respect for other people," Alan told him, barely restraining his anger.

Alan burst out of the bedroom, startled to find me in the hall, his body poised for a fight, red face and ears.

I ducked into the bathroom. I heard him explain the situation to Carol As they went back to the kitchen, I heard Jackie come down the hallway and ask Dennis about the argument.

I tried to be quiet so I could hear their conversation. Sound carried through that house like a whistle in a tunnel.

"Oh, Alan got mad because Brent opened their bedroom door this morning," Dennis said.

"Why was he mad about that?"

"I guess he thinks they're entitle to privacy in this house," Dennis said with arrogance.

Jackie laughed.

I was disappointed in them. They couldn't even teach their kids respect and consideration for other people. Their kids would grow up to be just like them. It was heartbreaking to think that they would likely be arrogant boors, just like their parents.

While I took care of business in the bathroom, I decided I would leave sooner than I had planned, right after dinner. The few extra hours waiting on my flight at the airport would be preferable to a family skirmish. I didn't want to get caught in the middle of another sibling war. Christmas somehow seemed to have lost its luster for me. It used to be so much fun In spite of having to travel, but it was becoming a dreadful experience. I wondered what the next year would be like. I'm not sure I wanted to spend it with Dennis' family. Then I thought about how selfish and rude that sounded. But then, I realized that Dennis' family *was* selfish and rude.

Our Christmas dinner was held on a happy note. Then, the remainder of the afternoon was spent listening to Dad tell stories he had told a hundred times before. We all knew them by heart. Aunt Verda and Aunt Vivian had joined us late in the morning. Dennis was blowing and going about his new job at some bank in Okemah. The kids had a good time, as well. No errant behavior. It was almost a record for the family.

After dinner, I helped Carol and Mom clean up while Brent and Becky ran helter-skelter through the house, yelling at each other. Dennis and Jackie sat in the living room with Dad, who was trying his best to ignore the brats. Teresa was following Vivian and Verda who were gathering tablecloths and napkins. Dennis and Jackie showed no signs of abating the racket or helping. That confirmed my decision to leave soon. Alan had gone into the basement to return some of the things Mom had used for the table setting. When he came up the stairs, he scowled at everyone. He looked at Carol and she nodded her head in agreement. They were planning to leave, too.

It's sad when families can no longer be together for more than a few hours. It just takes one family to disrupt the entire flock. I know Dennis wasn't raised the way he and his kids act. Where did that come from? He was never the considerate type, but hell, you'd think that as an adult he would have some idea of how other people treat him and how he treats other people. Sometimes I am so ashamed of my family. When my friends talk about their families, the compassion, the togetherness, the love between them, I feel like falling into a hole, some deep abyss where there is no one at all, and escaping.

I couldn't wait to leave the melee behind. The afternoon was progressing and it would be well after dark before I got home. I was willing to endure the stress of driving back to the airport in Wichita just to be home and away from everyone else.

****

I had a late flight, and while sitting in the airport I happened to talk to a woman sitting nearby.

"I guess you're going home?" she asked.

"Oh, yes," I said. "I've had enough family for one year."

She turned abruptly in her seat and looked at me, her brown eyes wide with interest.

"You too, huh?" She threw her head back, her blonde hair flying, and sighed. "Well, I've had enough family for a lifetime," she almost gushed.

I laughed. "Surely it can't be that bad."

"Listen, dearie," she said, waving her hand at me as if batting a fly away, "you have no idea." She took a deep breath and continued. "I have two sisters, both with kids. No, not kids." She paused. "More like brats."

I sharpened my gaze on her and leaned in.

"I'm not married," she confided. "I don't have kids. I like kids, but not those kids."

She let out a humph. "Does that sound awful?" She shook her head. "Well, I don't see how anyone can like those kids. They just drive me crazy, always yelling, jumping around, and getting into things they have no business getting into."

"I think I'm familiar with that," I said in sympathy.

"Oh," she said, her eyes in question. "Do you have kids?"

"No," I said, in a sigh of relief. "I'm not married, either."

Her brown eyes sharpened, and her face lit up.

"So, you've been visiting family?"

"If you want to call it that." I smiled. "It's more like enduring them."

"Say," she said, "I could use a drink. How about you?"

That's all it took for me to jump up. We headed for the nearest bar. After we got our drinks, she exploded into an exposé of her family's deportment in explicit detail.

"My sisters are absolute bitches," she said, her face becoming animated. "They have no consideration for anyone else. The only things important in the world are themselves. It's all about them," she said, dragging out the 'all.' "It's as if I'm not even alive."

I took a stiff drink. "That sounds like one of my bothers."

"Oh, dear," she said. "You have brothers?"

"Two of them."

"Sisters are bad enough. How on earth do you cope with two brothers?"

"Well, actually, only one is the problem. Dennis. He's a year older, grossly overweight, an arrogant boor."

"Oh, my god," she said. "That's Catrina, all over. Well, except for being overweight."

"What about your other sister?" I asked, taking another drink.

She downed her glass of whiskey and nearly slammed it on the table, then let out a huge huff.

"Cassandra is one of those trophy wives, you know, model perfect, makeup galore, self-centered, extravagant, and very high maintenance. I don't know how Roy, her husband, puts up with it all."

"I should probably introduce myself," I said, extending a hand. "I'm Susan Carter."

"Oh, yes, of course. I'm Bertha Haynes. I'm so glad I ran into you today. This wait would have been intolerable without you."

"Same here," I told her.

"Let me get you another drink," she offered, raising her hand for a waiter. "You said you had two brothers."

"Yes. Two."

What's the other one like?"

"That would be Alan. The enigma of the family."

"That sounds ominous."

"No, on the contrary, he's a good brother, for the most part."

She reared back in surprise. "You can't be serious."

"Alan is very complex. He can be sweet, charming, in his own way, and considerate. And he is somewhat of a snob. Well, about coffee and things like that. But that all comes with a price."

Our drinks came, she paid for them, and leaned forward to hear more.

"What do you mean?"

"Alan is a Vietnam vet. In addition to coping with our dysfunctional family, he has his own demons to fight."

"I'm so sorry. Is he…?"

I laughed. "No. He's perfectly fine. He just has moments of introspection that we have learned to respect. He's quite brilliant. An engineer.

"Oh, my. That's impressive. What kind of engineer?"

"Oh, he designs buildings. Well, at least he designs the structures for them. He built his own two-story log house. It's quite a showplace."

Bertha's face took on a peculiar expression, much like disbelief or skepticism.

"I've never known an engineer," she said, picking up her glass. "Is he…weird or anything like that?" Then she took a drink. "I'm sorry. I didn't mean—" She caught herself. "It's just that I've heard so many stories about engineers and how strange they can be."

I laughed again. "No, no. He's perfectly normal. Most of the time. He does stay pretty much to himself, though. I imagine that's because of Vietnam."

We continued talking at length about our families, me wondering what it would be like to have a family like hers, and, I suppose she was most likely wondering the same thing about my family. Considering what I had heard from Bertha, was our family really that bad? That far removed from the norm? I looked around at all the people sitting around me, and I began to suspect that maybe I didn't have it so bad, after all.

The announcement was for my flight. We said our good-byes and parted company. At least I had something to think about on the way home.

RECOVERY

March 2002

I hated hospitals. As if Mom's death wasn't enough, I remembered when Dad had his heart attack several years earlier. Mom was beside herself and was slowly succumbing to Alzheimer's Disease. She was already under the grips of Parkinson's Disease, and it just made it nearly impossible for her to get a grip on reality. Dad was having a difficult time coping with it all.

Then the bottom fell out of our lives.

The heart attack was a big one. The doctor said he needed a triple bypass. Mom, at least, was lucid enough at the time to call for an ambulance. Beyond that, she had little idea what she was doing.

I had just started a new job with no sick days or holiday time available, so going up to Winfield to help was out of the question. Alan had been sent off to Chicago for a conference with a client. Carol jumped in and went up to Winfield to stay with Mom. Dennis? Hell, Dennis and Jackie were "too busy," of course. Alan's company did allow him time to fly home to see his father in the hospital and get some things done for Mom.

Alan and Carol carried Mom through the difficulties with Dad's recovery. Dennis and Jackie showed up at the hospital the day before Dad was to be released.

Alan told me that while standing in his room, Dad went on

about how he was going to change his life. He was going to eat healthy food, exercise, and not worry so much about things. He also promised that when he got out of the hospital, he was going to give each of us kids ten-thousand dollars. Of course, Alan, in his own sadistic way, said that was just a ploy to make himself feel better. Alan was right. He never gave us a dime.

It wasn't until Dad had been home for a couple of weeks that I sweet-talked my boss into letting me get away and visit him.

****

"Dad," I said, rushing into the house. Where are you?"

I turned around in the entry and saw him sitting at the kitchen table, as stoical as he usually was, drinking coffee.

Mom hurried from the kitchen to greet me. She leaned close and whispered in my ear, "He's been on pins and needles waiting for you kids to come."

I nodded and said, "I don't see any cars. Am I the only one here?"

I followed her into the kitchen. She seemed alert and feisty. That was a good sign.

"Carol left yesterday. Dennis hasn't made it, yet."

"Hi, Pop," I said going over to him. "How are you doing?"

His face lit up and he leaned to the side, resting on his right elbow that was planted on the arm of the chair. A plastic device sat on the table in front of him to measure his lung capacity. "Huh, huh," he grunted. That was what he always did when someone asked him a question like that. "Oh, ah, pretty good."

"Sit down," Mom ordered. "The doctor told him to take it easy for several weeks." She paused, as if a thought had just occurred to her. "He'll have to be careful what he eats."

I took a seat across from Mom. Dad seemed to be recovering all right, and things would probably be okay, unless Mom drifted into one of her spells of disorientation.

"Carol told me Alan got to come see you," I said to Dad. "I wish I had been here sooner, but my new job is taking a toll. I finally just told my boss I was taking a couple of days off to come home. I told him he could pay me or not.

Mom sat slumped idly in her chair, here glassy eyes staring at something that was not obvious, not to Dad or me. I turned back to Dad. "I guess Carol took care of things while she was here?"

He sat up all of a sudden and leaned forward on the table.

"By God, she's quite a woman. I don't know what we would have done without her."

He told me that Alan and Carol were able to quell any disturbances that arose. I decided not to bring up Dennis and Jackie.

Yes, I thought to myself. Carol *is* quite a woman.

Dad *did* recover fully and things got back to normal, except for Mom, of course.

****

I was still at Alan's when Jackie called to tell us that Dennis' transplant went as planned and he was in ICU recovery. The news hit me like a wave of cold water. I was nearly stunned by the anxiety being washed away so suddenly. I could even see the relief in Alan's face, as difficult as it was to read. Carol seemed to perk up, too.

Jackie had said it would be a few days before he could have visitors, so the next two days were filled with anticipation, laughter, and reminiscing. Alan and I replayed many parts of our lives, much to Carol's delight. It helped get us through the hours of suspense and worry. I had taken two weeks of vacation and Alan had taken off work for a few days.

He and I had our beers and Carol had her wine.

"What really happened when Dennis lost his job at the bank in Oklahoma City?" Carol asked. "I never did understand that. He always talked like he was set for life there."

For all of the swank and swagger he had displayed to the world, Dennis' voyage on the high tide in the Good Ship Luck ran aground as he neared the age of sixty. True to the promise of the Peter Principle, he had been let go by the bastion of financial wealth to which he had dedicated several years of loyalty and more than his share of arrogance. It was with mixed emotions that the family greeted this development.

"He said he got laid off, but I suspect he got fired," Alan volunteered, taking a swig of beer.

"Well," I said, "I really think he did get laid off." I tipped the beer up to my lips and drank. "You remember the big hoopla at their house when the folks came to visit, just before I moved to Dallas."

"Oh, yeah." Alan nodded his head and took a drink of his beer. "Boy, Dad really gave him the evil eye. I can still recall that moment perfectly."

"Oh, so can I," I said.

****

"So, they just let you go?" Dad asked, his head turned slightly away from Dennis, and looking out of the tops of his eyes, as if he had already decided not to believe what excuse Dennis offered. Dennis leaned back in the chair, his bloated stomach rising with the effort, and pushed himself further back with his hands on the arms of the chair.

"Yeah," he said, with an imperious flair. "They cut back on the staff. A lot of folks got the axe."

I took this in with a dose of suspicion. I'm pretty sure Alan did, too. Dennis seemed to have skipped from job to job over the last two decades like a rock skipping over water.

"Well, what are you going to do?" Dad had asked, still looking over the top of his glasses, the doubtful gaze he always used when one of us was not quite telling the truth.

Jackie spoke up to save him.

"We're going to sell our house in the city and find a smaller place. And we can see what is out there for us to do. I've still got my realtor's license, so I can fill in while Dennis looks for something."

Dennis, that arrogant look still on his face, seemed content to let Jackie's explanation ride. He didn't volunteer anything else, a smart move on his part, because Dad would have asked more questions.

Carol moved closer to Jackie.

"Are you sure you're going to be all right, Jackie?"

"We'll be fine. Becky will be around to help out and Brent said he'd be available if we needed him."

Dad still held Dennis in his sights. Mom said nothing about any of it; just looked down at her glass. We all left it at that.

****

Dull, dark skies, the color of wet steel, seemed to pull all of the life out of the surrounding trees and pasture across the road from the house. It was the kind of day that left me unwilling to do anything, sucking all of the resolve and motivation from my mind. A do-nothing day. Even with the news about Dennis, I still felt resigned to lay back and let the day pass. The beer helped.

Then I saw squirrels playing in the big oak trees just outside the window. I suddenly realized that I was sulking, something I rarely do. I didn't know why. Dennis' transplant was successful, Jackie seemed to be coping well, and we were all safe in our distant familial camaraderie.

"He never did find anything else, did he?" Carol said, her wine glass nearly empty.

"No," Alan told her. "That's when they moved to Okemah and he got a job at that veterinarian's office taking care of the books."

"That's really kind of sad," she said.

"He never did make it back to the big time. He never did have any grand ambition. Oh, he still had a good store of arrogance and racism. No, I don't think he ever had ambition for anything but spending money. Even in Milton he never gave any hint of what he really wanted to do in life." Another drink of beer. "Except make my life miserable. It was the same after we moved to Ponca City's and I was in junior high."

I shot him a look of rebuke, not that it would make any difference. He could be such an ass.

"Alan…"

"I know, I know," he said. "But goddamn it, that son of a bitch never gave me a moment's rest."

"Alan," I said, standing, "give us a break. I'm getting tired of hearing your lament over Dennis and you."

He snapped his head toward me. "Well, Sis, how the hell did you like growing up with his crass remarks about *you*? And his disgusting habits."

"Yes, Alan. I know."

"Like trying to eat breakfast at the same table with him."

"What happened at breakfast?" asked Carol.

I tried to explain.

"When we lived in Milton, Dennis was in junior high and Alan was in grade school, we had this small breakfast room at the back of the house next to the kitchen. We'd have cereal one day, oatmeal another, French toast or pancakes, and of course, eggs and bacon. It was the eggs and bacon that really got to Alan."

"It was damned disgusting," Alan said with a bit of anger. "He just couldn't leave me alone."

I continued. "On mornings Mom prepared eggs and bacon, Alan would chop the fried eggs into small pieces with a fork, mixing the yolk and whites, then crumble bacon into it and stir it together. Dennis would say "blood and guts." Then he would gloat at his cleverness."

"It sounds pretty awful to me," said Carol. "I don't like yolks, anyway."

I chuckled. "Alan would glare at him with barbaric eyes. If I had to guess, I'd say he had wished for that meat tenderizer again."

"If I'd had the damned thing," said Alan, "I would have used it."

"Actually, Alan's plate did kind of resemble something that was the result of a massacre."

I looked at Alan.

"But you're right Alan. I always wished that I could have eaten alone just once."

"I don't remember any of us picking on any other," said Carol. "Well, my sisters and I picked on George a lot, because he usually got anything he wanted. We never got much of anything."

"Families are such fun," I said. "I think I'll go upstairs and check in with work."

****

Two days after the surgery Jackie called again with an update on Dennis.

Carol talked to her. She said we just wished we were there. Not that we could do much, but we could be there for her. This had to be traumatic for Jackie. After she finished talking with Jackie, she came over to the table where Alan and I sat.

"What about Brent and Becky?" I asked. "How are they handling it?"

"They're both there at the hospital. They're helping out with food and such."

Alan spoke up. "I'm glad of that."

He went to the kitchen to grab a couple of beers, then poured Carol a glass of wine.

After sitting back down, "It seems like ages since I've seen either of them."

"Well, that's a relief. I couldn't imagine them not coming. How long do you think Dennis is going to be in the hospital?"

"I imagine that's something they'll have to take a day at a time," said Carol. "Jackie said it just depends on how he responds to all of the medication they pour down him."

"Is it a lot?"

"It sounded like he swallows a small pharmacy every day."

"You're kidding?"

"No. Then they have to figure out which medication is working and which isn't and make adjustments. It might take a while."

I couldn't believe it was so complicated. I'd never thought about transplants. I doubt that many people have. Transplants are things other people do that we never hear about. We just seem to take our lives for granted. Boy, Dennis certainly did.

The next day Alan drove us all back to the hospital to see Dennis. Jackie met us in the hallway outside the ICU.

Standing there in smart pants and blouse, she looked fabulous. Her bright smile was a good sign and her eyes almost twinkled.

"Hi, guys," she blurted out with gusto. "The doc says he's doing great. He's in a real good mood today."

That seemed to relieve the knots in my stomach. Alan's posture relaxed and he raised his head as if in relief.

Carol headed straight for Jackie, and they hugged.

"Can he have visitors?" She asked.

She turned to Alan. "Why don't you and Sue go on in. I'll stay with Jackie."

Entering Dennis' room, I was stunned by his appearance. He looked so different. Both eyes open, color in his face, the haggard look gone, the forest of poles and bags was still there, but the mood was lighter.

"Hey, Bro," I said. "You look great."

"Yeah," said Alan. "Better than last time."

"I feel a lot better, too," Dennis said, his voice stronger than I expected.

Alan moved toward the bed and stood beside it.

"Listen, Dennis…"

An awkward silence passed between them.

"…I, ah…I'm glad you're all right. You had us all worried there for a bit."

Dennis smiled.

Then, "You son of a bitch!" Alan was leaning over him. "What the hell did you think you were doing? You had us all worried about your sorry ass. Don't ever have another heart attack."

Then Alan straightened up and started laughing.

Dennis tried to laugh. "Shit," he said. "It hurts to laugh."

"Serves you right," I said. "How long are you in for?"

Dennis looked at me. In a strained voice, he said, "At least a couple of weeks."

"Well, it looks like you're in good hands. I'm going out to talk to Jackie. You two behave yourselves."

While I walked back to the outer hallway, I thought about what had just happened. It was such a relief to see the two of them in good spirits. It had been a long time. I just hoped they could come to some reconciliation. If something like this didn't do it, then nothing would.

REVELATIONS FROM THE NEW MAN

March 2002

Dennis was recovering and we were all optimistic. I hadn't really thought about what it would be like if he had actually lived through this. I wasted my time dwelling on what life would be like if he had died. Big brother was going to make it. A tremendous weight fell from my mind.

He had been moved to a private room where he could recover in more comfort, if such a thing was possible.

The ward was busy, nurses scurrying about, phones ringing, monitors beeping and chirping, and the ambiance was the same as the rest of the dismal hospital. The antiseptic vapors were not kind to my nose, and the stark walls and ceiling screamed "institution."

I strutted into Dennis' room with Alan and Carol in tow and saw Jackie sitting in a corner of the room along with the forest of poles with bags and tubes, and an army of beeping monitors, little lines squiggling across the screens. In the middle of it all was Dennis, lying beneath the blanket, his bloated belly like an iceberg floating in a white sea.

Jackie looked up as we entered the room and a big smile broke out across her face.

"Hi, guys!"

I went over to her and gave her a hug. Alan and Carol went

to the side of the bed, Carol smiling and Alan with a serious look on his face.

"Hi Jackie," I said. "How's he doing?"

"He's doing great." She was almost bubbling.

"Hey," Alan said, moving closer to Dennis' face. "Nice to see you still with us."

Dennis half smiled and almost laughed until the pain stopped him. A week ago, he still had that pallor of post-surgery, but not serious. As I looked at him, it was all gone.

"Yeah," he said, "I'm still hanging around."

They looked at each other for a few seconds.

"How are you doing?" Alan asked.

"I feel like I've been kicked in the chest."

"Yeah, well, you look like it, too."

"Glad you came."

"I am, too. I wondered if I'd get to see you again."

"I know. I wish it wasn't like this."

"Maybe we should do something about that."

Dennis narrowed his eyebrows apparently pondering Alan's suggestion.

"Maybe you're right," said Dennis, a smirk on his face.

"That would be great, guys," Jackie almost shrieked. "I'd love to see y'all more often. Brent and Becky and Teresa could get together, too."

"It would be nice to go see them," said Carol.

"I missed Dad's burial," Dennis said with a somber tone.

"It's okay," Alan told him. "We took care of everything. There wasn't anything for you to do. Brent was there and helped with the concrete bases for the headstones."

Dad had died just before Dennis' ordeal. I'm glad it happened at that time. If Dad had been alive when Dennis had his heart attack, it would have killed him for sure. They rarely saw eye to eye, but I know Dad held Dennis in a special place in his stoical makeup. I'm not sure how it all worked, but there was something there beyond what he had felt for Alan or me. My thoughts wandered during the brief silence. Jackie finally broke the ice.

She looked at Dennis and said, "We've been doing a lot of thinking. We've decided to make a big change in our lives."

We all looked at her.

"We've talked to our minister, and he suggested some counseling."

I saw Alan's face tighten. He looked at me and rolled his eyes.

"That sounds wonderful," I said. "Do you have a plan, yet?"

"No, we'll discuss that with the minister."

"So, what do you think, big brother?" I asked Dennis.

He looked at me with a not so enthusiastic expression, a kind of smirk on his face.

"I think we can make it work," he said, reluctantly.

He looked over at Jackie and they smiled at each other, more tentative than real.

Dennis looked at each of us, pulled his lips taut and said, "I'm going to change my lifestyle."

I watched Alan, hoping for some sign of acknowledgement. Nothing.

"I'm going to be a new man."

Carol moved closer to Alan and took his hand.

"Well," she said, "I hope everything works out for you."

"So, how long are you going to be laid up?" asked Alan.

I wished he had let Dennis finish what he was going to say. I thought there surely would be more.

"The doctor thinks he might get to go home in a week or two," Jackie said. "They want to make sure the anti-rejection drugs work first."

"How long till you're up and about normally?" I asked.

Dennis spoke up. "That depends on how well the drugs work and if no complication set in."

Sounds like you're in for a long recovery," said Carol. "Is there anything we can do for you?"

That was Carol. Always thinking of someone else.

"No," said Jackie. "I think we have everything taken care of right now. The insurance is supposed to cover most of it, but we won't find out for a while, yet. Becky said she would help out if we needed her. And Brent is going to take some time off to handle things around the house that need doing."

"I think I'll get a computer," Dennis said. "And take a class at the vo-tech."

"Sounds like a good plan," Alan told him, loosening up. "When probate is settled, you'll have some extra cash to use."

"Yeah, that'll help a lot."

He looked at Alan with a stern face.

"I kind of left you holding the bag with probate and all."

"It's okay," said Alan. "I've got it all covered, the attorney is handling most of it. I've dug through Dad's files and found all of his investments. I don't think there will be any problems."

Conversation came to a halt, and I said, "We should go and let you rest."

"Well, thanks for coming by," Dennis said, sincerely, a look of anxiety mixed with anticipation on his face. "Hope I get out of here soon."

****

The trip back to Harrison was quiet. I mused about Dennis and all of the things I hadn't thought about during the episode.

I felt relieved that their kids were willing to be of some use to them. I had been worried about that. It wasn't that often that I got to see them, not that I missed those visits. Well, they *were* family, but good grief. Those two could really try my patience.

Things were looking favorable for Dennis and his family. I was so relieved. I just couldn't fathom what they must have been going through. Dennis must have been scared to death. And Jackie, well, she must have been worried sick over it all. Maybe I should be more proactive in my own life. I know I do stupid things, but hell, who doesn't?

And Alan? Oh, Jesus. That man will probably live to be a hundred. Yeah, one hundred years. What would that be like? A hundred years. People do it. What is it like to see a hundred years pass by your eyes? I wonder if Alan could even withstand the memories of Vietnam for that long. What was it like for him?

Trying to keep all of that horror in the past. How did he do it? How did Carol cope with it all? She seemed so secure and confident. How in hell did she manage to deal with Alan's torment? I know it must be torment. What else could it possibly be, living with the guilt of having lost his crew? God, I wish I had known. But what could I have done? What could Carol have done? Neither of us really understood what he went through. How could we? How could anyone who wasn't there?

And Teresa. Thank goodness she had been insulated from most of it. She had a full plate with her fellowship at the University of Oklahoma. I'll bet she still had some difficulties with it, although she seemed to be doing all right.

Enough. I had to quit worrying about Alan. He would have to fight his own demons. It was Dennis that needed our support.

****

Back in the sanity of Alan's house in Harrison, we gathered around the table in the large bay window to gorge on ribs and sandwiches from the local barbecue place. It had been a long time since I'd had the melt-in -your-mouth pork ribs and the hot beef barbecue sandwiches. The jalapeño peppers added a little zing.

"So, what do you think?" I asked, letting a bite of rib wallow in my mouth.

"I'll believe it when I see it," Alan said with a scoff of disbelief. He threw his head back and took a gulp of his beer. George Killian's Irish Red. I'm not necessarily fond of beer, but Killian's was pretty good.

"If it works, I say good for them," Carol volunteered, swishing wine in her glass. "I just hope they get some help to cope with this. It's going to be a hard battle. And probably a long one."

I read the empathy beneath the matter-of-fact delivery. I knew she'd had a lot more compassion for Jackie than Alan had. As for her feeling for Dennis, not so much.

Carol continued. "Jackie said they'd contacted the VA to see if Dennis could apply for benefits and get some help. I wonder if they've heard anything."

I nearly choked on my beer. "You mean he's never applied?"

"Not that I know of," Alan said. "I'm not sure he would be eligible."

"Why not, for god's sake? He's a veteran."

"What does it take to qualify?" Carol asked.

"I'm not sure," Alan said.

"What do you mean, you're not sure?" I figured any veteran would get VA benefits. "Aren't you in the VA?"

"Me? No. I've never applied, either," Alan said.

"Alan!" I gave him my how-dare-you look. "Why the hell not?"

He shrugged. "What for? I don't need it."

"Someday you might," I told him. I think I was almost shouting. It was just like him to be so blasé about it. He always had spurned any kind of help or assistance. I suppose I shouldn't have been surprised. He always wanted to do things by himself. Kind of a loner. I pulled back my hackles.

"What does it take to sign up?" Carol asked, again. "You should qualify, shouldn't you?"

Alan looked at Carol, then me. "I guess I should check it out. You never know. It might come in handy."

"You've still got all of your army papers, don't you?"

Alan looked at Carol. "If I can figure out where you put them."

I laughed. "You still move things around every so often?" I asked Carol.

"It's almost like coming home to a new house every night," Alan joked. "Drawing a map wouldn't help much. The positions change too often."

Carol leaned over and punched him. "Oh, I do not! I haven't moved anything in several months."

"A few months?" Alan said in feigned surprise. "All I can say is I'm glad everything's on rollers."

Carol sat back. "Well, it makes it easier. At least you don't have to help."

"Well, I think you should do it," I told him. "As a veteran you're entitled to it. And thank you for your service, by the way."

Alan looked at me funny, his eyebrows raised. "You know, that's the first time anyone in this entire family said that to me."

"Seriously?"

"Well, I damned sure didn't hear it when I came home. I've never heard it since. I've never even heard it from *her* family," he said, gesturing toward Carol. "Nobody seems to care."

"Alan, you know that's not true. A lot of people are grateful for what you did for your country."

"Yeah, well, I haven't seen any of them. And I'm pretty sure Dennis never heard it, either."

He sat there, a sad scowl on his face, his eyes angry. Just like he did when he used to pout when we were little.

"Of course," he continued, "he was never in combat. It shouldn't make any difference, though."

I bit my lip. "No, you're right. It shouldn't. Even Dennis' two years in the army counted for something. What was he, corporal or something like that?"

"Spec four," Alan said. "Same as a corporal, only in a technical MOS. He was an electrical technician, whatever the hell that meant."

"Electrical technician?" Carol said.

"Yeah. I assume he worked on radios and such. He brought home a bunch of field manuals for radio and a toolbox full of electrician's tools."

There was a subtle change in Alan's expression. If not envy, then maybe a bit of admiration.

"That was after Dad bought him that Plymouth Valiant to drive to his first assignment at Fort Leavenworth for boot camp. Boy, did we get some wild tales then."

"Yeah," I said. "I remember that. It was bright red. It had that slant-six engine. He was quite proud of it."

"I thought he had that pink Rambler?" Carol said.

"Oh, I got that when Dad bought him the Valiant," Alan said. "I must have been the laughingstock of college."

His face took on that look of embarrassment like it did whenever Dennis made fun of him.

"But at least you *had* a car," Carol said. "I never had one. None of us did. Well, except for my brother, George. He got about anything he wanted."

"Do you remember my old Henry J?" I asked.

Alan laughed and Carol looked perplexed.

"What's a Henry J?" she asked.

I laughed, too "It was a pathetic excuse for a car."

We both laughed again, Carol was still waiting.

"It was an ugly, slow, machine that Dad probably paid a dollar for. I can't imagine him paying much more for it."

Carol smiled. "What was it like? I've never seen one."

"You haven't missed much. It was black, faded, if you can imagine faded black, and it had a standard shift. It was kind of ahead of its time. It had a fastback and a front end out of the forties. I think I drove Dad nuts trying to teach me how to drive it. I actually grew fond of the poor thing."

Alan and I finished our beers and Carol sipped on her wine.

"So, do you really think Dennis is serious about this new man thing of his?" I asked.

Alan huffed. "About as serious as he is about losing that god-damned belly of his." Then he leaned back in his chair, satisfied with himself.

I let out an audible sigh. He just couldn't turn loose of it. He just couldn't give Dennis the benefit of the doubt for anything. Not one shred of support or encouragement. It was as if he had drawn the battle line and dug in his defensive position.

"Jackie seems sincere about it," Carol said. "She might encourage him to start going to church. At least, she said she would."

I nodded. "She did seem to be pretty set on it, having a minister lined up and all, and—"

"Y'all can think what you like." Alan interrupted, "But he won't last longer than three weeks."

Carol and I both gave him a sour look. He would never outgrow his contempt for Dennis. It was almost as if he were born with it. Sure, Dennis was a jerk, but he did have some good qualities. Alan just never stopped to think about them.

"We can at least give him a chance," Carol said.

The conversation fell into a lull, and I thought about what Dad would have thought about all of this. What would he think of his first-born in such a situation? Had he not died when he did, things would be very different, now. And then I thought about how he actually did die. I never got the whole story.

"Tell me, Alan, what actually happened when Dad died? What all went on then?"

He leaned back in his chair, sighed.

"After Mom's burial, such as it was, for the next several months we tried to look after Dad, but you know his ego. It was damned near impossible. Without Mom, he was lost and unable to fathom what he should or could do. I couldn't stay with him during the day because I had to work. I took him to the senior citizens center for lunch a couple of times. He didn't care for it. Carol had things to do, too, but she made an effort to look in on him several times a day. That worked until she and Dad had a confrontation one day about his treatment of Mom. Dad became belligerent toward her, and she refused to have anything more to do with him."

"I never knew him to do anything like that," I said.

"He changed, Sis. His whole attitude was different. Almost like he was mad at everyone."

"I never knew Mom's death affected him like that."

"Well, it did. By December, Dad had failed quickly. I went in to check on him one evening and found him sitting in front of an open oven, the heating elements glowing. I asked him what he was doing. He said he was trying to keep warm."

Alan chuckled at that. Carol almost laughed, as well.

"It was freezing in there. I asked him if the heater was working. He said he'd kept turning it up, but it keeps getting colder."

This time Alan let go with a real laugh.

"I looked at the thermostat. Dad had worked on it earlier and had put it back together wrong so that the temperature dial worked backwards. I turned it back the other way and the heat came on. His mind was losing its grip."

"Alan," I said, "I never knew about any of this. Why didn't you say something?"

"Why?" he said. "I knew you were busy with your job. I didn't want to interfere. Besides, we handled it."

"Still, I think I could have done something to help."

Carol put her hand on my arm. "There was nothing for you to do. We were perfectly fine."

"Anyway," Alan continued, "around mid-December, I'd check on him in the mornings before I went to work. Dad would be lying in bed on top of a pool of feces and urine. By that time, he was on oxygen and didn't have much endurance. He was barely able to get out of bed. I'd get him up and into the bathroom, clean him up, get him into his clothes, and fix breakfast for him. Then put the bedding in the washer and left for work."

"My god, Alan. You shouldn't have had to do that."

"Well, hell, Sue," he said. "Carol had her things to do, and I didn't mind. Hell, he was my father for Christ sakes."

"I know, but still…"

"Anyway, one morning, after our regimen, Dad complained of not being able to breathe. I got him into his car and drove him to his doctor. He took one look at Dad and said he had congestive heart failure and to take him to the hospital. The doctor would follow us is within the hour."

"I told Alan," said Carol, "to go on to work and I would go to the hospital to stay with him."

Alan leaned forward. "I called Dennis and you to let you know what was happening."

"Yes," I said. "I remember the call. I wasn't sure what to make of it at the time. I hoped it wasn't serious."

"Well, I was hoping the same thing. The second day in the hospital Carol called me at work and told me that Dennis and Jackie were there."

Carol learned in. "They showed up and caused quite a stir when they asked to see his medical records. Of course, since Alan had his Dad's power of attorney, the hospital staff wouldn't let them see them. Jackie told them she was a medical insurance claims processor and was an expert at interpreting medical records. Then, Dennis bragged about being an employee of a veterinarian. He said that he knew all about drugs and medical procedures. I just wanted to slap them both."

I couldn't believe what I was hearing. "Is this for real?"

"That's our big brother," Alan said.

Carol continued. "When Alan finally made it back to the hospital later that afternoon. Dennis and Jackie were still there, stewing over the row with the doctor and staff. Alan signed a consent form so Dennis could see the records. They stood by the nurse's station looking over the papers in the file. Dennis finally gave them back."

I just looked at them in. disbelief.

Alan said, "They went in to see Dad and left right after that, and I apologized to the doctor and the hospital staff."

"The next day, he passed away. Carol was with him. I was at work."

"I know," I said. "I know you took time off work to make all of the arrangements for the cremation, death certificates, and burial. But I don't understand why Dad didn't give his power of attorney to Dennis, since he's the oldest? I told him I don't want it."

Alan looked at me, surprised. "Hell, Sue, if Dennis had had it, Dad would have been broke by now. He couldn't keep a dollar in his own pocket, much less anyone else's."

"Yeah, I guess you're right," I told him. "I'm just thankful you were able to get though everything. I feel bad that I couldn't help. And Dennis wasn't able to, being in the hospital and all. I just want you to know that I appreciate everything you've done."

"Yeah," he said, "it was quite a hassle, but it got done."

"You know, I felt kind of guilty taking all of that money after probate. I'm sure you guys could have used some of it."

"No, Sue. You didn't want the trailer or car, so it was only fair you take a larger share of the investments. We're fine with the way it turned out. We sold the trailer and I socked all of my share away for Teresa's college expenses. That way we don't have to take out any loans."

"That's just like you, baby brother. Always socking it away. I remember Dennis borrowing money from you all the time when we were kids."

"Yes, I was his personal banker."

"Well, I took those investments and might let them sit for now. I think I might put some of that into the shelter. God knows there are a lot of things we need."

"You're doing good, Sis. I'm glad to hear it."

"Did you ever hear what Dennis did with his share?"

"The last time we were there in Okemah, we saw his new house. A fixer-upper. More like a money pit. He still has Dad's car. He also went out and bought this big ass RV. Said they were going to start traveling."

"Well, I'll believe that when I see it."

****

Dad's death really got to me that night. I found it difficult to sleep. For a time after the burial, I was not quite up to par at work. Familial musing took up much of my time. It was difficult for me to get used to not having parents alive. I couldn't call them. I couldn't visit them. I could no longer hear their voices or see their faces and laugh at their corny jokes. Of course I had never done any of those things very much, another stab of guilt. My coworkers sensed that I was not myself and tried to make the shelter more…affable. I love them all too much. It took me several months to get myself together.

I wasn't the only one deeply affected by our parents' deaths. Alan had his own demons to deal with. As if Vietnam wasn't enough, the stress of probate and Dennis' situation and trying to accept the deaths of Mom and Dad. I know Carol did whatever she could to comfort Alan and Teresa during that difficult time.

Dennis? Well, he and Jackie had their own issues to endure. I wondered if Dennis ever thought about our parents after that. I couldn't really see any indications of grief, regret, or respect for them. I suppose I shouldn't have been surprised. After all, their deaths weren't all about him.

After that, we all began drifting farther apart. Fewer phone calls, fewer visits. Our family was disintegrating, like a rusted bolt, slowly being eaten away by the environment in which it existed. Our parents raised us to be independent, to be able to stand on our own two feet and not rely on anyone else for help. Well, in that they succeeded very well. But what they failed to do was teach us how to be normal. How to be affectionate. How to be together.

I have always looked at other families and thought, why couldn't we be like them? Why couldn't we hug each other and laugh together instead of clashing? Why couldn't we feel happy for each other and share in each other's successes? What made it so hard for us?

Therein lies our real story. The story none of us wanted to know. The story none of us understood. I think, at times, that each of us, Dennis, Alan, and myself, have at one point broken through that shell of self-importance and made some stride toward becoming a normal human being, if there really is such a thing.

That's who we are. No one really has much choice of who they become. Some of it is luck. Some of it is a result of choices. I think most of it is what life does to you. Or for you.

Life must go on, and our lives are still moving forward through whatever is thrown at us.

****

After a restless night listening to the wind blow and rain batter the metal roof, which wasn't all that unpleasant, I awoke to the aroma of fresh coffee.

"Good morning," Carol said as I ventured down the stairs. "Do you want breakfast?"

The table was set with a carafe of coffee, scones, and jam.

"Oh, good. Scones," I said. "Where did you get them?"

"Alan makes them and freezes them." She brought me a cup. "He likes whole wheat scones. He likes whole wheat everything. We can't find them anywhere, so he makes his own."

"Whole wheat?"

"That's what he says. He won't use regular white flour. Bad for you, he claims." She sat down with her glass of chocolate milk. "I really don't see what difference it makes."

How fitting for Alan to be on a healthy food kick after lambasting his big brother for abusing his body with what he called, "deplorable food." In light of the current situation, I could see some validity to that state of mind.

"And I love this jam," I said, scooping a spoonful for my scone. "Black currant conserves. That's all Alan will eat."

"Well, he always did have strange tastes. In just about everything. I think that architecture school messed with his mind. And then the army and, well…Vietnam."

"I wish I had known him before that." Carol leaned toward me. "Vietnam, I mean. Except for the other day he never talked about it. I don't' know what to make of it. Or him. I've always been afraid to bring it up. At least now I understand how difficult it must have been for him."

"Well, don't hold your breath. He's never talked about it to any of our family, either. Nobody has ever had the nerve to ask him." I spread some of conserves on my scone and took a bite. Geez, it was delicious. I have to give Alan credit for his taste in food.

IN RECOVERY

March 2002

"Hey, big brother, how are you doing?"

Carol stood at the foot of the bed. "You look really good," she said, smiling.

"Hey," Alan volunteered, moving beside the bed.

'Hey, guys," Jackie said, from her chair near the head of the bed. "It's good to see y'all."

Jackie was cheery, many of her worries probably gone. I stood across from Alan at the side of the bed in front of her. Much of the high-tech equipment was missing, and there was room to move around. Dennis looked great, happy, full of life.

"You look like you're about ready to get out of here," I said.

"Hell, I've been ready for weeks." He pushed himself up in the bed with a little grimace of pain. "I'm ready to do something besides lay around."

"I'll bet you are," I said.

"We've been trying to plan what we're going to do," Jackie said. "Dennis has to make some changes."

Yes, the new man he was going to become. I looked at him, surprised, but apprehensive. I'd never known Dennis to make any change in his lifestyle, at least not since he left for the service.

"And just what kind of changes would those be?"

"I'm going to change," he boasted. "I got myself into this and I need to get myself out."

"That's right," Jackie almost shouted, her eyes wide with excitement. "We're going to start going to church. After this, we think Dennis has a second chance and the good Lord made it possible."

I looked at Alan. Not even he could hold a stoical face at that news, even if it was a look of suspicion. And Carol seemed...not shocked, but...I don't know. Disbelieving? As for myself, I was somewhere between here and there, wherever *there* was. If Dennis thought that it was the good Lord that gave him his second chance, well then, he must have been frightened out of his gourd, which I'm sure he was. I know I would have been.

Dennis got that little smirk on his face and nodded his head. "Church will be a start. I'll see if I can get my job back at the vet's office. When I get better, I'll start back to work on the house."

The "fixer-upper" in Okemah. Dennis had made an attempt to get it "fixed-up." It had not been going too well.

Alan seemed to have a glaze over his eyes. I'm not sure he was even listening to Dennis.

"I think going to church will be fun," Jackie said. "We'll get to meet a lot of new people."

I could only imagine how that was going to work. Dennis had never let anyone tell him what to do or how to do it, except Dad. I was fairly certain he wasn't going to afford a preacher such latitude with his life.

Dennis only grinned at us, as if he had another plan in mind. If I hadn't known him so well, I might have thought he was shirking off Jackie's plan, but I honestly believed he was serious about turning his life around. It might not happen just the way Jackie described it, but it would most likely happen to some extent.

Alan and Dennis chatted for a few minutes, even laughing at times. It was so good to hear that, a reminder of times long past.

I stared at the two of them and wondered what exactly had happened to our family. The cold emptiness of unsentimental relationships had left us remote and barren of real love, or at least the ability to express it. Mutual laughter had escaped us for so long. To hear my two brothers then charged me with new hope for us. I watched as they said their goodbyes.

****

I had planned to return to Dallas after that last visit. I figured Dennis and Jackie would work through it all and find what they were hoping for.

Back in the sanity of Alan's house in Harrison, we gathered around the table to gorge on pizza, a rare concession with Alan. He took it in good stride. I think he really like it, too, in spite of his health food regimen.

"So, what do you think?" I asked.

"I still don't believe it," said Alan. "It's just not like Dennis. I can't see him going to church. Hell, if he did, I can only imagine how many people he might offend."

"I'm not sure what I think," Carol volunteered, a glass of wine in her hand. "I just hope it works out for them."

I agreed with Alan, but Carol made a good point. I also hoped they could make all of this work.

"I just hope Dennis can get some help from the VA," said Carol. "The medical bills have to be astronomical." She looked at Alan. "Have you done anything about that, yet?"

"No," he said. "I'll look into that tomorrow. Hell, I ought to get something for what I've been through."

"I agree," I said. "That war wasn't exactly a total loss."

"It was close enough to one," Alan growled. "We didn't exactly accomplish a whole lot except to kill a bunch of soldiers."

"At least you defended our country," I told him. "I think it was very brave, what you did for our country."

"And exactly what did we do for our country?" He spat back. "The war was a farce, a waste of lives and money. I accomplished nothing but getting a lot of good men killed."

Carol and I sat there, startled by his comment. I had never heard him be so critical of the army. I wasn't sure that I didn't agree with what good the war achieved.

"I don't know about what good it served, but you were given an order and you did your duty. Right or wrong, it was your duty, and you did it."

He turned his head toward me, eyes studious, not angry.

"You know the country was all upset about Communism back then. That's what you went to war for. So, yes, thank you for your service. You might not have heard it often, but I'm saying it now."

"Yeah, well, I haven't heard it from anyone else. And, like I said, I'm pretty sure Dennis never heard it, either."

He sat there, a sad scowl on his face, his eyes angry."

"At least Dennis didn't have to go over there. He had a nice cushy time here. I envy him, now. I imagine basic training was as hard as he had it."

"Oh, my God!" I said. "Do you remember the first night he came home from basic? He tried to teach you Indian leg wrestling?"

Alan laughed, "Yeah, I remember that."

"He was so cocky. Then you flipped him over his head and Mom and Dad died laughing."

"I think he got mad at us."

"Yes, and Dad said, 'Old Buck just showed *you* something.'"

Alan grinned. "Dennis could dish it out, but he sure couldn't take it."

"I hope this experience changes that," Carol said. "I think he could be really fun to be around if he wasn't so arrogant."

"Well," I said, "he does have his moments."

Alan got up. "I think I'll go up and read for a bit."

"I think I will, too," I said. "See you all in the morning."

****

I heard noises from the kitchen early in the morning. When I finally got around to going downstairs, Carol was cooking pancakes, eggs, and sausage.

"My goodness," I said to her. "You didn't have to go to all of this trouble."

"Oh, I felt like a good breakfast, this morning. Kind of a celebration."

"Yes," I said, "it certainly is. I'll get plates."

As I was setting the table, Alan sauntered down the stairs.

"Morning," he said.

"A little late this morning, aren't you?" I asked.

He went to the coffee press and poured a cup of coffee.

"Naw, I was down earlier to make coffee. I was just shaving and such."

"I've got pancakes ready" Carol said over her shoulder.

He sat down with his coffee.

"Wonder how Dennis is doing this morning." he said.

Carol brought a dish of pancakes to the table. "I imagine he's doing pretty well. With his new heart and all, I think he'd be happy to be alive."

"Yeah, I suppose so."

"He'll be so glad to get home," I said, putting a dish of sausage on the table. "Hospitals are the pits."

"So, Sue," Alan turned toward me. "When are you planning to return to Dallas? Not that I'm rushing you off. We've enjoyed having you here. We don't get to see each other that often."

"I was planning on leaving today after lunch."

"Need help packing?"

"No, that's all right," I told him. "I can manage what little I have."

Carol had gone back for the scrambled eggs and we all dived in.

Alan looked at us with a smile on his face. Then he stared straight at Carol.

"I think we should take a trip."

Carol and I looked at each other wondering what we just heard him say. A trip? Now?

"Why do you want to go on a trip now?" asked Carol.

"I think we could both use a break." He took a sip of coffee. "The crisis has passed, and Dennis is going to be okay. I can work a couple of weeks to get things caught up again, and then I can take the rest of my vacation time."

"How much do you have left?"

"About a week. It carried over from last year."

"That sounds great, guys," I said. "Where are you going?"

"I don't know," said Alan, looking at Carol. "Any place you'd like to go?"

"Well. I hadn't really thought about it."

"I think you should go back to New Orleans," I told them. "That was your honeymoon, right?"

They looked at each other and smiled. Carol lowered her head.

"That would be nice, but how about someplace more local. Like…I don't know."

I understood her reluctance to take a major vacation.

"Where was that place Dennis and Jackie went several years ago?" Carol asked.

"What?" Alan said, "you mean Nashville?"

"Oh," I said. "Was that it? I thought it was someplace closer."

"No," said Carol. "It was Nashville."

"And they never let us forget it," Alan grumbled.

I turned to him with a puzzled look. "What do you mean?"

"Oh, remember when we met for a quick Christmas dinner with the folks a few years ago when Dennis was, as he put it, too busy to come to our Christmas get together. That's the year you moved to Texas and couldn't join us."

"That's right," I admitted. "I was so disappointed about that. I really missed seeing you all."

"We had just gotten back from our trip to Sea World in Texas. Teresa had a blast, there, watching the killer whales and dolphins."

Alan leaned forward. "We tried to tell the folks about it. Then Dennis and Jackie burst in with a rendition of their vacation in Nashville. It was non-stop talking about how great it was, it was better than any other trip could have been, and the Grand Ol' Opry, and Elvis' house, and anything else they could think of to dominate the conversation."

"Yes, I remember you telling me about that," I said. "They can be pretty intense."

Alan gave me a scowl. "Intense isn't the word for it. Every time we'd try to tell them about anything we had done or seen, they would take off on something they had done or seen that was a hundred times better. Bigger and better. It never failed. They didn't give a damn about anything or what anyone else had done. It was always all about them."

He finally leaned back and let the dust settle. Carol looked embarrassed, trying to bite her tongue. I let things lay as they were until I saw Alan relax a bit.

"Are you through?" I asked him.

"Okay," he said, nodding his head and looking down at the table. "I'm sorry. I didn't mean to go off like that."

He looked up at me. "But I just get so pissed off at them for being such jerks."

"I know, Alan. I do too. But can we just enjoy our time here and the fact that our brother is going to be okay?"

He sighed. "You're right."

Carol stood up. "What do you all want for lunch.?"

LIFE AFTER A TRANSPLANT

March 2002

That last afternoon at Alan's gave us all an opportunity to grasp the real impact of Dennis' survival. Each of us had his own idea of the future, and we shared our thoughts. We had just finished lunch and were still at the table in the bay window.

"You know," said Carol, "I've never been very religious, but I hope Dennis finds something there to help him."

"I haven't either," said Alan.

"Me either," I said, looking at Alan. "We both know Dennis wasn't."

"So," asked Carol, "Y'all never went to church?"

"Well," I said, "it wasn't like we hated it. It's just that we were indifferent. Especially Alan. Religion was just never an important part of our lives. Dad's, either. Mom was the driving force to get us all to church or Sunday school. If she said we were going, we went. Dad went along until he found he could use the store as an excuse to escape it. She tried for years to instill some inkling of religious fervor into us, but as we got older, she realized how futile it all was. She gave up about the time Dennis started high school. Of course, Dennis had given up long before that. It was just something to tolerate when around other people. Oh, he could play the part when faced with a situation that required some show of piety, and no one was the wiser, except for Nancy Mulligan. Remember her?"

"Hell, yes," said Alan. "She was that real skinny girl that acted like she was afraid of everybody."

"He dated her for a short time in his junior year of high school. It was that Easter Sunday."

"Oh, yeah," said Alan, laughing. "I remember. Nancy had asked him to go with her to Easter services at her church. Of course, he was head over heels into her and he agreed. He had no idea what he had agreed to."

I had to laugh, too. "Easter Sunday rolled around, and Dennis primped in the bathroom. The rest of us had to take turns in that small bathroom in the rear of the house where the washer and dryer were located. When he decided he was perfect and emerged from the bathroom, he almost strutted. His suit was the one he had worn only twice before and I don't know where he got the tie. He drove his pink Rambler to the church to meet Nancy."

"So how did that go?" asked Carol.

"Well, when he got home, the scowl on his face could have frozen icicles onto the Devil. Everyone stayed out of his way. Even Mom didn't say anything."

"Yeah," said Alan, "I remember him giving me a hateful look. I stayed away from him."

I chuckled. "Nancy was only a grade ahead of me in school and we saw each other sometimes and sat at the same table in the lunchroom. The Monday after Easter, I asked her how the date went. She told me it had gone fine until Dennis cracked a joke when the preacher got to the part about Jesus' resurrection, and the embarrassment was too much for her. That pretty much ended that relationship. She said she would never speak to him again. And as far as I know, she never did. And Dennis never set foot in a church again until he married Jackie."

Alan laughed again. "He just couldn't take rejection. Or any kind of ribbing. He wasn't all that bad, though."

"What?" I said. "You're actually applauding your brother?"

"Well, he did have a few good attributes."

Shortly after, I loaded my car and left for Dallas.

****

When I got home, I threw my bag on the bed and went to the living room. My good mood turned a bit sour when. I opened the curtains and looked out of my window at the barren streets, dirty gray concrete, lawns devoid of trees or any other vegetation except dry, brown grass. I thought back to the morning I had spent at Alan's house.

It was mid-morning and the expanse of lawn exploded in bright yellowish white under the low winter sun. I sat at the dining table by the large bay window that overlooked the front yard, one of two bay windows at the front of the house. Squirrels were running amok on the porch and playing around the huge oak trees in the yard. It was so damned peaceful there. No close neighbors, no lawn mowers roaring, little traffic on the gravel road that serenely passed by the house. Alan had done well for himself. And Carol and Teresa. I was stuck in a nondescript, lonely apartment in Dallas, a thriving hellhole of insane Republicans and gun-totin' idiots. How I longed to live someplace like that log house in Harrison. My present location was akin to the dusty, barren field.

Then I recalled a conversation I'd had with Alan and Carol at the dining table discussing the one subject that compelled us all. I think I will always remember our conversation.

"I remember one time," Alan said.

"One time what?" Carol asked.

"One time picking cotton."

"Oh, yeah," I said. "That was in Milton. We were in junior high."

"Yeah, Dennis was in high school. The only year I did it."

"So, what about it?" Carol asked.

He looked over at her. "One of Dad's customers was a farmer." Then he looked at me. "You remember. Old man Becker. He had a cotton field and was looking for kids to pull cotton." Then at Carol again. "It was kind of hard back then to find cotton pickers, so the farmers started recruiting kids. It got to be quite popular. In fact, they even closed school for two weeks in the fall so the kids could get the cotton crops in on time before it wasted away."

"They closed school?" Carol asked.

"Hey, it was a big deal. Cotton was a mainstay of the local economy. The cotton gin ran around the clock. It was big business."

"I remember you coming home all black with your hands bleeding," I said. "Mom just gritted her teeth and told you to take a bath. Then she would rub salve on your hands and make you wear those white gloves. You hated it."

"No shit," Alan said, nodding his head, his eyes wide. "That was hard dragging that damned bag behind me, grabbing those boles with the sharp points on them and stuffing them in the bag. It was hotter than hell and dusty as all get out. The water was back at the truck by the scales. When you got to the far end of the row, your mouth was dry and it seemed like those rows went on forever, and the bag got heavier every step. And bending over sure played hell with my back. I was sore for two weeks after all that shit."

"Did Dennis pick, too?" Carol asked.

"Some days he picked. We didn't see each other in the field. We were too busy picking cotton. But one time I went too far on the row and my bag weighed a ton. When I finally got it to the wagon to weigh it, I couldn't lift it up to the scales. Dennis happened to come up then and helped me lift it up. That's the one time I can remember him really being a big brother. I really wanted to look up to him. Well, without him finding some way to make fun of me."

"See?" Carol said. "He's not so bad after all."

Alan held up his hand. "There's more."

"What?"

"After he helped me weigh mine, which by the way was the heaviest I'd ever had, about seventy some pounds, I helped him weigh his, or helped as much as I could. He checked the scale several times and finally accepted the fact that it was ten pounds lighter than mine."

"Oh, God!" I said. "I remember that. When you two got home you started bragging about it and Mom started laughing. Then Dad said something like, 'Ol' Buck,' that's what he used to call Alan, 'kind of showed you up, didn't he?' Dennis started making all kinds of smart assed remarks. Then he pouted the rest of the night."

I was still laughing when Carol said, "how could you pull a heavy sack like that? I've picked cotton, too, and I know how heavy those things can get."

"Well, I was at the far end of a row with my bag almost full. I figured I didn't want to waste time going back to the trailer, so I just kept picking on the way back. My shoulder hurt like hell. It was red as a beet when I got home. I think I even had blisters on it."

I smiled at Alan. "You made really good money that year. I remember you squirreling it away somewhere. Mom was so proud of you."

"Yeah," he said. "Dennis went through his in no time."

"Well, money always did burn a hole in his pocket."

"I guess that's why he moved to Okemah, huh?" Carol said.

"I never saw their house, there," I told them. "What is it like?"

Alan and Carol had visited them once after they moved. He let out another heavy sigh.

"Well, I've seen rat traps in my time, but nothing like this. It was small, smaller than he was used to, and way under his preferred social level. It was so full of junk there was only a narrow aisle down the hallway. I think they tried to move everything they owned into that little house. It had a pretty nice back yard, though."

Carol laughed. "The house was pretty much a fixer-upper."

"Yeah," said Alan. "He'd tried to do some work replacing the sheetrock and wood trim around the insides of the living room windows. The last time I was there, he still hadn't finished it. That was quite a step down from his exalted station of self-proclaimed importance."

"Alan," I scolded, "I wish you wouldn't get sarcastic."

"Yeah, I know. But you know what he's like."

Yes, I knew what he's like, but I could never reconcile it with Alan's version of it. I looked at him, nodding my head.

"Okay, I'll give you that. But you can't keep berating him. He had some good qualities."

Carol's face fell into a half smile.

I got up to refill my glass. "Anybody need anything?"

They shook their heads.

"It would be nice to hear something good about him." Carol said.

I sat down across from Alan.

"Do you remember the blind date they set you up with?"

Alan rolled his eyes and leaned back in his chair.

"Yeah," he said, sheepishly. "The girl with the mustache."

"What?" Carol asked.

"A mustache," he said. "She had a mustache."

"So what," I said. "From what Jackie said she was a nice girl. Her sister was a friend of Jackie's."

Alan looked down at the table.

"Wasn't she?" I asked him.

"Okay," he mumbled. "Sure."

"And according to Jackie, you were kind of a jerk the entire evening."

Alan sighed. "I guess I was. It was New Year's Eve. I'd just got back from Nam for Christmas. I should have been a little more excited about it."

"Then," I said, "you drank too much and threw up on the table and you put you r napkin over it. Dennis didn't think anyone noticed except him. He took you to the restroom and got you squared away."

Alan's eyes nearly glazed over. "Yeah, I'd forgotten."

"Seems like you've forgotten a lot of things," I said, taunting him. "You've made your life so remote from your family you can't even remember what it was really like, except for your beef with Dennis of course."

Carol looked at him, her eyes accusatory but concerned. I'm sure this had been a subject of contention between them for some time.

Alan breathed deeply, blew out a gust of air, and fell back into his chair. He looked at me, embarrassed. Then he looked down again.

"Yeah." He played with his glass on the table. "You're right, Sue." He looked at Carol, his face flushed, then back to the table.

"I guess our lives have been pretty much a shit-show, haven't they?"

"Well," I said, "I wouldn't go that far. I know what you went through. I kind of did, too. It was like a competition between you two. Yes, Dennis is a jerk. But he's our brother. I think brothers are entitled to some degree of exploitation of siblings. Maybe he took that a bit too far. But it wasn't life-threatening. You survived and so did I."

The table fell into silence for a moment.

"And," I continued, "you know what?"

They both looked at me.

"Dennis has had his own share of problems that we probably don't even know about."

Alan blinked, his eyebrows narrowed, gazing through the window into whatever.

"I'll bet he had," said Carol. "Jackie has always tried to make excuses for him, and I always thought he was at fault. But you're right. I never stopped to think what problems he might have had in his life."

Alan finally brought his mind back to the table with another deep breath.

"I was never really competing with him."

Carol and I waited for his explanation.

"I just wanted to prove to myself that I could be better than what he thought I was." He looked up. "That's all," he said shaking his head. "It was never about being better than him. I didn't care about that. What I cared about was my own confidence. Why the hell do you think I stayed in ROTC and joined the army? Hell, I hated it. But I had to know that I could do it. And I did. If Dennis is jealous of that…well, that's his damn problem."

I sat there at the table, stunned. Carol was staring at her husband as if she didn't recognize him.

"You said you liked working at the dam with the Corps of Engineers," Carol said. "You always talked about the new things you got to do."

"I thought you liked the army," I said. "You were so proud when you graduated from college and got your commission. At graduation, you pranced around in that uniform like you were God's gift to humanity. And when you got back from Vietnam and were assigned to the Kaw Dam, I thought you loved it."

"I don't know why the hell you thought that," he said. "Yeah, I was proud of my commission. Hell, I worked hard enough for it. And, yeah, my time at the dam was great. A dream assignment.

But I didn't like the army. I didn't like people telling me what to do and how to do it. My ambition was to be an engineer."

Carol and I looked at each other with raised eyebrows. A moment later we burst out laughing.

Alan's mouth fell open and he looked at us, astonished.

"What the hell is with you two?"

"Alan," I said between laughs, "you are such a dweeb."

"What do you mean?" he asked, clueless.

"I'm sorry, Alan, but I can't help thinking that you're being a bit dramatic."

"Dramatic?" he said. "What's so dramatic about wanting to make my own decisions?"

He had a point. All of his life he had been the "good son." The one that did what he was supposed to do. The one that the parents could point to and say, "That's our boy." The one who never created problems for Mom and Dad. Well, except for a few minor infractions. The one who met his parents' expectations. What could I say?

"You're right, Alan." I looked him square in the eye. "I'm sorry. You had every right to leave the military."

We all took a moment to think about what we had said. Then, I had another thought.

"You know, if you'd stayed in the army, you'd probably be a general by now."

"I'd never have made it that long. I spent seven and a half years in college working my ass off to be an engineer and that's what I was going to be."

"Well, I'm glad you're happy with your decision. It probably would have been hell having to move all of the time, anyway."

"To be honest, it wouldn't have bothered me that much, but it wouldn't have been good for a family."

****

I still remember him sitting there looking me in the eye and saying that. I never really knew he had been thinking about a family at the time. It was just him. A loner, like he always was. It was probably a good thing he hadn't been married when he went to Vietnam. I think Carol would have been strong enough to endure it, but I'm not so sure about Alan. It's hard to tell how having a family back home would have affected him. His stoical nature might have let him shove them to the back of his mind, but I know he couldn't have done that. Not Alan. In spite of his apparent reticence, he has very deep feelings for Carol and Teresa. That much I *can* read.

I couldn't help thinking about Dennis and Alan. I knew this was difficult for Alan. Hell, it was difficult for me. It must have been hell for Dennis. They'd spent their entire lives in a contest. Dennis, the lazy, carefree arrogant braggart had been all about Dennis. He rarely gave me the time of day. The only time he really paid me any notice was to make fun of me for being a girl. I had still idolized him because he was my big brother, not that he ever acted like it. I was just an annoyance to him. Even so, I had still felt obligated to help him whenever he found himself in a tight spot. I arranged dates for him, I lent him money which he sometimes paid back, and I even lied for him to spare him parental wrath. I suppose I only wanted him to offer just a bit of attention and respect to me as a sibling. After he married, I rarely saw him. I would call him on holidays or special occasions. He never called me.

I suppose I was never aware of how I really felt about it all. I just never stopped to think about it. I was busy with my own friends and life. Dennis was merely a series of brief interruptions. Now I think about it all the time. Why had I given in to him? What was I afraid of? Or *was* I afraid?

I suppose I just wanted him to be happy. And I wanted Alan to be happy. It was damned hard trying to do both.

Alan and I arranged to go visit Dennis and Jackie after he'd had time to adjust at home. We figured a month or so would work.

****

I got word from Jackie a couple of weeks later that Dennis had been released from the hospital. Her sprite voice seemed to soothe the coarse twang that drove us all crazy. It instilled energy in me, too. After all, my brother had escaped death. Suddenly, all of my memories flooded back. The good ones. That's all I thought about. The good ones.

We had all suffered through the anguish and were left with strained expectations. Carol had been the calmest of us in spite of her emotional tendencies. Alan had appeared calm, but a ubiquitous storm was brewing beneath his stoical facade. I had no idea how he would eventually come to terms with it all.

Although the doctor assured Jackie that Dennis was recovering fine, doubts still lingered in my mind. I didn't know that much about the transplant process, but I knew it was complicated. Seeing him there, so chipper with Jackie before I left the city, I was excited for them. Their future. He got a second chance.

The test would be what he would do with it. Turning toward the church was a good start, especially for Dennis. He was never one to idolize religion. In fact, he often ridiculed it and those who were believers. I guess we all did in some ways.

SURPRISE VISIT

March 2002

After our visit to the hospital, Alan and I decided we would visit Dennis at home a couple of weeks later. It was another long drive for both of us, but we figured he deserved that.

I ventured into the town of Okemah just after lunchtime on a Saturday. I found the house, a nondescript white clapboard affair, small, with a detached garage and a decent sized back yard on a corner lot. The white paint had started peeling off the siding and the shrubbery needed some attention. But overall, a decent house. Alan's Jeep Grand Cherokee was parked on the street in front of the house. I parked behind it.

Jackie opened the door before I even got to it.

"Hi, Sue," she said, bubbling over with enthusiasm. "I'm glad you could come. Alan said you'd be here."

"Yes, I said, I'm anxious to see how the patient is doing."

She led me inside to a dark living room, the windows covered with blinds. It smelled old, like an ancient building, almost musty but cloaked with some kind of air freshener. It wasn't bad, overall.

"He's doing great," she said, looking at him, slumped in a recliner in a corner. "I just have to keep his medication straight."

Dennis perked up when he saw me and pushed himself up in the chair.

"Alan said you were coming. Glad to see you."

I turned around and saw Alan and Carol on the sofa.

"Good trip?" He asked.

"Just long and boring," I told him. "But it was worth it to see you two."

"Hi, Sue." Carol smiled at me. "It's good to see you again."

"You too, Carol."

"Sit down," Jackie ordered, pointing to the sofa by Alan.

She took the armchair beside Dennis' recliner.

"I see you're still moving in," I said, looking at the trove of boxes lining the hallway.

"Yeah," said Dennis. "We got to find a place for everything. The house is quite a bit smaller than what we had."

"It looks like you have a nice back yard."

"The corner lot is perfect," said Jackie. "I'll have a lot of room for planting things."

I tried not to look at the worn carpet. God knows what all was living in it. Then I noticed the trim missing from around the windows.

"Looks like you're doing some work on the windows."

"Yeah," said Dennis. "I started to put up some new trim, something that looked better, then all this shit happened. Kind of put a halt to everything."

"I bet Alan could help you finish that," I said.

Then I saw a change in Dennis' expression. Very slight, but it was there.

"I'm going to finish it when I get recovered enough," he said with authority.

Alan gave him a barely obvious smirk.

"So," I said, "how have things been going for you?"

Jackie spoke up. "The doctor's really happy with the way things are going. He said Dennis should be able to get back to work in a couple of weeks."

"Are you still at the vet's office?" Carol asked.

Dennis put on one of his silly grins. "Yup. They kept my job open."

"That was damned nice of them," said Alan. "A lot of places wouldn't do that."

"Well, this is a small office and we all get along pretty good."

Jackie stood. "Anybody want something to drink?"

"I'd like some tea, if you've got it," said Carol.

"Me, too," said Alan.

"I'll take a refill," Dennis added.

Jackie looked at me "Sue?"

"Sure."

Dennis pulled himself up out of his chair and slowly made his way to the small dining room between the living room and the kitchen. He plopped down in a chair and grabbed one of two large pill boxes, the, kind with little lids that opened over compartments.

I followed him into the dining room and stood beside him.

"What's this? Your personal pharmacy?"

He looked up at me with a smirk "Yeah, that's what it is."

"God, how many pills do you take?"

He opened the lids of the box and started removing pills.

"I take twenty-two three times a day and…Jackie, how many twice a day?"

"Fourteen," she yelled from the kitchen.

Alan and Carol had joined us, sitting at the table. I took a seat, too. Jackie brought the drinks and we all watched as Dennis began swallowing pills, washing them down with his tea.

"What is all of that stuff?" asked Alan.

Dennis pointed to the various compartments.

"I've got anti-rejection drugs. They lower my immune system, so these pills fix that. And blood a thinner and one of them is for nausea. I'm not sure what the rest of them do."

Alan sat shaking his head. "Dear Lord, how do you do that every day?"

Dennis shrugged. "Just do it," he said. "Hell, it keeps me alive." He laughed.

Jackie joined us, and conversation drifted from subject to subject. Then I could sense a change.

"The hospital called and asked us if we would be interested in meeting the family of the donor."

"Oh, that would be so nice," said Carol. "I imagine they would be interested in knowing who got the heart."

Dennis snorted. "Hell, I don't want to meet them. I don't know them, and they don't know me. I don't want to be involved with them."

Alan, Carol and I sat there, not sure we heard what he had said. The remark was such a sharp dismissal of any acknowledgment that someone had donated a life-saving organ so that Dennis could survive. It sounded so selfish, so…I don't know. How could Dennis not show some gratitude for the benevolence of that young man who had died? At least an acknowledgment to his family that he was grateful for what he had done.

I caught the redness in Alan's ears, the tightened jaw, the narrowed eyes. I just hoped a squabble didn't erupt.

"Why do you have to be involved with them?" said Alan. "

Dennis got that annoyed look on his face. "I just don't want to have to deal with them. I don't know them, and they don't know me."

"That's just the point," I said. "Why don't you want to just meet them?"

He turned his head toward me. "I just don't," he snapped.

"Did you start at the vo-tech, yet?" Carol asked.

"Yeah," Dennis said. "I've been going a week. So far, I'm ahead of everyone else in the class."

"Well," I said, "look at you."

"It must be going pretty well, then," said Carol.

"Yeah, it is. I'm learning spreadsheets. I can use that in my job at the vet's office."

Alan leaned forward over the table. "Has the VA said anything about helping?"

"No," said Jackie. "We haven't heard anything, yet. I hope they say something pretty soon. The bills are starting to pile up."

"Are you in the VA?" Dennis asked Alan.

"No, I'm not. I'm thinking about it. I'll look into it next week."

"Hey," said Dennis, twisting his noisy chair toward Alan. "What ever happened to Dad's tool chest?"

"Which one?"

"The big gray one."

"It's in my garage."

Dennis got a perturbed look on his face. "I thought I was supposed to get that?"

Alan's face turned serious, eyes narrowing a bit.

"As I recall, we never discussed the tool chest. You took what tools you wanted and left me the rest. Including the chest."

Dennis slid his mouth to the side, a sign of impending trouble.

"I could have sworn we agreed that I would get it."

Alan leaned back in his chair.

"Well, we didn't."

"You know," said Dennis "it just doesn't seem fair."

Alan looked at him questioningly. I began to wonder where all of this was going. Carol, bless her heart, was a bit on edge at the skirmish. Jackie was looking on in avid interest.

I mean," Dennis continued, "that trailer and the garage had to be worth more than that car. And all of his tools on top of that."

"You said you didn't want the tools," said Alan, shaking his head.

"Well, what about the trailer and garage. Dad paid for those, didn't he?"

"Yes," said Alan. "He did."

"What did you get for the trailer when you sold it?"

"Around sixteen thousand. About what the car was worth."

"What about the garage?"

"Well, obviously we didn't sell that. But it cost around four thousand to have built."

"See, you're up four thousand dollars."

By this time, Alan's ears were turning even redder, and his jaw tightened.

"Yeah, so we're up four thousand. But we're also out a ton of sweat and our own money to get that place ready for them to move in. I finished out the inside of that garage myself. I dug all of the ditches for utilities myself. I installed the utilities myself and then filled in all the ditches by myself. Where the hell were you when all of this was going on? In view of the circumstances, I'd say Carol and I were entitled to a little more. And the fact that we cared for them without any help from you."

"And I agree, Dennis," I said. "Alan worked himself to death on that place."

Dennis turned around to scowl at me, a look that must have been painful for him.

"So, you're taking his side?" he said in a hateful voice.

"It's not about taking sides," I told him. "It's about being fair. Alan put in the work for our parents' place, and I think he deserves everything he can get for it. And, by the way, big brother, where were you when they moved to Harrison? You didn't help one bit in the garage sale, cleaning out the house, and moving all of their things down there. You just gave us your standard excuse that you were too busy. I call bullshit on that, Dennis. I know better. And so do you."

Jackie had finally had enough.

"Okay, stop it, y'all. I've had enough. It really doesn't matter. It's over and done with. Just…just leave it be."

Carol let out a big sigh and looked at Alan.

"I think we need to go, Alan."

Alan closed his eyes and nodded his head, then got up from the table. Carol rose and they headed for the door.

Jackie popped up and followed them.

"I'm sorry, guys. Please don't leave."

"I think it's best that we do," said Alan. "I'm sorry."

I went out to their car with them.

"Alan, please don't leave like this."

"Sorry, Sis, I'm not playing this game with him. He's screwed me over enough as it is."

And then they were gone. That was it.

I went back into the house and sat down beside Dennis. I looked him in the eye.

"Dennis, all of this bullshit was totally uncalled for. We all had an agreement on how the folks' property was to be divided. It was fair and you agreed to it. Why the hell do you want to bring all of this up now?"

He sat, there sulking, a sour expression on his face. He made no effort to respond.

"I'm so sorry, Sue," said Jackie. "I wish this didn't end like this."

I looked at her. "I know, Jackie. I do too. I think I'll head out as well."

With that I left them to their misery.

THE WOMEN'S SHELTER

March 2002

When I got back to Dallas and went in to work Monday morning, it was as if a riot squad had been there and completely traumatized the place. The staff were flustered, having been bombarded with conflict between residents, and the residents themselves were on edge. I found Marsha and asked her what had happened.

"Boy," she said. "You should be glad you were gone."

I motioned her to my office.

"What in the world went on here?"

"Well, yesterday evening one of the residents reported some items stolen from her room."

"Which one?"

"Sherrel."

"Brenda and I started checking around and we found the stuff in Alice's room. The other residents demanded that we call the police. They carted Alice away."

It was upsetting, of course, and Marsha filled me in on all that had happened. But there was one issue that they hadn't addressed, yet.

"Megan Walker's father is going to have a heart transplant. It's for tomorrow afternoon."

My heart almost stopped. Another heart transplant.

"Does she have a way to get to the hospital?"

"The problem is her ex-husband had threatened that if she tried to see her father, he would see that she never saw him again."

"Oh, my god! For real?"

"For real."

I knew her dilemma, since my own brother had just undergone the same thing. I went to her room to talk with her and her eight-year-old son.

"Hello, Megan. Can I come in?"

She nodded her approval.

"I'm so sorry to hear about your father."

"Thanks," she said, a coy grin flashed across her face.

"When did all of this begin?"

She went into a lengthy tale of abuse and near tragedy and a graphic description of the harm her ex had done to her son. I'm sure she had relayed this story to the agent who admitted her, but sometimes it helps to talk about it. After her neighbors called for the police, she found herself in court asking for restraining order at the urging of her attorney, which only added to her financial predicament.

"As long as you're here, you're safe. We have the police nearby and we won't let anything happen to you or your son."

I don't know why I made those promises. If her ex came back in a show of force, I wasn't sure we could stop him before the police arrived. But the relief on her face outweighed my guilt. I'd tackle the son of a bitch myself and strangle him if I had to.

I then went to visit with Sherell, the woman whose property had been stolen.

"Sherell," I said, sitting down beside her on the bed, "I'm sorry this happened."

She looked at me, tears in her eyes.

"I know it probably makes you feel violated, somehow."

She nodded her head. "I just feel so vulnerable," she said, her voice wavering.

"Well, we found all of your things. I'll see that they are returned to you."

She gave me a smile and wiped tears from her eyes.

I gave her some pointers on how to keep certain items secure. I even offered to buy her a padlock for her locker. After our talk she showed signs of relaxing a bit and started socializing with other residents again.

I strolled back to my office, scrutinizing the residents' rooms as I drifted by their doors. All seemed to be in order. My desk still had a mound of paperwork, as in incident reports that would have to be reported to our superiors, invoices, letters from city officials requesting information on our operation and praising us for the excellent service to the community, but with no special accolades. Form letters we received like clockwork. Most of them went into the wastebasket.

"Sue."

Marsha entered the hallway ahead of me.

"What is it, Marsha?"

She pointed to the lobby. "There's a Detective Barnes to see you."

I detoured to the lobby to see a large, man dressed in a wrinkled blue suit and scuffed black shoes, an unbridled mop of black hair on his head.

I approached him, extending my hand.

"Detective Barnes?"

"Miss Carter, I assume," he said, grasping my hand in a smarmy grip.

"Yes. How can I help you?"

"Miss Carter, I am investigating the ex-husband of one of your residents. Ah…a Megan Walker."

I was glad to see that the police were taking her story seriously.

"Yes. Her father is to undergo a heart transplant soon."

"That's precisely why I'm here, Miss Carter."

"Perhaps we should talk in my office."

I led him back to my office and gestured for him to sit.

Once he had dropped into a chair, his face became stern, focused.

"Miss Carter, we have reason to believe that Mrs. Walker's husband is involved with national socialist group that has been harassing the Latino communities."

That made sense, because Megan had immigrated from Mexico some years ago with her father.

The detective continued, matter-of-factly in his resonating deep voice.

"We have been tracking him, but we lost him early this morning. I wanted to warn you that he might try to gain access to this shelter. I will have officers posted outside around the clock until we can locate him. We believe he is armed and dangerous."

Dear lord, that's all I needed just then. I was no stranger to the police taking charge of people in our shelter, but the danger factor was not necessarily great. This news from the detective scared the hell out of me. We were not equipped to deal with that kind of situation.

"Detective, do I have reason to be concerned about the safety of our other residents?"

He looked down at the floor for a moment, then raised his eyes to me, "I'm afraid so, ma'am That's why we have officers posted outside."

"Tell me, Detective." I looked him straight in the eye. "Just what are we talking about here? What makes this man so dangerous?"

He took a deep breath and slowly let it out.

"Ma'am, Mr. Walker has a history of criminal offenses. After serving in Iraq, he was dishonorably discharged from the army several years ago."

"I see," I said, leaning back in my chair. PTSD. The only thing I could think of was PTSD. Is that what it was? Was that part of Alan's problem? He wasn't violent, though. At least not that I ever knew.

"Miss Carter?"

"Sorry. I was just thinking about something else."

My mind began working on how the hell we could deal with that kind of threat.

"Are there any precautions we should take to assure Mrs. Walker and her son are safe?"

"Just keep them confined to this shelter and keep the doors and windows locked."

"And just how are the other residents supposed to go about their business if we do that?"

The detective appeared to be annoyed at my questions.

"You will have to have someone on duty to lock and unlock the doors as your residents come and go."

During the momentary lull, I stared at Detective Barnes with a mixture of trepidation and gratitude. I was glad that the police were doing their jobs, but I dreaded the thought of Mr. Walker causing any kind of trouble and putting the residents in danger.

The detective rose.

"Well, if there is nothing else, I'll be on my way."

He dropped a card on my desk.

"If you should encounter any trouble, please call me right away."

"Thank you, Detective Barnes," I said, shaking his hand again. "I'll be sure and call if any trouble arises."

After Detective Barnes left, I assembled the staff and assigned shifts so that two of them would be on duty for each shift throughout the night. I paired myself with Marsha on the last shift. It would give me an opportunity to start the day at the center early. I did not sleep well that night, thinking about Mr. Walker and Dennis.

****

The night passed smoothly with no altercations. Shortly after nine the next morning, Detective Barnes called to tell me that Mr. Walker had been apprehended and was in the county jail. I immediately went to talk with Megan. She nearly fainted with relief when I told her what had happened. I worked with her to get her to the hospital to see her father. I told her we would look after her son in her absence.

And I thought about Dennis. What had it been like for him? At least he had his family there. Megan's father had no one that I knew of. How awful to be secluded with no family around.

I had to quit thinking about it. My own family drama was enough for me to handle just then. But then, I remembered my visit to Dennis in Texas some years earlier. Good intentions aside, it exposed a rip in the fabric of our family.

VISITING DENNIS AND JACKIE

April 1986

Dennis and Jackie had lived in several homes. Their first, just after they were married, was a tiny two-bedroom apartment in Winfield, barely large enough for a sofa in the living room. They shared the apartment with a large German Shepard named Spook. Such humble beginnings. Alan was on summer break from college, and they invited him to spend the night with them. He wound up on a cot in the "extra" room that was filled with boxes, barely enough room for Alan.

Then came the larger house once Dennis got a job at a commercial credit outfit. Then the houses got bigger and better.

The house they'd bought in Dennison, Texas, several years ago came to mind. I'd had a conference in Oklahoma City on a Thursday and Friday. I would drive back home through Dennison. I'd planned to stop by Dennis' house and say hi. I hadn't seen them and their kids for months. I wanted to see how much Brent and Becky had grown. The last time I had seen them was at their house in Oklahoma City the year before when we had our family Christmas get together at Dennis' house.

Dennis had been a vice-president of a bank, there, and he and Jackie had a nice house not far from the bank. Having Christmas at Dennis' house was an anomaly, since we usually had it at the folks' house in Winfield. Alan had suggested that we have our two aunts, Verda and Vivian, there, since they no longer drove long distances and hadn't been to a Christmas dinner for some years. Alan volunteered to drive to Winfield and pick them up. Dennis said he would take them home the next day.

That had been one of the best holidays we'd had.

The next year, in his race to the big bucks, Dennis landed a job at a large bank in Dennison, Texas, as the vice-president of something or other. His status as a bigwig fed his ego with a rich diet of swagger and sway. He had bragged to the family about his new house, there, and to hear him talk, it was the gem of the neighborhood.

Dennis has always been good at bravado, even when he was in junior high. It was something the family got used to and learned to give token accolades in order to cease the flow of boasting.

Of course, they were all too happy for me to visit.

It was Friday afternoon, and when I found the street, it was easy to find the house. A two-story tract house just like every other one on the block, except it was on a corner lot and the color, a drab beige with uninspiring brown trim and the token evergreens in front like every other house, gave it a depressing curb appeal. It looked neat, though, and it did have some trees around it.

Jackie met me at the door with a broad smile. I liked that about her. She had a wonderful, full, white-tooth smile, not like the bland, unrevealing smiles so many folks have.

"Hiya," she said, her eyes alive with sparkling vigor, like they were plugged into a wall outlet. "Come on in. Dennis is still at work, but he should be home soon."

She ushered me into a high-ceilinged living room stocked with the furniture they had brought with them from their house in Oklahoma City. The cacophony of color was startling, the greens, blues, pinks, and browns swarming around the room in confusion looking for order. I wondered if they couldn't afford new furniture or if the unsettling effect didn't bother them. Neither of them possessed a sense of style or aesthetics. I sat in an armchair, the one I remembered with a blaring blue and green floral brocade and dark wood accents, and waited for Jackie to make her move.

"How about some tea?" she finally asked.

"That would be nice," I said. "Thank you."

As she turned to go to the kitchen, I said, "This is really a nice room. I love the tall ceiling."

Jackie's face lit up. It always did when someone complimented her. "Oh, we love it. It makes the room seem so much bigger."

She came back with the tea and sat on the sofa, a companion to my armchair, a few feet away. I glanced at the huge, pretentious dining room set across the room. The hutch, an overly ornate dark hunk of wood sat against the wall as if holding it up in a grand gesture of might and power.

"I guess Brent and Becky are still at school?"

"She should be home anytime. Brent went home with a friend."

"How's she doing?"

She seemed to sigh, then got a look of frustration. "She's having trouble with math, but mostly she's doing good."

"Is she in any activities?"

"No, she just hangs out with her friends."

I heard the door open, and Becky blew in.

"Hi, Mom."

Then she saw me.

"Oh, Aunt Susan."

"Hello, Becky. How are you?"

She looked at me with her pretty brown eyes and a gorgeous smile, unlike any other eight-year-old girl I had seen, and said, "I'm fine. Are you going to stay a while?"

"No, sweetie, I just dropped by to say hi."

"I wish you could stay."

She pulled her face into a mask of sadness and turned to look at her mother, who confirmed the news.

"Aunt Susan has to get back home. She has a lot of important work to do."

Becky would have almost been a charming child had it not been for her snotty attitude. She could be almost belligerent, which her parents seem to have cultivated. Much like her brother, Brent, another unbridled bundle of energy.

Jackie shooed Becky off to some other part of the house, and we talked, mainly about her and her family, not one bit of curiosity about me or Alan's family. It was all about her.

Jackie had taken up an interest in art. Well, not paintings and such, but trying her hand at small sculptures, the kind that comes in kits from hobby stores. I have to say I was impressed by her initiative to do something for herself. The previous Christmas, Alan had given her a kit of a Don Quixote statuette she had completed. It was quite good, an excellent complement to the carved wooden flatware she had obtained from Mexico on their last visit down there.

"I see you finished Don Quixote. He looks good."

"Yeah, I had a lot of fun with that. Alan got me interested in that kind of thing."

It wasn't long until Dennis arrived. I watched the grin form on his face, a pleasant break from his usual smirk. I was surprised that he approached us with an air of humility, so unlike him. Of course, his big belly was leading the way, straining the buttons on his shirt. "Hey, Sis, when did you get here?"

"I'm on my way home from a conference in Oklahoma City. Thought I'd drop by and say hi."

"You staying the night?"

"No, I need to get home. I've got to study some proposals for our center this weekend. We're having a meeting with our supporters Monday morning. If all goes well, we can get funding for an expansion."

Dennis plopped down in a recliner and looked at me with his goofy smile, the one that gave him all of his charm.

"So, how's things in Dallas?"

"Busy. We're full up and still have women waiting for a space. That's why we're having our meeting Monday."

"You keep kids, too. Right?"

"Yeah. Most women have families. It stretches our resources, but we make do."

"Are all of these women really in trouble?" He focused his eyes as if interrogating me. "I mean, do they all need to be there? Like, aren't some of them just freeloading?"

I should have expected that, given his borderline misogyny. I'd heard it too many times, the tirades against women in his workplace, his mocking of women drivers, his disdain for any legislation favoring women.

"Yes, Dennis. All of these women have been abused by their husbands, neglected by their families, or they have no families for support. Our shelters are some of the few places they can go for protection and care. We don't have any freeloaders there."

He sank farther into the chair and said, "So, what happens to them?"

"We help them with necessities, arrange for schooling for their children, arrange for legal and psychological counseling. And we help them find jobs. Those kinds of things."

"Who pays for all of that?"

The skepticism in his voice was unmistakable.

"We apply for grants and take donations. We have several prominent donors that keep us afloat. And of course, we receive a little funding from the city, but don't worry, brother dear. Our imposition on the sanctity of your precious taxpayer dollars is probably less than it costs to keep the street clean."

I didn't want him to start in on his "bleeding heart liberal" shit again.

Jackie got up. "I guess I'll fix something for supper. You're staying for super, right?"

I got up and followed her to the kitchen.

"I'm glad you're doing that shelter thing," she said to me, opening the refrigerator. "I've known so many women who need that kind of help. There just wasn't that much help available to them. I wonder if there are any shelters, here?"

"I'm sure there are. They're all over the country."

"I don't think Dennis goes in for that sort of thing."

"I know," I said. "What did you have in mind to fix?"

"I'm going to cook some ground beef and make spaghetti."

"Hmm. Sounds good. What can I do to help?"

While Jackie and I prepared supper, Becky watched television and Dennis read the newspaper. Jackie's expertise in the kitchen surprised me. I knew she was a very good cook, but I hadn't realized her efficiency in the kitchen. She had learned a lot from her mother, also a good cook. For all of her apparent innocence, she was a marvel at meal preparation. And I got to know a bit more about her and her family. Aside from her loud voice and harsh laugh, she was really quite charming.

Brent had found his way home and went directly to his room. I had no idea what he did up there. Dennis interrupted us to take me out to the back yard to show off the swimming pool. The descending sun pulled the heat from the air, and it was too cool to go swimming, thank goodness, but I expressed my admiration and watched him strut around it like a peacock. I have no use for a pool, myself, but I don't hold it against those who do. I like to swim occasionally, but I don't have any use for the trouble and expense of maintaining a pool.

I noticed a dog in a part of the yard that was fenced off, looking sheepishly through the wire, his fur matted, cowling as if it had done something wrong. Behind it stood a decrepit doghouse in tall, overgrown grass.

"What's the dog's name?" I asked Dennis.

"Tyco.'"

"Tyco? What kind of name is that?"

"It's just a name."

I opened the gate to go over to Tyco and pet him. His tail began flailing, excitement in his eyes, and his entire body quivering. I reached out to him, patting him on the head, then scratching behind his ears. The dog stretched as tall as he could to meet my hand, whimpering. The poor thing had been starved of attention.

I wondered if anyone in the family ever played with him or just kept him company. Then I felt the bumps in his coat. Ticks. Big dog ticks. He was covered in them.

"Dennis, did you know that your dog is covered in ticks?"

He looked at me, his face puzzled while Tyco writhed and fidgeted under my hand.

"These ticks are eating him alive. Don't you ever check on him?"

He got that perturbed look on his face and stomped over to the dog. Tyco seemed to want to back away from him. He bent down to look, then seemed puzzled again.

"You need to get those off of him," I said. "It's a wonder the poor thing is still alive."

Of course, Tyco, in the midst of this attention, was alive with glee, his head twisting about in excitement. I helped Dennis pick ticks off.

"I didn't know he was this bad," Dennis said.

"Does anybody ever play with him? Or is he just another of your possessions?"

Dennis snapped his head up and glared at me. I had overstepped. I didn't need to say that. But since it was out there, I continued to rub it in.

"Hell, Dennis, if you're going to have a pet, you're obligated to take care of it, not neglect it."

His lack of response told me it was time for me to go back into the house.

By the time I got back into the kitchen, Jackie had dinner on the table.

"How'd ya' like the pool?" she asked.

"It's looking nice. I wish I'd brought my swim suit."

"Oh, I imagine it's a bit cold for swimming right now."

"You're probably right. The table looks amazing."

"I hope you like spaghetti."

"I love it." I lied. I never cared for it, even when Mom made it when we were kids. Alan and Dennis ate it, of course. Hell Alan would practically eat anything if it was halfway healthy.

Dennis came in, an agitated expression on his face.

"Jackie, what's the name of that vet we met at that party?"

"Why?" she asked. "Is something wrong with Tyco?"

"He's covered with ticks."

Jackie dropped her mouth. "Where did he get ticks?"

"Hell, I don't know," Dennis said with a bit of displeasure. "I guess they're in the yard someplace."

While they mulled over the issue with Tyco, I found a seat at the table. The rest of the family joined me for a quiet and uneventful dinner.

After eating I went into the living room and found Becky sitting by herself on the sofa.

"Hey, Becky," I said, sitting next to her. "How's school this year?"

She turned her round little face up toward me, her mouth open like a fish going after a baited hook. "It's okay."

"What subjects are you taking?"

She sighed and looked back down at her hands in her lap. "Oh, just the same old stuff."

"Like English and math?"

"Yeah."

Do any of your friends live around here?"

She looked at the television. "No."

"You mean there are no other kids that live around here?"

She looked up at me with cold eyes and said, "Well, there's a nigger girl that lives two houses down, but I can't play with her."

Her brazen tone shocked me and I sat there, speechless, for a moment until Jackie came in.

"Oh," she said, "there's a black family that lives down the street, but we don't allow our kids to play with their kids."

"Why not?" I asked.

"Dennis doesn't want our kids hanging around with them."

I thought for a moment. "Well, is something wrong with them?"

Jackie looked at me as if I had just crawled out of a bottle. "They're black," she said, an incredulous look on her face.

"So, why is that bad?"

Becky was looking at me with the same look as her mother.

"They're black, Sue." She shook her head in disbelief. "They're different."

"Different, how?"

She let out a small gasp. "Sue…they're…just different. You know…"

"No Jackie, I don't know. Just because their skin is black doesn't mean they're bad people. They're just like you and me."

Her eyes widened and her mouth flew open. Becky tilted her head, shaking it from side to side.

"Well," she said in her authoritative voice, "you don't have kids. You don't understand."

"I think I understand perfectly," I said, standing my ground. "You're racist, aren't you?"

She pulled back, apparently shocked at what I had said. "Why, no," she almost yelled. "I'm not a racist. I have nothing against black people."

I narrowed my eyes at her. "Then why don't you want your kids associating with them?"

Dennis came back into the room with one of his puzzled looks on his face. He had so many, it was difficult to know what prompted it.

"Associating with who?" he asked, heading toward a recliner.

Jackie laughed and said, "Sue thinks we're racist." Then she continued laughing.

"We are," he said, pushing back in his chair.

Jackie's face turned a bit red; her eyes held a look of surprise.

"Hell," Dennis continued, "all these damn niggers around here just bring property values down." He put a satisfied look on his face and said, "I don't want my kids anywhere near them."

I hadn't noticed the fire raging inside me until I tried to speak. I just didn't know what to say. I had always suspected as much of them, but to stand there and actually hear Dennis admit it. I felt as if he had been an implant in our family, not really one of us. I could hardly bring myself to admit any relation to him.

"What's the matter, Sis?" he said. "You bleeding-heart liberals think them niggers are special, don't you? Hell, they'll steal you blind and stab you in the back."

I looked at him, my eyes probably glowing with embers. "Dennis, your hatred for anyone who is not like you transcends even the weakest of human compassion. I know Mom and Dad were not keen on minorities, but they didn't hate them. I'm ashamed to even admit that I'm related to you, sometimes."

I picked up my coat and purse and headed for the door.

"Sue," Dennis almost yelled. "Don't go. Don't be like that."

"Thanks for dinner," I said.

I left, shutting the door a bit harder than necessary. The thought of a member of my own family being so crass and bigoted just turned me inside out. I shouldn't have been so surprised.

I'd heard him go off on minorities before, but never with such blatant conceit. It was as if he was a stranger, someone I had never known. That couldn't have been what he really thought. How he really felt. It just couldn't. Mom and Dad raised us better than that. But then, I thought about Mom and how she thought it was awful that Alan and Carol let Teresa play with black kids.

I sat in my car for a moment while I cooled down. I felt my pulse raging against the steering wheel while I stared through the windshield at that corrupted house. It took on an almost evil presence, an aura of hatred and doom. To think that my own brother who I had grown up with, who went to school with native Americans and black kids, inhabited that…that hideous attitude.

Dennis appeared on the porch, and I hastily started my car and backed out of the driveway, then almost left rubber behind as I shot down the street.

The entire visit was such a shock. Why had I even decided to stop? I damned sure didn't need that.

I drove back to the interstate and headed home, all the while thinking about Dennis and my relationship to him. Our lives had always been trying. We had never shared the same beliefs, likes and dislikes. We had never been what you would call close. Hell, none of our family were close. Mom's family was, but that was it. Dad's family always kept a comfortable distance emotionally and physically. Just like we did. But how could Dennis have become such a bigot? What had happened in his life to turn him into someone like that? I would never know.

ALAN'S VISIT

April 2002

When I got home from the shelter, tired and relieved, I poured a drink, collapsed on the sofa and replayed that visit I had made to Dennison. Depression crept in and I held a glass of Scotch in my hand, contemplating why people do the things they do. What turns someone into a bigot? What drives a person to gorge himself to death? What happens to a person who primps in his youth to make him completely neglectful of his physical well-being later in life?

Then Alan came to mind. Why hadn't the same things happened to him? He turned out so differently from Dennis. And me. It defied explanation. Where Dennis had shrouded himself with his ego, Alan had blossomed into a compassionate soul, although not without problems.

And Jackie and Carol? Boy they were an ocean apart. The kids, too. And I was caught in the middle of it all.

I looked at the Scotch in my hand. I smiled as I remembered how Alan had encouraged me to try it. I thought it would be putrid, but I fell in love with it just like Alan did. I thought about the first time he and Carol visited me in Dallas.

****

About two weeks after my stay in Harrison, Alan called.

"Hey, Sis. How are you?"

"Alan. Nice to hear from you. Do you have news, or is this a social call?"

"News, I guess," he said. "Listen, we're going to be in Dallas next week for a conference. Mind of we drop by?"

"That would be great. You can stay here, if you like. I have room."

"Actually, we need to stay at the conference hotel. But thanks."

I was both disappointed and glad. I would have had to clean the apartment and try to find sheets and such for the extra bed. Living alone, I'd never fixed up the guest room, because I had few, if any, guests. But, bless his heart, he made that unnecessary.

"Tell you what," I said. "How about I pick you guys up after the conference and bring your over here for supper?"

"Sounds like a winner," he said. "The conference is over at five on Thursday. We have a short meeting on Friday then we go home."

"Okay. I'll see you at five on Thursday. Where will you be?"

"The South Marriott."

"Good. See you then."

They had been to my new place only once before. That was several years ago just after I had moved from my previous apartment that had been demolished and replaced by a parking lot. Dennis had never visited me. Ever. I wasn't surprised. He never seemed to think of me unless he wanted something from me. Like money. Or help babysitting his little darlings. Of course that hadn't happened in several years. Not since we both moved away from the Winfield area.

I hadn't moved that often. Only twice. That had been enough for me. I don't have that much furniture, but still, trying to cram all of my stuff into my Camaro was a challenge. Dennis seemed to move quite a bit, always chasing the dollar. Ever since he left the consumer credit type shops. He seemed too consumed with making it big. There was always another job with a higher salary and more perks.

Alan had moved around a bit, too, but for job advancement, not for the money. I thought about all the times Alan had moved around, and I wondered how he had managed it. He seemed to float around the country like a tumbleweed in the wind. Of course, at that time, engineering jobs were very competitive, companies raiding other companies for good structural engineers to handle the increasing building boom by offering advanced positions in the company. I had suspected while he was still in the army that that would happen eventually, but not until he married, if he ever did.

****

Thursday at five-fifteen I saw spotted them walking toward me from the main entrance.

"So." I said as I pulled into traffic, "how was the conference?"

"Boring," said Alan. "I thought they'd never quit talking."

I looked at Carol.

"What did you do all day while Alan was in meetings?"

"Oh, I walked around town and looked in the store windows. And I worked crossword puzzles."

"Well, I'm sorry you had such a boring day. Maybe we can fix that," I said on the short drive from the hotel.

I parked in front of my apartment and led them inside. Alan still had on his slacks, coat and dress shirt, without a tie. I couldn't help but think how remarkably professional he looked. He'd always been fit and trim, and the clothes seemed to accent that. Carol wore smart slacks and a light green blouse. She could have been a colleague from work. They made me feel comfortable and, in a rare sense, confident. But then, I usually felt that way around Alan.

"Wow," said Alan. "You've done some decorating. It looks good."

"Thanks. At least it's not barren."

In a break from his phlegmatic cocoon, Alan seemed high-spirited and excited. Carol was laughing, I suppose, at something Alan had said. I guess getting away from Harrison agreed with them. It certainly did me good to get away from Winfield, in spite of the fact that it had been my home for so many years.

"How about some wine Carol?"

"Sure. Have you got white?"

"As a matter of fact, I do."

Alan started to speak.

"I know what you want Alan. I'm on it."

I poured Carol and me some wine and she made herself comfortable on the sofa in the living room. I call it that because it's the largest room I have. It also serves as a dining room and office. The place wasn't large, but it was comfortable. And I could afford it.

"You've really got this place looking nice," Carol said, scanning from wall to wall. "This isn't your furniture, is it? I don't remember it."

"No, the apartment came furnished."

"Well, it's pretty nice furniture for an apartment. The owners have good taste."

"Yes, they do. The rent is reasonable, too, for this area. The shelter is just a few blocks away."

I poured Scotch for Alan while I watched him roam around the room.

"Sit, Alan. You're making me nervous."

"You nervous?" he asked. "You've never been nervous in your life."

"Oh, come on, now. You know I was a nervous wreck before my final exams in college. Even in high school. You and Dennis both made fun of me."

"Yes. The biology test in Mrs. Byler's class. I hated biology. That and history. I tried to read all of the assignments and studied my ass off, but I still had that sinking feeling that I didn't know anything about biology. Of course, you and Dennis sensed my anxiety and the floodgates opened. You made corny jokes with sympathetic overtone. But Dennis made me feel like an idiot. I was so mad at him. Then, after the test, he asked me how I did on it and congratulated me as well as his insensitive heart would allow Then he would be so nice to me for about a week."

"Yeah, well, it *was* kind of funny," Alan said with a smirk.

"So, what's the conference about?" I asked, taking a sip of wine.

"Some new-fangled techniques for testing seismic loads on buildings." He sat beside Carol and swirled the Scotch in his glass "A local company had developed new analysis techniques for measuring the various factors that contribute to seismic loads."

"Hmm, sounds like it's deep. I never liked science."

"I know you didn't. I'm disappointed in you, too."

"Well, I didn't care for it, either," said Carol. "I was never good at it."

Alan shook his head. "You know, if it weren't for science, we'd still be traveling by horseback or mule and pulling our two-wheeled carts behind us."

I cast my eyes at him with a tiresome look. "I know. You say that every time anything to do with science is mentioned."

He had that shit-eating grin of his. "Well, I guess it hasn't soaked in yet, has it?"

"No, Alan, It never will. I'll just take my conveniences for granted, thank you very much."

"That's the problem with science. These kids in school end up having to unlearn what they think they know about it and relearn it correctly. I guess you never took the trouble."

Carol turned toward me. "How is the shelter getting on?"

"We're full up and still have women asking for space, as always. I just don't know what we're going to do. There's no room to expand and more and more women are finding it hard to get in a shelter. We had a couple of incidents recently that brought the police in."

"Anything serious?" asked Alan.

"As it turned out, no. It could have been, though."

"Your shelter always seems to be full," said Carol. "Are they all full?"

"For the most part, yes. My boss has been trying to negotiate with local building owners to let us use their buildings as annexes."

"Can you do that?" asked Alan.

"Well, we're trying. We haven't met any roadblocks yet, except the owners' concerns about liability. Our attorney is looking into what we can do about that."

"It sounds complicated," Carol said. "Any time an attorney is involved, it gets complicated."

A momentary lull filled the room.

"Well," I said, "anybody hungry?"

"As a matter of fact," Alan said, draining his glass. "I'm starving. The food at the conference sucked."

"How about ordering in a pizza?" Carol offered.

"Great idea," agreed Alan.

"Pizza it is. Any preference?"

"I'd go for the works," said Alan.

"That would be okay with me," said Carol.

I made the call.

"By the way, Alan, I wanted to ask you."

"What?"

"Oh, another drink?"

"Damned right."

I poured the Scotch and set it in front of him. "How many times did you move while you were in the army?"

He took a good sip. "Well, in the army, there was the move to Fort Belvoir, Virginia, then to Fort Wolters, Texas, then Fort Rucker, Alabama, then back home. Vietnam really wasn't a move. More of a pain in the ass. Then back home, again. After that, I went to Ponca City."

"How did you move all of your stuff?"

"Well, hell. In my car."

"You must not have had much."

"I didn't."

"I guess that wouldn't have been so bad, then."

Carol asked, "Where did you get all of the things you had when we married? I mean, you didn't have that much, but it seemed like a lot at the time. I didn't have much of anything."

Alan shrugged his shoulders. "I bought it."

Carol was still curious.

"You had that little station wagon?"

"Yeah,"

"Is that what you had before the MG? I know all of your things wouldn't have fit into that little thing."

"Oh, well, I didn't have the MG until I got back from Vietnam and moved to Ponca City to work on the dam. I had this Rambler American station wagon. A sixty-four, flat head four-banger piece of shit. One of Dad's cheap finds."

"You had that pink Rambler before that?" Carol asked.

"Yeah. It used to be Dennis' until he went into the army, then I inherited it when I started college. God, I hated that thing. Me, with a pink car. At college I was the laughing stock of the dorm. By the time I went into the army, it was getting old and Dad thought I needed a different car."

"So, the pink one was your first car?"

"Yeah."

"That's when Dennis got the red Plymouth?"

"Yeah," Alan said, "he was kind of hell on cars."

"He didn't take care of them?" Carol asked.

"Oh, he tried. He maintained them. He just wrecked two of them. I think he did pretty good until he got the big head when he went to work for that big bank In Texas."

"Well," Carol said to me, "I remember you complaining to Dennis about working on cars. You were having a fit about having to change oil in the Jeep."

"Yes, and Dennis told me, 'Hell, I have it done. I'm too important to bother with working on cars.'"

I couldn't help but laugh. That was so Dennis. He always wanted to be Mr. Big.

"Sue," Carol said, "have you heard any updates on Dennis?"

"As a matter of fact, yes. Dennis actually called me last week."

They both looked so surprised.

"He said he was recovering really well. His medications are working, and his doctor is happy with all of it."

"Is he able to get out at all?"

"Oh, yes." I paused a bit. "Let me tell you about that."

Alan suddenly perked up and looked at me.

"Jackie took him to his doctor's appointment and on the way back, a car rear-ended them."

"Oh, my god!" Carol said. "Was anyone hurt?"

"No, but the rear bumper was damaged."

"That's going to cost a bit," said Alan.

"Dennis said it was a 'goddamn Mexican' who hit them. He said the guy backed up and took off, waving at them and smiling."

"No shit?" said Alan.

"Yes, and when he called the police to report it, they kind of waved him off. Told him that kind of thing happened all the time. The guy probably didn't have a driver's license and no insurance. It wouldn't be worth their time to look into it. He said he should just file with his own insurance company."

Alan smirked. "Boy, that's a crock."

"Then Dennis said, 'Damned Mexican trash, they ought to send them all back to Mexico.'"

Alan let out a huff. "Well, so much for his better man shit."

I really couldn't argue with that.

"So," Carol said, "I guess he's doing all right, then?"

I drained my wine glass. "Yes, he seems to be. I talked to Jackie for a few minutes. She seems really excited for him."

The doorbell rang. I jumped up. "Ah, the pizza is here."

I saw Alan reaching for his wallet.

"I've got it, Alan. You can buy dinner next time we get together."

"Deal. Let's eat."

I opened the box and we all grabbed for a slice. It didn't take long to devour it all.

"You know," I said, "Dennis also told me he wanted us all to get together at his house. I'm not sure if he was feeling guilty about something or if he was serious about changing things between us."

Alan sat motionless, the near empty glass of Scotch in his hand, a question on his face. Carol seemed to brighten a bit and looked at me, I guess, hopeful.

"I imagine he'll call you, Alan. When he does, I hope you take time to listen to what he has to say."

He put his glass down on the table.

"Huh." He sat back. "He really said that?"

"Yeah. I think he was really serious."

"I will look forward to that," said Carol. "I mean, I've never been too…well, I always thought Dennis was a bit much. But I hope we can get together."

A bright spot had just opened in my life, and I suspected in Alan's, too. It was time for our family to get over ourselves and move on. Each of us needed a change. A way to look at what we *could* be and not what we had become.

I looked forward to the reunion. I knew Alan would be receptive and I had every hope that the two of them could come to terms with their differences. What was left of our family was in tatters. I could only do so much to keep it patched together. It was as if neither Dennis nor Alan wanted to do anything about it. Dennis was just Dennis. He wasn't going to change. Alan was… well, not quite the Alan I grew up with. Vietnam had changed him so much, not to the point of being a completely different person, but enough to know that he saw things differently now than he used to. I wasn't sure that any change in our family was in his nature, either. He seemed hardened, skeptical, vengeful. I didn't know how to deal with that. It was sweet anticipation.

REUNION

November 2002

Several months had passed since Alan's visit. We were both busy with our jobs and Dennis and Jackie were working on his rehabilitation. He hadn't been able to return to work, but he had taken classes at the local vo-tech school in computer programming. He believed he could use those skills to earn some income. They were doing okay with Jackie's new job at the local community college and the future was promising.

Tuesday, I had just gotten home from work. It had been a bitch of a day. Two women at the center got into a catfight over a bottle of Diet Coke. We finally had to call the police before it spread to other areas of the building. They were carted away with scratches and bruises and such profane language even *I* was repulsed. Then another pair of policemen came and arrested one of our clients for shoplifting. Her kids were taken as well, I suppose to be assigned to Child Protective Services. We all just wanted to die.

The Scotch was calming my nerves as the light from the large widow across the room was fading into a dull, lifeless gray that seemed to instill death throes on the world outside. It seemed like this winter would be another depressing one. The atmosphere inside my apartment was little better. I thought about turning on a light, but somehow, I relished the empty and dispassionate feeling that coursed through my body.

After I had finished the glass of Scotch, I felt nothing. Nothing at all. There should have been bliss, freedom, harmony, but I wasn't aware of it. There might have been sadness, but I didn't feel that either. I breathed in deeply, savoring the fullness of my lungs, the captured stale air somehow comforting me. I happened to look up at the picture on the wall. The one of Alan, Dennis and me at a family Christmas from when I was ten. What a grand time that was in Milton. I was so happy, then. We all were, except Dad. And maybe, Mom. And Alan was happy, most of the time. Those were trying times for the folks, but we kids were so carefree, oblivious to whatever burdens had befallen our parents. Except for not buying a bunch of things we wanted, the folks never put their worries on us. They harbored them all, even to the point of near despair. Alan and Dennis had not yet regressed to warfare, and I had a lot of friends to occupy my time.

But something had happened to us. Where had all of that familial togetherness gone? The distance between us seemed to grow farther every year. Except for calls between Alan and me, I hardly hear anything from my family. Dennis never called. He has never called. Well, one time after his surgery. I visited him once. He has never visited me. That's why when the phone rang, the call I got from Dennis was so surprising. It had been nearly eight months since I'd seen him.

"Hi, big brother," I said, with a bit of cheer. I was glad to get the call, to hear his voice, but I waited for the bomb to fall. "What's going on in your world?"

"Hey, Sis."

He sounded hesitant, as if he wished he hadn't called.

"Listen, you remember our talk?"

"When, last April? We haven't had that many."

"Yeah, that would be about right. You remember I mentioned getting together this Christmas?"

"Yes, I remember. Are you having second thoughts?"

"No, no. I've been thinking about our last get together. You know, the one where Alan and me got into it. I mentioned it last time we talked."

"Yes, something like that is hard to forget."

"Look, I know I acted like an ass. We both kind of said things that we shouldn't have."

I waited through a pause, wondering if he was drunk or overcome with another illness.

"Anyway, I wanted you to know that I called Alan and we talked."

Another pause. The surprise interrupted my mind, and I began to think that maybe he was serious.

"We apologized and I think we're good. We still want to get together this Christmas."

My mind stopped for a moment. First, Dennis calls *me*, then says he called Alan, then he says he still wants to get together. I was confused and elated. To have us all together again would be fantastic.

"Sue?"

"Yeah, Dennis, I'm here."

What else could I say?

"Sure. I'd love to get together again. When and where?"

"How about the Saturday before Christmas? At my house.?"

"Okay. I'll make plans to get to Okemah."

"Oh, Sue?"

"Yeah?"

"You don't know. We've moved to Oklahoma City."

"What? When?"

"A couple of months ago. It's closer to my doctors and we have a nicer house."

So, you sold the house in Okemah?"

"Yeah. I got rid of that RV and we used some of Dad's money to put in on a house. I'll send you the address."

After Dad had died just before Dennis had his heart attack, Alan had worked his ass off getting probate taken care of and tracking down all of the investments. Then he got the taxes filed. That all took about six months. When Alan began distributing the funds, Dennis bought a huge RV. Just like him to squander his money. Couldn't wait to spend it. At least now he had sense enough to get into a decent house.

"Dennis, I'm so happy for you. How is Jackie?"

"She's loving it. She's working as an insurance transcriber for the hospital. Making good money."

"How about Brent and Becky?"

"Brent has a job with a telephone company. He does new installations. And Becky is with an advertising company. They're both doing fine."

"Well, it sounds like things are coming together for you."

"Yeah, they are. So you'll come?"

"I wouldn't miss it. It will be good to see you guys again."

"Brent and Becky won't be able to come until Christmas Day."

"That's a shame. I would like to have seen them."

"Yeah, sorry. They're both working that weekend."

"Well, I'll look forward to seeing you guys."

"Okay. Thanks, Sis."

I knew that I heard Dennis say what he did, but my brain had difficulty registering that as reality. Maybe he really *was* a new man. If that was the case, this reunion could be one for the record books. No more battles. No more anxiety. Oh, I knew Dennis would anger easily, but he would never stay mad for long. His temper was like a dust devil, stirring up a small storm for a bit then disappearing in the wind. I was glad that he had called with the invitation, but at the same time, I wasn't sure what would be waiting in Oklahoma City. And why not meet on Christmas Day?

I immediately called Alan.

"Sue. What's up?"

"Alan, did Dennis call you recently?"

"Oh, did he call you, too?"

"Yes. I just talked to him."

"Yeah," Alan said, a tone of surprise in his voice. "You were right. He wants to get together this Christmas."

We both let that sink in for a moment.

"So, what do you think?" I asked.

"Well, he did apologize. And I apologized to him. I know we both got carried away. He didn't really deserve all those things I said. So, yeah. We'll be there. I hope you can make it, too."

I was almost shocked to hear Alan say what he had. Maybe there was hope for them, yet.

"Okay," I said. "I'll make plans to be there. Dennis said he'd moved. He said he'd send me his new address. I can't wait to see their house. God, it's got to be better than that rat trap they had."

"I'm guessing he still had some of the inheritance left. Maybe he got rid of that stupid trailer. I don't see much hope of them using it, now."

"He did say he sold it. Let's just hope that a lot of things have changed."

I heard Carol in the background asking him about the shelter.

"So," he said, "how's the shelter doing this winter?"

I looked up at the murky environment inside the apartment. It suddenly didn't look quite so depressing. Anticipation always brightens my day.

"There were some altercations, today. A couple of residents got arrested. It's busy as hell. There's been a big increase in domestic violence, here in Dallas. Not sure what it is, but we're full up and still getting women in looking for help, like always. We've had to double up on rooms and we're about at our limit. I don't know what we can do after that."

"I'm sorry to hear that, Sue. Isn't there any other agency that can help?"

"Well, there's always the Salvation Army and several other homeless shelters around town. But they aren't secure. It would be better than nothing. At least other people would be around."

"I don't suppose there's anything I can do to help?"

"No, Alan. There's absolutely nothing you can do except make a donation to our cause. But I wouldn't ask you to do that."

"Damn, Sis. It sounds like you're in a real pickle."

"We're trying to get more funding from the city, but that will take months or years. We've also applied for other grants. We'll just have to weather the storm. It can't last forever."

****

It would have been nice to be at Alan's for Christmas, but the thought of being with both brothers was undeniably preferable. If they both were committed to reconciling their differences, then I couldn't do anything to jeopardize that.

I made plans to drive the four hours to Oklahoma City. I could think about how I would handle what might happen. Optimism. That's what I had to keep in mind.

****

It was suddenly December, the weekend before Christmas. I was on my way to Oklahoma City, a long early morning drive, but worth the trouble to see both of my brothers.

The red brick house stood out from the painted houses along the block, large trees filtering the low winter sun through their spiny branches. A nice house. Neat and trim. Alan's Jeep was in the driveway. I pulled in beside it in front of the two-car garage.

Jackie was out of the door to welcome me before I even got out of my car.

"Sue," she yelled. "It's so good to see you. Did you have any trouble on the way?"

I shut my door and opened the trunk to extract the presents I had brought.

"No, no trouble. It was a pleasant drive, but long."

"Let me help you with those packages."

She was lively and high-spirited, her smile wide, her eyes sparkling, and her hair in a kind of retro style, or rather perm like Mom used to wear. It was so Jackie.

Between the two of us, we managed to get most of the presents into the house. I'd have to go back for my overnight bag and the casserole I had brought. We dumped the packages beneath the Christmas tree, and I turned around to find Dennis sitting in a recliner laughing at me, his big belly jumping up and down.

"Hey, big brother."

He pried himself out of the chair to stand and smirked. "You didn't have to get that many present for me."

I laughed and said, "Well guess what. I didn't get you anything. These are for everyone else."

"Hey, Sis." Alan was sitting on a sofa across the room. "How was the long drive?"

I looked at him with a smile. God, it was good to see him. And Carol and Teresa sat beside him. Teresa looked so grown up, but then, as a legislative assistant for a U.S. senator, I guess she really was.

"Well, yes. It was long. But a nice drive. It's not quite so barren here as it is around Dallas, right now."

Dennis plopped back into the recliner. He had a cheery disposition, a satisfied look on his face, and a lively lilt in his voice. It looked like he might have lost a bit of weight, but it was hard to tell. My apprehension about the reunion seemed to begin melting away.

"You look great, Sue," Alan said. "I guess you're weathering the storm okay?"

"Sit down," Jackie said. "I'll get something to drink." She turned and stopped. "Coffee, iced tea?"

"They don't have Scotch," Alan said, but the whiskey's good."

"That'll work for me," I told her, moving toward a chair. It was almost noon, close enough for happy hour.

"Well, hell," said Alan. "If you're having one, I'm having another one, too."

He got up and walked toward the kitchen where Jackie was headed. Dennis got up, too, pressing down on the arms of the chair, finally forcing himself erect and followed Alan into the kitchen.

Dennis' stride was solid and steady, a good sign he had been behaving himself. He looked good, color in his face, and he seemed to handle himself pretty well. I guess Jackie had taken good care of him and Dennis was following the doctor's orders.

I turned toward Teresa.

"Teresa, how are you?"

"I'm fine," she said, coyly. "I'm glad to be away from D.C. for a while."

She had just graduated from college, a doctorate degree, no less and had started work in Washington, D. C. In June.

"Why is that? I thought you like it there?"

"I did at first. But D.C. is the kind of place no one is from. Everyone is just a temporary resident."

"How's your new job?"

"I like it," she said, somewhat excited. "It's going to be very interesting."

I asked Carol, "When did you get here?"

"Oh, we've only been here about a half hour. Dad was so excited about coming."

"I was, too. I wanted to see Dennis' new house. It looks nice. A lot better that that thing they had in Okemah."

"Isn't that the truth. I'm so glad they got out of that."

The others returned from the kitchen and sat down, Jackie with a brilliant smile and drinks for me and herself, Alan with a healthy glass of whiskey, and Dennis with a glass of iced tea along with a grin on his face that gave me the impression he was genuinely happy we were all there together. Jackie handed me a glass of whiskey. "Done anything else on your house?" Dennis asked Alan, looking at him with honest interest.

I saw a flash of puzzlement on Alan's face in the instant just before it disappeared. God, don't let it start.

"No, I really haven't. It's been too cold, and I've been too busy."

What a relief. No antagonism. I could really get used to this, a real family sit-down.

"I've got several projects lined up, though," said Carol. "When the weather gets better, it needs to be stained again and a few repairs made."

Dennis cocked his head. "Doesn't that house take a lot of maintenance?"

"Hell, yes," replied Alan. "It's a real maintenance hog. But there's nothing like coming home to the smell of wood and all the trees around there."

Jackie made her contribution. "It's such a beautiful; setting. It seems so peaceful."

"That it is," said Alan. "Watching the deer cross the pasture and, sometimes through our yard. And the birds are everywhere. Then there's the armadillos we have to keep running off, and the moles and gophers. And the goddamn squirrels."

I had expected Dennis to make some remark about shooting the deer, but for some reason he didn't.

"What's wrong with the squirrels?" asked Dennis.

"Hell, they're chewing up the place. They even gnaw on the treated wood deck. They get into the bird feeders, and they chew up the cushions on our chairs out front. I've tried trapping them and taking them down the road, but I think they got wise to that. So, I've just been shooting the bastards."

That brought a hoot of laughter from Dennis. He almost choked on his tea. The sound of laughter was music, the cheery air an absolute delight. I sat stunned as Alan and Dennis exchanged tales of their childhood and small barbs that left all of us laughing.

"Remember when I hid in your bedroom?" Dennis said to Alan. "I waited until you got into bed, then moved my hand under the covers. When I touched your leg I thought you were going to jump out of that bed."

He reared back in a fit of laughter. Alan turned a bit red but grinned, just the same.

"I remember that," I said.

"When was this?" Carol asked.

"I was in high school," Alan volunteered. "It was a pretty mean thing to do."

"And Sue," Dennis continued, "you were talking on the phone with your boyfriend, and I stopped by you and farted."

Another roar of laughter.

"And," said Alan, "I still remember when you dislocated your elbow."

Dennis suddenly withdrew and got a shocked look on his face.

"He was on the football team," said Alan, "and during one game he was sitting on the end of the bench. The players scooted down to make room for another player and pushed Dennis off onto the ground. When he fell, his elbow was dislocated."

We all broke down in hysterics. Well, all but Dennis, who had a sheepish grin on his face.

"I remember that," I sad. "They took him to the emergency room. He wore a cast for a few weeks."

"I still think about the trips we took," I sad. "The long one we took one fall to Colorado."

"Yeah," said Dennis, "I remember that one. We spent the nights at creepy motels. Verda was with us. One day we packed up in the morning and drove a ways before we stopped to fix breakfast."

"Why didn't you eat at the motel?" Asked Carol.

Alan jumped in. "Most motels back then didn't have restaurants. And keep in mind that our dad was a cheapskate. It was probably bad enough spending money on a trip like that. Mom had this little notebook she kept and wrote down every penny we spent on the trip. She would pack food in an ice chest and Dad would pack up his portable Coleman gas stove. We'd stop by the side of the road and cook eggs and bacon and toast."

"That sounds like fun," said Jackie.

"It would have been," said Alan, "except that it was colder than hell up there in the mountains. There was even goddamn snow up there where they decided to stop. Mom and Dad set up for cooking and put up an old army cot for us kid to sit on."

I laughed. "And Alan was so cold. When Verda gave him his plate of food, he was shivering so much he couldn't even keep scrambled eggs on his fork."

Everyone broke out laughing. It was amazing. We hadn't laughed like that in decades. I even remembered Dad's corny laugh.

"You know," I said, "I miss Mom and Dad."

Dennis kind of grimaced and said, "Yeah, I do, too. Dad was right about a lot of things."

Alan looked up with cold eyes and clenched jaws.

"He was wrong about a lot of things, too," he said sternly.

"What do you mean?" I asked.

Silence fell on us while my eyes met Alan's. He had that fierce look, as if he were staring down a bear. The alarm put a sour feeling in my stomach. What now?

He lowered his head.

"I've never told you about some of the things that happened when they were living with us in that trailer."

"Like what?" I challenged.

"Well, you know they were always at odds. Mom had no idea what was going on most of the time, and Dad had no idea what was going on with Mom. He didn't understand her disease and had no inclination to understand it. He thought she was doing all of the outlandish things she did just to get back at him."

196

"We all knew that," I said.

"One night we heard the awfullest noise coming from the trailer. I went over to see what might be wrong. Before I could knock on the door, I heard Dad almost yelling at Mom in the bedroom. I thought I'd better check it out before I went in. The curtains on the bedroom windows were never closed. Just the sheers covered them. I went over to the bedroom window and saw Mom sitting on the edge of the bed, cowered down with a blank look on her face. Dad was trying to get her nightgown on. And you know what that son of a bitch said?"

No one made a sound, all of us waiting for Alan to reveal what he had heard. Carol's face was full of surprise. Dennis leaned forward, eager for Alan to go on.

"He told her, 'You're a lot of trouble, you know. I should never have married you. You're just too much trouble.'"

We all sat there, stunned.

Alan looked up.

"What kind of man says something like that to his wife?"

No one had an answer. The revelation took us all by surprise. Dennis' eyes narrowed. I could tell he wasn't sure about what Alan had told us.

"Why didn't you tell me?" Carol scolded.

Alan looked at her, a forlorn look, lost, a deficit of words. Yes, why hadn't he said anything about that to any of us?

He looked back at each of us in turn, focusing on Carol.

"Because, at that time, I thought I understood why he said that." He dropped his head, then looked up again. "Sure, I felt sorry for Mom. She was in a place that she couldn't escape from. She had no control over anything."

He stopped talking for a bit, the rest of us wondering what else he was going to say.

"But I also felt sorry for Dad. He was in a bad place, too, one he didn't know how to control. His refusal to accept Mom's illness only made it worse. He was tired, frustrated, angry…"

Carol took his hand.

"Yeah, I understand why he said those things, then. But now, after all these years, I realize it was so wrong. I know they loved each other but Dad never had the courage to face problems like that."

He looked at me.

"Hell, Sue, he ever try to console you when that halfwit boyfriend of yours tried to make a move on you right there in our driveway? As I recall, he just asked if you were okay and grunted."

That memory really stung. I thought I was going to be raped until I grabbed my umbrella and beat him over the head with it. Mom was so furious. Dad just didn't understand.

"Did your boyfriend really do that to you?" Jackie asked.

I looked at her and nodded my head. Dennis gave his token grimace of disapproval and Carol looked so sad. Poor Teresa looked so confused, an almost unsettled look on her face.

Alan's sudden confession, completely impossible to have anticipated, released a strange fear in my gut, that kind of fear that you don't really know you have until something happens. Was Dad really like that? What the hell went on down there after they had moved to Harrison? Why the secrecy?

"Well," said Jackie in a lively tone, "who's ready to eat?"

We made our way to the table and sat. The food looked divine, as I would have expected. Jackie was a whirlwind in the kitchen, as long as it was her own.

The meal went off without a hitch. Conversation was upbeat and everyone was content to just talk. We all decided to exchange gifts that evening. It would allow some of us to leave early in the morning to get back home. I know Alan and Carol were having her family's Christmas dinner the next day.

The next morning, we all parted on good terms, and I started back to Dallas. It would be late when I arrived, but I was pumped up, that nagging feeling about Alan and Dad. I wondered if Dennis would approach Alan about it after I left. I was certain that Carol would.

A SHOCK TO THE FAMILY

February 2006

Several years went by filled with phone calls and visits between us three. I felt as if the entire world had changed, and I no longer agonized over our failed family relationships. It was a second chance for each of us. A second chance at life for Dennis, a second chance at our family coherence for all of us. Life seemed happier, my apartment became more inspiring, and I lost my distrust of the future.

In the last few months, I had started talking with one of detectives who often dropped by the shelter. He was really nice, good looking, and had a great sense of humor. He finally asked me out. At first, I had no idea what to do. How does a woman my age date? What does she say? How does she act? My worries had been for nothing. James, that was his name, was understanding and knew just what to say and do. He was a widower. His wife was killed in a car crash some years ago. We'd been dating for a few months and the thought of marriage had finally crossed my mind.

I went to bed that night with a bright outlook for the next day. Even a brisk January morning would be welcome. I had just gotten into bed. Then the damned phone rang. What time was it? It was Jackie, again. Ten-thirty-three at night. She was crying, her voice dark, somber.

"Dennis passed away tonight," she sobbed. "He's gone."

It took a minute for her words to register. She'd told us that Dennis had been having some problems, lately, but it was nothing serious, or at least she didn't think so. I had been to see him two months earlier and Alan and Carol made a point to visit him every couple of months.

And he died tonight? Why tonight, of all nights? Things were going so well for us.

We were happier than we'd been in decades.

"Oh, Jackie." I took a deep breath. "I'm so sorry."

"Thanks, Sue." I heard a shaky breath. "I know I shouldn't be so upset. We both knew this would happen one day. I just didn't think it would be quite this soon."

A few sniffs. At least she was rational.

"Are you all right?"

"Yeah," her voice wavered. "I'm okay."

"What happened?"

"Well, he got a cold a couple of weeks ago. It wasn't bad, just sniffles and runny nose. Then yesterday he started having trouble breathing. I found him hanging by his hands from the top of a door frame. He said he couldn't breathe. I called for an ambulance. When we got to the emergency room, his whole chest was hurting. They said he had pneumonia. He went unconscious and never came back."

"God, Jackie. I hate that this happened. How are Brent and Becky?"

"Oh, they're all right. I think they had expected this, too."

The raging wind outside filled the silence on my end of the phone, and the raging thoughts in my head filled me with fear and anxiety. How could this have happened now? After all Dennis had gone through. The frightening heart attack, the transplant, the drugs, the hope of a new life. His reconciliation with Alan. How could all of that be taken away?

"Jackie," I said, finally, "is there anything at all I can do?"

A sniff. "No. I'll get with the kids and work things out."

"Have you called Alan?"

"No. I wasn't sure what to say. How to tell him."

"Tell you what. I'll call Alan. Have you made plans for a service?"

"Well, we decided not to have a funeral. Dennis wanted to be cremated, no funeral. So, I'm just having a small celebration of life in Okemah. Just close friends and relatives. Jason, you remember him?"

"Yeah. Our cousin. He has a production company in Okemah."

"Well, he's going to be at his studio with a CD of songs he's going to produce for Dennis. That's where the celebration will be."

"How nice," I said. "I haven't seen Jason in ages. What a great idea."

"Oh, Becky's here. I'll call you later with the time, okay?"

After Jackie hung up, I looked at the phone in my hand. I dreaded the next call. I had no idea what to expect from Alan. It would be a shock, but what would his reaction be? I just hoped he didn't take it hard.

Three rings. Four. Five.

"Sue?"

"Alan."

After a slight pause, "What's up? It's…almost eleven. I didn't know you stayed up this late."

"Alan, Jackie just called."

I listened to dead air for a moment.

"Shit. Dennis?"

I took a deep breath. "Yes. He—"

"Is he all right?"

I took another deep breath. "Alan, Dennis died a little while ago."

"Oh, Jesus."

I heard him trying to wake Carol, then he came back. "What… what happened?"

"Complications with pneumonia."

"Pneumonia? I didn't know anything was wrong with him. Is Jackie all right?"

"She sounded like she was holding it together."

I heard Carol in the background. He was trying to tell her about Dennis. I heard her ask about the funeral.

"Have any arrangements been made? Like a funeral or something?"

"She said she'd have a celebration of life at Jason's studio in Okemah. Just a few people. Jason will be there. Something about a CD he's making for Dennis.

"God, I haven't seen Jason in years. I didn't even know he lived in Okemah."

"She said she'd call later with the time."

"What about Brent and Becky?"

"Jackie says they're fine. Becky was just getting there when she called. I can't imagine that they would be okay, but that's just me."

The silence that followed concerned me. What was he thinking?

"Alan?"

"Yeah."

"Are you okay?"

A pause.

"I'm not sure," his voice low.

What did he mean by that?

"I'm sorry, Alan."

Another pause.

"I know," he murmured.

"This leaves just the two of us."

"Yeah. You and me."

"Is Carol there with you?"

"Yeah. She's right beside me in the bed."

"Well, at least you've got her. And Teresa."

"Yeah."

I heard him sigh.

"And what about you Sis? Is there anyone else in your life?"

I wasn't expecting that. I paused a moment to think about how to answer.

"I'm seeing someone," I said, in a matter-of-fact way.

I could hear him smile. He always let out this little huff through his nose when he smiled.

"I'm glad."

"Well, nothing serious, yet. We just like each other and are very compatible."

"Good for you. You deserve that."

I was thinking what to say next, and I imagine Alan was, too. We drifted through the silence in thought.

I took a chance. "Was he really that bad?"

I waited for his answer.

"You know, I've spent most of my life trying to overcome what happened. I know all of it wasn't his fault. I know I shouldn't blame Mom and Dad, either. Now I have to stop and think about what my life has been all about."

"Alan, it's been about you and your family. Carol and Teresa. You should be proud of your daughter. She's a real gem. I'm envious."

"Thanks, Sis. I'm proud of you too. The shelter, I mean. All of those women and children. I can't imagine what hell they have been through. At least they have you to lean on."

That was the first compliment anyone in our family had given me for decades. I wasn't sure how I felt about it.

"Yes, I suppose they do."

"Listen, Sue…"

I waited.

"If you hear anything about the service, let me know."

"Yes, Alan. I will. Go back to sleep."

****

I certainly wasn't going back to sleep. There was no way in hell that was going to happen. I got up and headed for the kitchen. The bottle of Scotch loomed in the nebulous glow of a night light, a murky beacon of respite to clear my head and contemplate the late-night intrusion of…what? Shock? Sadness? Apprehension? Worry? What was it, exactly, that had happened? Dennis. Dead. As I thought about it, I wasn't sure just where my mind resided; in reality or in some abstract form of it. It was as if I couldn't bring myself to accept it, but that's what the phone call had told me.

I poured a shot, doubled it, and went to the living room, turning on some music, Dave Brubeck Quartet playing "Take Five." I plopped in my recliner and let my mind wander.

What was it like, I wondered, to lose a husband? One like Dennis. In a family like theirs. Dennis had been demanding, selfish, and arrogant. Nonetheless, he still provided for his family. Not that either he or Jackie knew squat about raising kids. They didn't. I wasn't married and even I recognized the mistakes they'd made. Both of the kids were very much like their parents: arrogant, self-absorbed, and apathetic to anyone else's difficulties. As small children they had been wild hellions, unrestrained and spoiled. Except for the fact that they were their grandchildren, Mom and Dad almost hated to see them coming. Alan could barely stand to be around them. Carol tried her best to be friendly toward them, but her efforts were largely met with indifference.

The few visits I had made to their home had been short and trying. Jackie's culinary skills she had learned from her mother, and she could spend all day in her kitchen baking and cooking delicious meals. It was the rest of the family that made mealtime disappointing. The eating habits ranged from gross to downright disgusting. They seemed to try to see just how much food they could shove in their mouths at one time.

After dinner, Dennis and Jackie would brag about their latest acquisitions, which were always the biggest and best available, or their latest trip, or any other for that matter, that had been more grandiose than trips taken by anyone else. Or if I mentioned that I had been somewhere, they would, without fail, brag about having gone somewhere bigger or better. It was infuriating and I now understood why Alan got upset when they did that to him. I felt sorry for him and Carol trying to talk about things they had done. Aside from our recent reunion, I never spent the night at their house. I don't think my sanity would have survived.

Alan's family, on the other hand, was almost a model American family. Being mostly shy…no. Not shy, reticent. Alan never bragged about anything and was always ready to compliment me on anything worth a compliment. Carol was the sweetest thing. They were both decent cooks and their meals were healthy, for the most part, and gave their guests a taste of different types of food. Evenings were very pleasant, being quiet and affable.

Their daughter, Teresa, was a little sweetheart. Bright, curious, and very adept at learning. She was her high school class valedictorian and had been selected as one of fifty Oklahoma academic scholars. Alan's family had more credentials and achievement than most other families I was acquainted with. Not to say that Alan ever bragged about any of it. He never did. Even his tour of duty in Vietnam had been kept under wraps for so many years. They were all very unassuming and low key. My visits with them were always satisfying and inspiring. And I had spent many nights at their house.

But then, there's Alan. That stoical reticence of his just drove me mad. I got so tired of him being so overly modest, never boasting, never tooting his horn, even though he has more to brag about than anyone else in the family. It's as if he was trying to play the martyr, always acquiescing to everyone else. Carol's the one who toots his horn for him, since he won't do it himself. He was incorrigible.

So, what had happened? What had led to the final straw that killed Dennis? He had really changed his lifestyle. I don't know about the church thing, but he and Jackie certainly looked at life differently.

Then I caught myself. There I was, praising Alan and vilifying Dennis. I started to cry.

****

I arrived in Okemah a bit later than I wanted. What was left of our family was all there. Brent had grown taller and very handsome, just like a young Dennis. Becky had put on a bit of weight but still had that engaging, devilish face that made you want to like her. And Jason, tall and burly, with a beard. Alan and Carol arrived late. Teresa was in Washington, D.C., at the time, She would not be there.

The small room held recording equipment, cases filled with tapes, and shelves overflowing with papers and files. We all exchanged greetings and small talk until Jackie called it to order with her booming, grating voice.

"I'm glad y'all could be here. It means a lot to me, and I know it would have meant a lot to Dennis."

She glanced at the urn in front of her, a tall pewter affair, quite pretty. Her eyes watered.

"We lost a husband and a father. He loved his kids so much. His sense of humor brought us through some tough times. He always laughed when he couldn't do anything else. And we laughed along with him. We decided not to have a funeral. Dennis didn't go in for that sort of thing. In fact, he hated them. So, we just wanted to meet so we could say goodbye."

Jackie continued for a short while with a very touching tribute. I was proud of her for doing that. Dennis deserved it. Even Alan had succumbed to the moment. I could see his eyes watering, his face tense and his hands clasped. Carol was dabbing her eyes with a tissue. My own eyes were flooding. Brent sat in his chair, solemn, unaware of anyone else. I figured he had been stunned by his father's death. Becky was also sniffling, dabbing at her eyes.

Jason then spoke.

"Dennis always liked country and western music. The few times we'd been together, we always listened to it. I put some of my favorite songs on a CD in memory of him. I've got copies for each of you."

The group chatted for a bit before breaking up to leave. Alan talked with Brent and Jason for a bit, and Carol and I chatted with Becky and Jackie. Then we paid our respects to Jackie and her kids. We got in our cars and left. I followed Alan and Carol back to Harrison.

****

The silhouette of the big log house loomed eerily against the blue-black moonlit sky. The naked branches of the huge oak trees that stood like sentries in front of it formed a black ragged border against the blackened sky. Lights from the house twinkled between branches as we approached. The effect gave the house a majestic look, imposing and grand. Alan had done right good for himself.

In spite of the late hour, Carol headed for the wine cabinet while Alan laid a fire in the fireplace. I headed for the Scotch. Carol took her wine to the sofa, I took my Scotch to a chair by the fireplace. Alan poured a Scotch and sat down beside Carol.

"At least Teresa is in D.C.," Carol said. "I just wish I were there with her."

Alan turned to face her.

"Yes. You don't like funerals."

Carol sipped her wine.

"No, I never have. They're so sad."

The crackling fire filled the silence. I was surprised to see Alan slumped on the sofa, his eyes straight ahead, chin lowered, detached from the reality of the evening. I wasn't sure what was going through his mind. How had Dennis' death affected him? Except for his watery eyes at Okemah, I hadn't seen much evidence of any emotion. Nothing at all. If it weren't for his slouching, it would almost be as if nothing had even happened.

Carol was staring at him, perplexed, as was I. She couldn't read him, either.

"I hope Jackie will be okay," I said. "It could be tough on her for a while."

"Alan," Carol said, "are you okay?"

He dropped his head a bit lower and stared at the floor.

"I honestly don't know."

So, it *had* affected him. I wanted him to turn loose and let it all come out, to yell, scream, whatever. I wanted him to show some emotion, some element of grief. Some sign that he had just lost a brother. Anger, rage, sadness, grief, anything. There was only that blank, empty stare, as if he were a million miles away, detached from us all.

"I'm sorry about Dennis," Carol said softly. "I know you don't like to show your emotions." She kept staring at him. "But it's okay. I understand."

I set my glass down on the table by my chair.

"Alan, this is kind of hard for me, too. All I have been able to think of lately is all of the good times we used to have. Playing, laughing. The trips we took. I still remember that time in Ponca City. It was Christmas eve at Dad's store. We were all there helping out with the Christmas rush. You, Dennis and I were standing in the aisle and Mom came up and said, 'The man who just left dropped a penny in that basket of toys.' You and Dennis look down at it, then at each other, and both of you dove in and threw all of the toys out, fighting for the penny. I'd never seen Mom laugh so hard. Dad came around and started laughing, too. I thought I would split a gut at you two."

Alan stared up at me, a sheepish expression on his face with an unforced smile.

"I remember that. We were in high school. Dennis was home on Christmas break from college."

He looked back down at that floor.

"We were kind of brothers, then."

Carol and I waited, expectantly. He took a sip of Scotch.

"You know, we did a lot of things back then. Things that brothers do."

"What kind of things?" asked Carol.

"There was this theater in Winfield. The Fox Theater." He looked at me. "Dennis and his friend, Larry, you remember him?" looking at me. "We walked those few blocks to the Saturday matinees, me trotting along behind. We were happy as larks. We watched Hopalong Cassidy, Superman, hell I don't know what all."

We sat silently still, stunned by what was happening. The fire had caught, and I could feel the heat radiating out from the fireplace, warming me, chasing away the chill. A catharsis of sorts. An awakening of what Alan and Dennis might have had as brothers. Alan went on.

"You know, Dennis even stopped by my mobile home when I was stationed at Ponca City at the Kaw Dam. He was on his way back home from some client he had seen in town there. I had just gotten the trailer a few weeks before. Didn't have much furniture. Didn't need much for just me."

He looked over to Carol.

"It was just before we were married. I didn't even have a bed. I had ordered a water bed and got it that afternoon. I filled it up and put the sheets and cover on it. I was looking forward to a good night's sleep. But I decided I'd let Dennis have first crack at it. I slept on the mattress I had in the living room."

He smiled.

"In the morning, he came out of the bedroom scowling. He said, 'I froze my ass off on your goddamned bed.'"

He started laughing again.

"I hadn't realized that the water was still cold from the faucet. I laughed my ass off."

We all shared a good laugh.

"I remember when you first got that mobile home," said Carol. "And I remember trying to sleep on that crappy water bed. It *was* cold. And if I rolled over, the bed swished and swished. I could have gotten seasick."

I felt as if I was dreaming. Alan seemed to have found the thread that connected him to Dennis. A very fine and fragile one, but one that led him to realize what Dennis meant to him. And to me. It was like I was sitting on a cloud. The revelation took me completely by surprise. I'm sure it did Carol, too. Maybe Dennis' death served some purpose that none of us had been aware of. I had never believed people when they said, "Everything happens for a purpose." Well, maybe they did, after all.

Later that evening, Alan went for a walk toward the lake. I imagine he needed some solitude to process what all had been happening. I know *I* needed it. I put on my coat and sat on the front porch steps, the cold air stinging my nose, and stared across the gravel road at black silhouettes. The pasture, the trees, the black sky punctured by a bright, nearly full moon. I didn't pay attention to any of it. It was just hard to accept that Dennis was gone. Just like that. No chance to say good-bye. No final touch. No final words. Just…gone.

What would happen to us, now? Would we still be a family? *Could* we still be a family? I felt so sorry for Jackie. She definitely had a rough road ahead. I just hoped that Brent and Becky stepped up to help. I was never sure just how close they had been as a family. I never heard Jackie or Dennis mention them visiting. Hell, ever since they left school, I had never heard from them. I had sent money and presents on their birthdays and Christmas but never heard a thing out of them. When I got home I would reach out to Jackie and offer my help if she needed it.

So, what would I do with myself? Alan and I were as close as anyone in our family had been. Now it was just him and me. And Carol and Teresa. I didn't think Jackie and her kids would have wanted to be included in our coterie. We should make the offer, but I was fairly certain she would decline.

And Alan? Oh, hell. What was I going to do about him? I was sure Carol could handle his issues better than I could. At times he seemed so…lost. Withdrawn from the world. Of course, he'd always been that way to some extent. Dennis' death had really shaken him. It was not that obvious on the surface, but beneath all of that stoical facade was a man in need of something. As if Vietnam wasn't enough, now he had to endure this. My own stability was shaky, just then. I couldn't imagine what torment he was going through.

And Teresa. What of her? Would her father alienate himself from her and Carol? But then, Teresa was smart enough to know what was going on. She and Carol could surely keep him grounded and in some state of sanity.

The crunch of gravel drew my eyes toward the road. Alan's gait was slow, troubled, his hands in his coat pockets. I could not guess what on earth he might have been contemplating. There were just too many possibilities. I watched as he lumbered toward me, completely unaware of my presence. About four feet from the porch steps, he stopped suddenly, startled, moonlight outlining his form, his eyes locked onto mine.

"Sue," he said, his eyes narrowing in confusion.

"Alan," I said, softly. "How was your walk?"

He blinked his eyes and shook his head.

I patted the step beside me.

"Sit down."

He let out a breath, then slowly removed his hands from the pockets and lowered himself to the step, forearms on his knees. We sat in silence for a few moments watching wisps of our breaths float into the brisk air, then I turned to him.

"You okay?"

He lowered his head and clasped his hands between his legs.

"Honestly?" He took a deep breath and blew it out. "I don't know anymore."

I waited in case there was more. There wasn't. It was my turn to say something.

"He did it to himself, you know."

He closed his eyes and clasped his hands tighter.

"That's just the way he was," I said. "No one could have changed him. It's just so tragic that it had to end this way."

He opened his eyes and stared across the road into the darkness.

"Tragic?" He let out a small huff, a small cloud shooting into the coldness. "I guess that's one way to put it."

I let him mull that over. I wanted him to open up. Tell me what the hell he was thinking.

"I guess tragic pretty well sums it all up," he said. "Just like our whole damned family. One giant tragedy."

Here we go, I thought. Back to the family.

"Alan, do you really think our family was that bad? I mean, look at all of the other people we know. Look at their families. They've all had their share of problems."

I thought I saw his jaw clench.

"Look, we might not have had perfect childhoods. We might not have been the best we could have been. Sure, we had some rough times. But look at all the good times we had."

After a couple of minutes, I noticed his body relaxing a bit. His shoulders fell and his hands moved to the tops of his thighs.

"And look at your own family. What you've accomplished during your lifetime. Are you going to sit there and tell me that with such a wonderful woman as Carol and a special daughter like Teresa, that you're not happy with that?"

He slowly looked at me, his eyes in question, glistening in the darkness.

"Yeah," he mumbled. "It's so easy to forget those things."

He looked back across the road, a stern expression on his face.

"You know…I did a lot of thinking when I walked. I thought about things I never really thought about before."

He let out a small huff and looked down at the steps, taking a deep breath. An arm pulled back as he turned to face me.

"I'm really as big of a jerk as I thought Dennis was."

I sat back not wanting to interrupt. He turned back toward the road, sitting erect in perfect military posture.

"I've been blaming him and the folks for everything that I thought was wrong with me. I always believed Dad thought I was a sissy, that that's why I rarely got to spend much time with him."

He took another deep breath and slowly and exhaled, vapor billowing from his mouth.

"But I realize now that neither did Dennis. Dad just wasn't in tune with kids." He gave a small snort. "Kind of like me."

I wasn't sure where all of this was coming from, but I wasn't going to stop it.

"And Mom. Well, she kind of looked out for me, but within narrow confines. She had no idea of the frustration and anger I went through when Dennis was harassing me. It never occurred to her that I was really helpless in those situations. There was nothing I could do to stop it. Nothing except fight him."

He looked up at the silhouetted trees and surveyed the land-scape.

"I suppose I could have tried to fight."

He smiled. "Can't imagine how bad he could have beaten me."

He shook his head.

"But I didn't want to fight. I didn't see the point of it. Brothers shouldn't have to fight. I just wanted him to accept me as his brother. I still looked up to him. That's why I didn't want to fight."

Even in the moonlight, the longing was visible in his eyes. Like a dream that had never come true.

"I guess I've wasted my entire life trying to put all of my shortcomings on him and the folks. I think now I see what Dennis had been going through. He let himself go with that belly of his. He was never a top-notch student. I made mostly As and Bs. He was always broke. I always had some money socked away. He dropped out of college and had to finish up nights after he was married. I earned a master's degree. He spent two years in the army as a SP4. I made captain and served in Vietnam. He was pretty much of a shade tree carpenter. I built my own house."

Then he turned and looked at me, eyes almost squinting.

"Why did we turn out so different? What caused him not to care?"

I laid a hand on his, our cold flesh surprisingly warm to the touch.

"I don't think it was because he didn't care. He just never knew what he wanted out of life."

"You know, you must think I'm a real asshole."

He leaned forward, resting his arms on his thighs again and stared back at the trees.

"I mean, anyone who looked at our two lives would think that we actually *were* competing. Now, I don't really know anymore."

His head fell again.

"Alan, look." I placed my hand on his arm. "It's not about who was better. Or who accomplished more. It was never about that. It's just the way you two were. Dennis was spontaneous, looking for a good time, and yeah, maybe a bit lazy. You were always so...serious. So...driven. It's like you knew from the time you were born that you knew what you wanted to do." I squeezed his arm. "What you *had* to do."

I heard Carol at the far end of the porch. I looked at her and smiled. She made her way toward us.

Alan's eyes watered, the moonlight sparkling from them.

"I always wanted to be closer to him, you know."

"Yes. I always knew that. So did I."

"It seems like he intentionally kept me away. He never really opened up and showed any sign of wanting to close the gap."

"Yes. I know that, too."

"I guess I really didn't, either. And now it's too late."

Carol stood on the lower step. "Can I sit down?"

Alan patted the step next to him. Carol sat down and he put his arm around her, pulling her to him.

Alan did his little huff, again.

"I've been such a fool."

"No," Carol softly told him. "No, you haven't."

He looked at her, bewildered.

"Alan," she continued, "as long as we've been married I know you. I know you're no fool."

"She's right, Alan," I said. "I grew up with you, remember? You've never been a fool. You were always there for me. And, besides, how would a fool have accomplished all you have?"

He nodded his head slowly and narrowed his eyes.

"Your platitudes are off base."

I waited for an explanation. What the hell was he thinking?

"I should have been the one to make the effort," he finally said. "I knew he would never have done it. I should have."

I was afraid he was going on a guilt trip. He could try to blame himself for all the wrongs in the world, but it wasn't going to change anything. It would only drive him deeper into depression.

Carol, with her nurturing nature, hugged him.

"You can't blame yourself. Dennis had every opportunity to do what was right. He chose not to. There's not much you could have done about that. He was just an abrasive, arrogant person."

I looked at Carol and her worried gaze met my eyes. She might have her hands full for a while. It would take Alan some time to come to terms with Dennis' death. I just hoped he *could* come to terms with it.

I later found myself upstairs in bed, the small light on the nightstand throwing a golden glow over the log walls, the big ceiling beams protecting me from above. I listened to the owls call to one another outside the windows. God, what a fantastic place that was. I wished I could have lived there. If there was ever a place that fostered contemplation and renewal, this was it.

It was going to be difficult to get used to Dennis not being around. Well, probably not that difficult. He wasn't exactly *around* when he was. I hardly ever heard from him. Unless he wanted something. Any attempt I made at inviting him down to Dallas was met with some hare-brained excuse like he always gave. Even family gatherings were not in his scheme of things, unless they happened to fall on some day when he could give no excuse, or unless it would benefit him somehow.

Jackie will probably be all right. I think she has enough smarts to get through this. In spite of her kids' arrogance, they will take care of her.

It was Alan I was worried about. I knew he felt guilty for some reason. And there's Vietnam on top of that. I had no idea how to help him. That would fall on Carol and Teresa. They were both strong and determined. I was sure they would know what to do.

I couldn't help wondering what other families would do in this situation. I knew our family was screwed up, but I couldn't help thinking other families were just as bad. They just didn't show it. Did we? Did we show it? From looking at our family photos one might think we were just the typical American family, enveloped in a cloak of happiness and the American dream. What a farce. The more I think about it the more I believe there are no families like that. We were all fucked up.

THE MENDING

February 2006

The next morning, I awoke to the sound of the coffee grinder. How lovely. Alan was up. The morning light was trying to breach the blinds. I opened them and let it in, but the sun was not quite there. An overcast sky loomed overhead, a shadowless landscape beyond the windows.

After a quick wash I hurried down for a cup of Alan's fresh coffee. I wanted to get home before dark, but some issues lingered in that house, and I was determined to resolve them. By the time I had poured my coffee, Alan had disappeared. I found him bundled in his coat sitting on the steps of the front porch, staring into the world, much like he had the previous evening.

"Good morning," I said, clenching my coat and sitting down beside him, coffee cup in hand.

He turned his head and regarded me.

"Yes, I think it might be."

The gloomy sky, the color of dirty concrete, seemed to be held at bay by a filagree of tree branches across the front yard. A cold breeze teased the flag on the pole in the center of the yard. Blackbirds screeched from the large oaks, fluttering, perhaps content with the austerity of the morning.

"Wow!" I sat back. "This from a man who finds every morning clogged with disapproval and generally disappointing. I'm surprised you're happy with this gloominess."

He gave me a smirk.

"Let me ask you something," he said, lowering his head and grasping his coffee cup a bit more tightly with both hands. "How do you feel about Dennis' death?"

He looked up at me. "I mean, really." He took a sip of coffee.

That turn of the conversation caught me off guard. I had never stopped to consider my own feelings about it. My real feelings. The ones that defined me, the real me. I had been too busy trying to figure out everyone else's feelings. And of all things for Alan to ask. He had never opened up like that. Not even when Mom or Dad had died. He never shed a tear when they passed. The sudden hint of emotion from him left me flailing in my own mixed-up thoughts.

"I mean," he continued, "how to you reconcile his death with our lives? What we are really like? All of the conflict between us."

I put both hands around my mug and looked at him, my eyes serious.

"I honestly don't know. I haven't figured that out, yet."

We both stared at the herd of deer meandering through the early morning haze in the field across the road between tree lines, slowly and gracefully, step by step, pausing every few steps to search the surroundings. Such beautiful creatures. Graceful, innocent, resilient. So different from us, fragile, emotional humans. We carry baggage. A lot of it. Memories, most of which obstruct our paths to happiness and leave us full of regret. I believe our family had more than our share of baggage. I happened to look back at the house and saw Carol watching from the window. I winked at her.

"Alan, I'm not sure it's possible to do that. Our history has been filled with so many inconsistencies that defy the nature of a close family. The indifference, neglect, rivalry, and…abuse. But, at the same time, we had love, in our own fashion; respect, although stifled by our own pride; and a sense of integrity not that any of us were angels."

He took a sip of coffee and looked at me, his piercing green eyes, curious, blinking.

"Do you really believe all of that?"

"Yes, I do. Why do you find it hard to accept?"

He looked back down at the steps.

"I just can't, that's all."

I turned on the step to face him.

"Look." I set my cup down. "We all had our problems. But each of us had our strengths. Mom and Dad? They were hardened toward affection by the depression. And rationing during the war. They learned what a person is capable of. They paid attention to survival and preparing for the future. Sure, it probably denied us some of the luxuries we thought we were entitled to. But look at us, now. I have a good career helping people who can't help themselves. I love it. It gives my life meaning. And Dennis didn't do so badly, either. A good wife, two kids. He might not have been a raging success, but he survived as long as he did, and his family is going to be all right. He even got a second chance at life."

Alan huffed.

"And we did, too," I told him.

He froze for a moment. He blinked his eyes and turned toward me.

"Yeah," he said. "I guess we did."

Then he nodded his head. "You know, we *did* have a second chance. I've waited my whole life to be able to sit with Dennis and just talk."

He nodded his head, again.

"And you know?" He smiled. "It was worth it."

I was almost euphoric to hear Alan say those words. Words I never imagined I would hear. It was as if the puzzle pieces of our family were coming together. Maybe I would have a chance to put my own life in order without having to play referee between the two of them.

"That's right, Alan. Dennis died a brother. Of all of our accomplishments, this was the best. I just wish Dennis hadn't had to pay for it."

We both turned to look across the road, the deer having moved on.

"And now, I still have you. My hero."

He smirked. "Well, we all have had a good run., We each had our accomplishments."

"And you, baby brother. You are the crown jewel of this family."

He snapped his head toward me, a stern look of contrition.

"The fuck I am," he almost barked. "Just stop it."

I wasn't prepared for his anger or the tone of indignation, if that's what it really was.

"What's wrong with that?"

"It's just not true. Don't make me out to be something I'm not." He pouted. "Never have been."

"Okay," I said, "I'll admit that you are an arrogant shit, you have this perpetual need to play the martyr, and you're so aloof that you can't seem to relate to anyone who doesn't think like you do."

His face turned red, then almost white, his lips pulled into his teeth.

"That's right Alan. You know, you and Dennis were alike in more ways that you think."

He just sat there, dazed by my assault on his ego.

"But," I continued, "you're still the best thing this family has produced."

He turned back to stare at the woods in front of us.

"You're so full of shit."

I almost felt venom in his words.

"Alan, you have accomplished—"

He cut me off with, "Don't, Sis," he spat. "Don't you dare do this to me."

"But I'm not, Alan. Don't you realize what you have meant to this family? Haven't you wondered why Mom and Dad never criticized you? Never stood in the way of anything you tried to do?"

I watched a puzzled look appear on his face and waited for him to say something. He didn't. I got up and stood in front of him.

"You don't have a clue, do you?"

His brow furrowed and he looked up at me as if I were some kind of deviant from another world.

"Look, Alan, Dennis made some bad choices during his life. He was impetuous and arrogant, a bad combination. Yes, he teased you. Verbally abused you. And he never really focused his life toward anything productive until much later. And Mom and Dad knew that. That's why they questioned most of what he did. Oh, he was smart. He was good at figuring things out. Mechanical things. But he couldn't figure out people, especially, you. He wasn't a bad person. He just never recognized the opportunities that were there."

Alan relaxed somewhat, slumping back on the steps.

"But you. You had a gift, Alan. You are a fast learner. You sat back and watched, observed. You learned from his mistakes. You had this...this thing for knowledge. It was like that was all that mattered to you. That and trying to excel where Dennis failed."

"No," he shouted. "It wasn't like that. It never was."

"Then, what was it like, Alan?" I shouted back.

"It wasn't that at all. I never tried to compete with Dennis. I always looked up to him. I thought he was setting an example when we were young. I never wanted to cross him or make him mad. I wanted him to like me as a brother. To *be* a brother. But he always looked down on me, treated me like some puny wimp that had no value to him or anyone else."

He picked up his cup and took a sip of coffee, but it was cold. He threw the rest of it into the yard and set the cup back on the porch.

"I guess it was when we moved to Ponca City that I finally realized what was happening. I knew he was jealous. I always got better grades in school. I managed to do things he never did good enough to satisfy himself. I still looked up to him, but I no longer expected him to ever recognize me as a real brother. I just made my own way and left him behind."

I watched him close in on himself. It was like some kind of drama was taking place inside him."

Alan took a deep breath and let it out.

"He always made me feel insecure. Worthless. Incompetent." Anger came back to his face. "That's why I focused on education. I knew that was the only tool I had to combat that. When I got to college, I discovered ROTC and what it could do for me. That's why I joined up and stayed in the advanced course. Then, there was Vietnam looming over my head. I knew the minute I graduated I'd be drafted and sent over there. That's the way my luck usually ran. I figured as long as I was going, I wanted to go my way, on my terms. And I wouldn't have to deal with Dennis. So, I signed up for flight training. Hell, it was free. It only cost another year on active duty. What the hell did I know about that?"

I sat back down and just let him vent. He was finally unloading. It was more than I had ever wished for. Except for his confession about losing his crew, Alan had rarely bared his soul to anyone. Well, maybe to Carol, but I wouldn't know about that. `

"And you know what?" he said, looking me in the eye. "I happened to be very good at ROTC. I was able to absorb all of those additional hours and still keep up my other grades. I made friends in ROTC. Friends like me. We were close. We respected each other and confided in each other. That's something I'd never had. Not like that. I didn't like the army that much, but the friendships made it all worthwhile. When I went to flight school I loved flying. I had found another way to prove to myself that I was better than Dennis thought I was. Better than *I* thought I was. I always wondered what Dennis really thought about me, then."

I had never really known why Alan had chosen to enter the army. I knew he liked airplanes, but I didn't know he liked flying that much.

I leaned toward him and put my hand on his arm. "Dennis admired you, Alan. He was so proud of you. Jackie said he would brag about his smart brother war hero."

He gave me one of his snarky looks.

"Bullshit."

I gave him my big sister look.

"Listen, you uppity, sanctimonious asshole." I scooted nearer to him, and he pulled back in surprise. "Don't pretend that you didn't know. He loved you, Alan. Sure, maybe he wasn't the best brother in the world, but who the hell is? You weren't exactly spot on with that, yourself. But our brother is dead. Does that not affect you at all? Does his death mean nothing to you?"

I saw his jaw clench, his entire body becoming rigid. He jumped up off the step and walked two paces into the yard before whirling to face me, his body a knot of anger and contempt, his fists clenched.

"Death?" He shouted, his arms shooting out to the side. "You want to talk about death?"

His green eyes were on fire, like blazing emeralds.

"Do you even know what death is?" He lunged forward nearly screaming at me, pointing a finger at my chest. "Have you ever seen it?" His fists beat his chest as he stood, erect, like a board. "I've touched it." Thud! "I've Lived it." Thud! "Smelled it." Thud!

He raised his head and breathed heavily for a moment, deep forceful breaths, then he began pacing back and forth in front of me. His sudden explosion scared the hell out of me. I had wondered if this was a PTSD episode, or some abstraction of his life that had emerged from Dennis' death. I didn't see anything good happening.

"I've seen so much death I started to believe I might have been one of them." He turned and started in the opposite direction, his hands upturned in front of him. "Men blown away, or cut in two with bullets, blood pouring out of them."

He stopped and turned to the side, dropping his head and letting his arms fall to his side.

"Vietnam showed me what death is. All it is, is an escape from the hell you live through. Death means nothing to me." He turned to stare at me. "I wonder if it ever did."

His shoulders fell, his head sank.

"I'm sorry, but I don't know how to feel like everybody else when someone dies. How do you do that? Does that mean something is wrong with me? How do I fix It? What do I have to do?"

I remembered the funerals we'd had in the family. Alan stayed pretty much to himself. Never shed a tear. Never said a word to anyone. Now, I wondered what had gone on in his head all of these years.

Was this the way he had always been and none of us ever realized it? His drive to join the army and fly helicopters in Vietnam. That just wasn't like him. I know it shocked Mom and Dad. Did they know? I could understand, then, why Dennis had reacted as he did after Alan came home. The jealousy, the need to distance himself from Alan. Dennis had always thought it was a competition between the two of them, and Alan's bravado damaged Dennis' ego. It wasn't that at all. It was merely Alan's way of dealing with what Vietnam had done to him.

He stood there, tears streaming down his face, looking up at the sky, breathing in huffs. We let the silence fill with birds shrieking and squirrels scattering across the yard. Finally, he lowered his head, again.

I watched him stand there, muscles tightening, jaw clenching. I went to him and put my arms around him.

"You know," he finally said, "I saw men die from bullets they never saw coming. Lost their lives. Lost everything. Good lives. Trying to do the right thing. Do their duty. God, I hate that. I feel so sorry for them. For their families."

His arms enfolded me, and we hugged for a long time. God, that felt good. The warmth of his body, the strength of his arms, the smell of him. We finally broke apart.

He put his hands in his coat pockets, turned away, and looked at the ground.

"Dennis." He looked up at the sky. "He just threw it away."

He faced me again and stared. A strained look, full of regret. The pain inside him must have been tremendous. I could see it. I could smell it. I could feel it permeating the air like the sudden drop in pressure before a storm. He looked down again.

"He just threw it all away. What did he accomplish? What did he leave behind except family?"

I didn't know what to say or do. I had questions, but I didn't know how to ask them.

He turned and walked toward the road, then stopped, his back to me.

"You know what he left behind."

Not a question.

"A couple of spoiled, selfish brats and an obnoxious wife."

I couldn't remain quiet.

"Alan, that's not fair," I almost yelled.

He whirled around to face me and took three steps to stand in front of me.

"The hell it isn't."

I stood up right in his face.

"Listen, you hateful, arrogant prick. There's nothing wrong with his kids. Hell, half the country is like that. Jackie isn't obnoxious. Not if you look beyond her brash laugh. There's a real caring person in there. Probably more so than in here," I said, poking him. In the chest. "A person doesn't have to achieve great things to live a good life. Dennis served his country, too. Maybe not in the same manner as you, but he served. Get off your high horse and come back down to Earth. We need you, here, not out there on some lofty plateau looking down on everyone like a god. I loved Dennis. I love you. That's all that matters."

He froze, apparently shocked by what I had said. I saw the jaw slacken and his body slump a bit. He stood like that for a couple of minutes, walked away, then turned and walked back toward the house. He plopped down on the step, staring across the road. I sat beside him.

"You know," he said, "in the army, I knew who I was." He looked at the ground. "What I was." A little huff. "Hell, I wore it on my chest. On my collar. I had a purpose in life."

He looked up again. "After my discharge, I lost that. I was...I wasn't sure who I was. What I was. Even when Carol and I married I was still working on it. Of course, I was still in the army at the time working on the dam with the Corps of Engineers. It was easy to put Vietnam aside. But it was still there. All the doubts, regrets, self-deceit, guilt. I just wanted to do the right thing. I just didn't know what that was."

Alan took a deep breath and leaned back on the step behind him.

"Then I was discharged and went back to college. It was a little tough and Carol put me through. It was all her. I learned to contain most of my insecurities, but I was never the same as I was before Vietnam. Carol had no idea because she never knew me before Vietnam. Thank God for that. She didn't get left behind wondering if I would come back."

He looked at me and smiled, then turned back toward the road.

"I guess that's when Dennis and I kind of drifted farther apart. His snide remarks when I came back from Nam just didn't sit well with me. Maybe he was just trying to be cute, as usual; but his jokes were personal. They weren't a generic manifestation of his humor. They were personal and they hurt. I just couldn't bring myself to respect him after that."

We sat there in silence for some time, me glancing at him occasionally, and Alan staring at his feet. I never knew how he had really felt about his experiences, but now that he had opened up, I can't say I wasn't surprised at it all. I have no idea what he went through over there, and no one else in our family did, either. I know Dennis didn't, but that didn't stop him from spouting off his rude comments. That must have been very painful for Alan. The Vietnam War was not a popular one, and a lot of folks didn't consider it worthy of recognition. He finally spoke.

"The army educates you. It trains you. You become a soldier."

He put his elbows on his knees and rested his chin on his hands.

"But what is a civilian? How do you define a civilian in meaningful terms?"

He sat back up and looked at me for a moment as if expecting an answer. He looked out toward the road.

"After my discharge, I became a civilian. But not just a civilian. Not like everyone else. I was a veteran. I'll always be a veteran. I'll always have part of the army inside me."

He lowered his head.

"I guess that's why I had high expectations for Dennis. He was a veteran. But he never acted like one. He never treated *me* like one. But then, neither did anyone one else. Of course, they're civilians. They wouldn't have known."

He sighed and nodded his head.

"Dennis. I expected more from him. Understanding. Respect. Compassion."

I had to say something. "But he did, Alan. He *did* show you those things."

He fired right back at me with a glare.

"Not to my face, he didn't."

I started to say something else, but he cut me off.

"I tried to ignore it, but goddamnit, that's just something I couldn't do. I suppose that's why we grew so far apart."

"I don't think that's all of it," I said. "Dennis and I grew apart, too. We all did. You see, it's not just you or me. Dennis played a part in it, too."

We both stared at the road, neither of us knowing what to say next.

"Did I ever tell you about me trying to get Dennis to go to our high school reunion?" I asked.

"No." He gave me a puzzled look. "I never knew you tried."

"Remember when one of your friends called you and invited you to one of your Milton reunions? You went and had a great time. I started going to my class reunions, too."

We both smiled.

"I asked Dennis why he didn't go to any reunions. You know what he said?"

"I can't imagine what came out of his mouth."

"He told me, 'Why should I? No body ever called *me*. If they wanted me to come, they could have called me. I don't give a damn about those people.'"

"Yeah," Alan said. "That's Dennis. It was always about him."

"He missed out on so much," I sighed. "He and Jackie could have had a really good time at these reunions. I Know Jackie would have."

We sat in the gray silence for some time, the brisk breeze cooling our noses. I could sense Alan mellowing a bit, jaw slackened, his breathing slower. I just wished he could come to terms with our past, his mistakes. Our mistakes. Our tendencies to reduce everything to familial transgressions.

Yes, Dennis was an arrogant bully. But Alan was an effete snob, looking down his nose at the rest of us, torn between two lives: a middle-class patriotic civilian and a combat veteran, neither of which seemed to be the dominant character role for him. I suppose all combat veterans have that same problem. At least

Alan didn't suffer from PTSD, or at least, I don't think he did. I'd never seen any signs of it. Of course, that doesn't mean he didn't.

Finally, he sat erect, almost alert.

"Forty years. Forty goddamned years. And I never made a real effort to be a brother to him. I think it was my fault that he kept his distance."

The change of subject alarmed me, but I decided not to interrupt his thoughts. I hoped he would explain.

"Hell, Sis. I haven't even been a brother to you. You've been kind of a savior to Dennis and me, always stepping in to stop a battle before it starts, keeping our hackles at bay. I'm grateful that you were there to do that."

"No, Alan."

He turned to look at me.

"That's not true," I said. "You've been every bit of a brother to me. All of our lives you have been there for me when I needed you. When I moved to Dallas, you and Carol drove down to help me find an apartment. You loaned me the money for the down payment on a decent car. You've listened to my dreadful confessions about the awful things that happen at the shelter. I couldn't have expected more of you."

He picked up a twig from the ground and twirled it between his fingers.

"Forty years." He snapped the twig in two. "And now it's too late."

"We all have our regrets, Alan. But this wasn't all because of you. We all had a part in it. That's the way we are. Dennis had his share of blame, too. And me."

We both played over what I had said.

"I wish things had been better between all of us, too," I said. "But, you know what? They weren't. We can't change that. It's over. Yes, I feel bad for Dennis. I feel bad for his family. I feel bad for you. But life can't stop. We work our way into the future one day at a time. We can choose to be miserable while we think about all the things we wish we had done differently. Or we can move forward and make the most of what we have left."

What else could I possible say?

"And, besides, we still have each other. You have a family that needs you."

I heard light coughing from the far end of the porch. I looked over and saw Carol slowly making her way toward us.

"You heard?" I asked.

"Yes," she said as she walked past me down the steps and sat with Alan.

She put her arms around him and he turned to wrap his arms around her.

"Why didn't you ever tell me?" I heard her say.

He pulled back to look into her eyes.

"I just never realized what was happening to me. I've tried to forget Vietnam so hard. To be normal. But it never really goes away. It's always there. It follows me. Never lets me out of its sight. I guess it finally found me, again."

Carol laid her head on his shoulder. "But you have me and Teresa. We can do this together. Now that I know who you really are."

The morning was getting brighter, the cloud layer thinning. I got up and left them to reconcile themselves to their future. A second chance. I needed to reconcile myself to my own future. It was a short flight back to Dallas. I planned to leave in the morning. I needed to let the office know. I went inside to call.

We hope you have enjoyed reading *Second Chances* by Marc Cullison. Please continue reading for a free preview of *The Other Vietnam War - A Helicopter Pilot's Life in Vietnam*, an autobiographical work by the same author that is ranked in Amazon's top 20 Biographies of the Vietnam War.

THE OTHER VIETNAM WAR

A Helicopter Pilot's Life in Vietnam

MARC CULLISON

INTRODUCTION

In 1971, I was among the many who, for the promise of glory or the threat of fear, followed the call to arms. We were swallowed by the evil and goodness, the wretched ugliness and amazing beauty, the despicable sins and glorious honor of war. A war that wasn't urgent, a war against no real threat to America, a war undeclared by our government. A war with only three possible redeeming qualities: it was a war that would make pacifists drunk with arrogance, humiliate the hawks, and place a shroud of humility around the United States of America.

It was many things to many people, but to the soldier, it was a chance to come to terms with his own doubts, beliefs, and frailties as a human being. While in Viet Nam, he grew up, became broken, or died.

The male college student in the late sixties was screwed. If he had a clean nose, he could avoid the draft with a college deferment. But even a minor academic mishap could erase that and he would be on his way to see the world, courtesy of Uncle Sam. That's what they said in the commercials: "Join the army, see the world." Hell, I hadn't even been anywhere but Kansas and Oklahoma. I had 49 other states to see in North America. I didn't give a rat's ass about the rest of the world. Not then, anyway. But as a student, I suspected Vietnam was inevitable.

Unless a guy had a shitload of luck, if he weren't in college, he was probably already on a plane headed for Vietnam. Another option was a medical deferment. If you were gung-ho, you had no interest in that. If you weren't gung-ho and had the money and knew the right doctor or congressman, you could buy one. Then there was always Canada.

Those of us who had enough drive to seek an education and the integrity to do what we thought was right ignored the ranting of our fellow students and peers who opposed the Vietnam War and pursued commissions as officers in the armed services. That was ROTC, the Reserve Officers Training Corps. All eligible freshmen and sophomores were required to undergo four semesters, or twelve credit hours, of ROTC training. Since it was a bona fide course, ROTC counted toward a student's grade point average. For those who loathed military training, this was a thorn in the saddle of education, at least to the students who were in college to actually get an education. To those who weren't, it was even more so, because they could easily jeopardize their draft deferment with low grades in ROTC. To the few who were gung-ho, it was a cushion for their grades.

The draft was not a fair business, but without it, our nation's defense might have suffered. A strong military seems to deter aggression by other countries. So, I can't be too hard on the draft. It was a necessary bit of awkwardness that we had to go through. I don't begrudge our country taking young men to fight for it. I was glad to do it. That's not quite all there was to this scenario, though. It's what we were sent to fight *for* that's the problem.

Since advanced ROTC was optional, after the sophomore year, most of the fellows dropped out of it. Enrollment in advanced ROTC meant you belonged to the military machine. You were one of *them*. You studied two more years, got your degree, and along with it a commission as a second lieutenant. Then you served your time, usually two or three years on active duty before being released. Well, you were still subject to being called up for active duty again, but that didn't happen very often.

Those of us who didn't drop out knew what was coming down the pike and figured that instead of allowing the military to tell us that we were going to be grunts sloshing and slashing our way through the rice paddies and jungles of Vietnam, we would select our own means of risking our lives and satisfying our military obligation. Well, there was a slight chance that you might escape the draft lottery. All the dates of birth of all eligible men were put into a pool and the dates were drawn, supposedly, at random. If your birth date was the first drawn, you would be the first to be called up for service. The first 120 dates were almost assured of being drafted unless that person had a deferment. Because I already had an education deferment, I had no idea what my number was and I really didn't care. I'm sure I saw it on the notice I received from the Selective Service Board, but I paid no attention to it. At that time, it didn't matter. But if I graduated, I would lose my deferment and if my crappy luck held, it would be the only time in my life that I would be close to number one. I made sure that didn't happen.

I've always wondered, though, what my number would have been. And what kind of person I would be now if I were number one and didn't finish college? But all of that aside, I am who I am now because of what happened during that time in my life.

As I look back, the Army wasn't so bad. It could have been a lot worse. As you will discover after reading this book, I was not a career officer, and I damned sure wasn't out to be a hero or win any medals, even though the Army gave me some. I'm not the bravest sort, and I don't have a death wish. Never did. Sometimes a guy gets put in a situation that makes him do things he wouldn't ordinarily do. That's what Vietnam did to me

I didn't know it at the time I signed up for flight training, but statistics now show that a helicopter pilot in battle in Vietnam was twice as likely to be injured or killed as a soldier fighting on the ground. The statistics also show that one out of eighteen helicopter pilots in Vietnam never made it back. Somehow, I survived. I figure I was damned lucky.

We were essentially brainwashed by the military and the government to believe the Vietnam War was a worthwhile endeavor. Oh, there was the threat of Communism, all right. But I can only blame myself for caving in to the shallow arguments we heard in the ROTC classroom about how the South Vietnamese people were oppressed by the communist aggression from the north and how the government of South Vietnam pleaded for our assistance to drive the communists back. I'm sure they were and it did. But the government was corrupt to begin with and the people of South Vietnam suffered from their own government's leadership. I'm willing to wager that if given the choice, most of the South Vietnamese would have gladly accepted the Communist regime only to be rid of the burden of the corrupt South Vietnamese government.

We were hedged by visions of duty, honor, and country. Those that resisted did not necessarily do so because they were smarter. I imagine some of them just didn't want to get their shit blown away. Well, I guess in some respects, that was damned smart. I can't blame them for that. I never have. Others just thought it was wrong, but they chose to run away instead of facing the problem like men. At least I don't have to live with that embarrassment. I don't hold anything against those folks, either. They did what they thought they had to do, and that is what I have always tried to do.

My ambitions? Different now. Regrets? Sure, I have a lot of them. Would I do it again? I would do my homework first, but knowing what I know now, no way in hell would I do that again. Not for the reasons we were given. I don't regret having served in Vietnam. It showed me what I was, and made me what I am. I proved to myself that I was as good as anyone else. And it also taught me humility and opened the door for the courage I never knew I had. I'm glad I went, but I wouldn't go again.

If you're expecting to read about white-knuckle exploits and heroics, or aggressive air battles, or blood and guts, you will probably be disappointed. That's not what this book is about. If you are easily offended by profanity and vulgarity, then this book is damned sure not for you. It's about an American serviceman's life in Vietnam. Many soldiers were profane and vulgar, but so was the Vietnam War.

So many books written by helicopter pilots in Vietnam elaborate on such themes. I'm not at odds with these books. I consider many of them to be well written accurate historical accounts of the war we fought, and I salute the brave souls who endured the hell of that country and lived to tell their stories. I also salute those who did not survive the experience.

This book tells the story about the other war in Vietnam. The personal war I, along with each of the other soldiers, fought with myself trying to adjust to the caustic environment, trying to fit in with the other guys who were waging their own personal battles, and trying to figure out how to survive so I could return home in one piece. The day-to-day trials, the challenges, the predicaments, and the choices I made were the results of struggles with my conscience, my ego, and the oath I took as a commissioned officer in the United States Army. After forty years of wondering about it all, I finally was able to make sense of most of it. Some of it I still don't understand and probably never will. I'm fortunate to be able to tell this story. I'm lucky. I didn't realize this until just a few years ago. That's when I began remembering all the shit that happened. The gullibility, the courage, the stupidity, and the luck. They were all there, for all of us. How we negotiated them determined whether or not we made it home.

A lot of books have been written about Vietnam, many by soldiers, especially helicopter pilots. Most of them are good. They tell it like it was. But many of them dwell on the violence, killing, and battles. There was much more to that war. There was the self-doubt of the soldier that played hell with his courage. There was the drudgery and tedium of waiting, with plenty of time to think about if he would get it. When would it be? Where would it happen? Could he face the danger and act like a soldier? And then there was the ever-present question: what was he actually doing there? And why?

As a commissioned officer, I did more than just fly helicopters. The warrant officers flew. That was pretty much it. They didn't see much of the behind the scenes nonsense and politics of command. They were given missions and they accomplished them. Commissioned officers were different. We had the burden of suffering through all of the shit that was necessary to make the unit work. The administrative functions, the supervisory details, all of the crap that those above thought necessary for our presence in that war. No one ever tells that story. The one about conscience, morality, mortality, and faith, if there really is such a thing in war.

So, this is my story. Of course, the names of the people are different. If you hadn't served in Vietnam during the war, you probably might not believe much of the account, but that I leave to you to deal with. What is certain is that you can have no idea of the day-to-day dangers, tedium and dilemmas we faced. I WAS there, and I still have to think about the reasons for the things I did or did not do.

It's like believing your coach when he tells you that you're going to go out and win the big game. Well, maybe you will, and maybe you won't. Hell, he doesn't know one way or the other. I don't think most of our presidents knew one way or the other about the game in Vietnam. Each of them had to make decisions and that's what he did. It's just too bad that they screwed up. Life isn't always fair. You take what you can get and endure the rest. You can't control most of what happens to you. All you can do is adapt and learn from it and strengthen yourself to meet new challenges. Just like Vietnam. Once you are army property, you do what you're told to do. You might not agree with it, but that's your job and you do it. I didn't think about what I did when I did it. I just did it. Now I do think about it. I don't like a lot of it, but I did it, just the same. If I really did do something bad, I'll have to live with it. I just don't know what that is yet.

This story is not the whole truth because truth can't be told in a story. Only the experience can. I have to convey my experiences in Vietnam the way I lived them. That's why I'm telling the story in my own way.

JANUARY 1971
A NEW LIFE BEGINS

LEAVING HOME

Bitter cold swept in from the Kansas plains, blasting every house in Derby. It was like I walked outside naked. My light-weight khakis and flight jacket made me look good but were otherwise practically worthless. I got into the car, one of those behemoth Oldsmobile 98s that would suck gas from any fuel pump within fifty feet, and settled back into the posh seat, prob-ably the last one I would sit in for the next year. My mother, her tiny four-foot-eight frame practically hidden behind the dash-board from other traffic, backed the car out of the driveway. The icy chill from the windows grabbed me by the balls, and I knew my life going to change. I just didn't know how.

My mother's silence on the way to the airport was as threat-ening as I imagined a bullet screaming toward my head would be. My father, a stoical relic of my youth, was at work. After all, his job as a tool and die maker fabricating parts to support good old capitalism was far more important than seeing his son off to Vietnam. So what if we might never see each other again? Good for him, I thought. I didn't need his indifference there in the car with us. The silence was trying enough. I just thank God, if he exists, that my brother wasn't there. I couldn't possibly imagine what kind of humiliation he would have put me through. The thought that I might never have to see him again left me with mixed feelings.

I had received orders in November, having successfully com-pleted advanced rotary-wing aviator training. That was the most challenging thing I had done in my life. Learning to fly a helicopter, that is. And being good at it. Well, I thought I was pretty good. The certificate I received said I was in the top five percent of my class, 70-40. The white hats. My head was pretty big then, too, but my hat still fit.

I didn't listen to newscasts about the Vietnam War much. I didn't listen to news about anything. I was in a world of my own, isolated in my own thoughts. I really didn't think about Vietnam too seriously, but it was always in the back of my mind, waiting for me to realize I would have to face it soon enough. Hell, the army training shoved it down my throat twenty-four hours a day, and I sat through those talks with my head up my ass, thinking about something else. My folks and I never talked much about it, but I could tell it was eating at them. There was this distance between us, as if I were a stranger. We weren't the huggie, lovey family that some were. We were somewhat stoical about the whole thing. I was just trying not to think about it.

I never kept in contact with the fellows in my flight class. We all went our separate ways and I never heard from any of them again. I suppose if I had, it would have put a severe obstacle in my path to survival in Vietnam. I would always be thinking about how so-and-so got it and I would worry about how I would get it. I was not married at the time, either, so I didn't have the problem of leaving behind a wife and kid. I never worried about much of anything except making a fool of myself.

During that short drive my mind kept drifting to the thought that I might never see my family again, but only as short impulses that flitted through my head. It wasn't like I actually believed that I would never come back. My twenty-four-year-old brain didn't understand that notion. Not that I knew what was in store for me. The ROTC cadre, the officer's basic staff, and the flight instructors had been vague about that. We can only put things into the perspective of events we have already experienced, not those that are foreign to us. What I was about to do would be as foreign to me as my first day at school.

It was January 12, 1971. I was supposed to be in-country by January 14. Allowing for the International Dateline and the twelve-hour lead in South Vietnam, my tickets were for the twelfth. I was surprised that Uncle Sam paid for my flight to California.

The folks in the terminal stared at us, or maybe just my uniform. There were a few smiles and pointing fingers, but mostly blank stares. I couldn't tell if it was because they were impressed by my stature as a soldier who was sworn to defend the country against all aggressors, or if it was because I was a symbol of the controversial and unpopular war raging in Southeast Asia. It could have been either. It wasn't like I was coming home. But that wouldn't have made much difference. I was targeted by a lot of scowls, as well. Those I just ignored. That's all I could do.

My mother walked with me to the gate at the airport while everyone stared at us. No kiss, no hug. Just a few words of parting, not that I remember what they were. I waved as I went through the door and didn't look back. I have no idea how long she might have stayed there, but I'm sure she watched me cross the concrete ramp and board my flight to San Francisco. I knew what she was thinking, and she might have known what I was thinking, but I doubt it. I was gone. Out of there. My own man. Free. And heading toward glory. Or death. Then I remembered how fortunate I was not to have to say goodbye to a wife. And I felt so alone.

The flight was short enough that I didn't spend a lot of time thinking about where I was going. The smoke from my cigarette filled my lungs and erased what I was trying not to think about. I just wanted to get my ass to the plane at Travis Air Force Base on time. I damned sure didn't want to start out my army career on the wrong foot, even if it did mean I might get killed. Well, hell, that was going to be my job anyway. Maybe getting myself killed, I mean. The flight attendants seemed to take special care with me. I'm not sure why, but I hoped it was out of respect for my uniform. It made the flight more pleasant when I thought of it that way. The plane landed before I could become too distracted from it.

I took a bus from the airport at San Francisco to Travis Air Force Base. The bus stopped some distance away from the gate at the airfield, so I lugged my two-ton duffle bag and gear along the sidewalk toward the gate. I had no idea what I was doing and a young black man watching me apparently knew it, too. He offered to carry my bag for me to the gate, and I remember thinking how thoughtful of him. I was about to change my opinion of the folks in California because my arm and shoulder were getting sore from the dead weight of the bag. But just as we neared the gate, the fellow slammed my bag to the sidewalk and said, "That'll be five dollars."

I had just been had. It wasn't the first time. I was just too stupid to wonder why the fellow was lurking around an airport terminal with no apparent means of transportation and no one else around. I paid him the five dollars. It was worth it to save the wear and tear on my shoulder. I lugged my bags around the corner and inside the door.

I was processed through customs with over a hundred other souls who were as clueless as I was. We were herded onto a Boeing 707 and off we went to Anchorage, Alaska, bound for Vietnam.

We made a quick fueling stop at Anchorage, and most of us disembarked to the terminal to smoke. We all looked out the windows through the darkness at the lights shining on the snow and ice. I had never seen so much snow in my life. It was deeper than most cars. It could just as well have been the Arctic. I wouldn't have known the difference. Then, back onto the plane.

I pretty much remember what I was thinking when I looked out that little window by my shoulder and saw the lights of the United States of America retreating into the distance. I know I had this sort of excitement about seeing a new country, but at the same time I was dreading actually getting there. You know how it is when you're excited about leaving on a trip to a new destination, but you're not sure what's going to happen when you get there. Well, I damned sure didn't know what would happen. After hearing all of my military instructors harp on the dangers we would face, I thought to myself, would I be killed? Would I perform some superhuman feat of bravery? Or would I piss my pants and be a coward? I had never been in combat and I'm sure none of the other saps on that plane had, either. I imagine the army did its best to prepare me for the possibility of killing and being killed. I had never done any of that. It's not like something you can practice. So I wondered if I'd be a hero or dead. I had about twenty hours of flying over the Pacific to think about it.

Interested in reading this Amazon best seller further?
The Other Vietnam War - A Helicopter Pilot's Life in Vietnam,
is available today in paperback, hardback, and audiobook!

Amazon Barnes & Noble Kobo

ABOUT THE AUTHOR

Marc Cullison is a baby-boomer who grew up in an era when education was everything and duty to country was a responsibility. After receiving a bachelor's degree in architectural engineering at Oklahoma State University, he was commissioned as a second lieutenant in the United States Army Reserve Corps of Engineers through the ROTC program. During his four-year tour of duty, he served as helicopter pilot with the 129th Assault Helicopter Company in II Corps, Vietnam, in 1971. He returned from overseas to an assignment as a military assistant to the resident engineer at Kaw Dam and Reservoir near Ponca City, Oklahoma, where he met the woman he would marry there. After two years in Ponca City he was honorably discharged and returned to Oklahoma State where he received a master's degree in architectural engineering and honed his technical skills as a professional structural engineer. Then into quality control at a manufacturing plant which led him into computer programming. His most recent career was a math and science instructor at Connors State College in Warner and Muskogee, Oklahoma, from which he retired in 2014. He lives with his wife in a self-built log house near Sallisaw.

www.mcullison.com

OTHER TITLES FROM IMZADI PUBLISHING

www.imzadipublishing.com

A NOTE FROM IMZADI PUBLISHING

We hope you have enjoyed *Second Chances,* and the free preview of *The Other Vietnam War - A Helicopter Pilot's Life in Vietnam,* both by Marc Cullison. You, the reader, are the backbone of the publishing industry; without you our industry simply would not exist. As such we depend upon you and your feedback.

Please take a few moments to leave a book rating and review for the book you have just read. It is not necessary to write a lengthy review, a few words will do. Reviews are remarkably difficult to obtain and we are incredibly grateful for every single one.

Happy reading!

Printed in the USA
CPSIA information can be obtained
at www.ICGtesting.com
LVHW010007250824
789166LV00013B/384